PUTIN'S ASSASSIN

A MYSTERY THRILLER

Victor Malarek

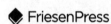 FriesenPress

One Printers Way
Altona, MB R0G 0B0
Canada

www.friesenpress.com

Copyright © 2024 by Victor Malarek
First Edition — 2024

All rights reserved.

Author's photo by Jeff Crider.

ISBN
978-1-03-831395-9 (Hardcover)
978-1-03-831394-2 (Paperback)
978-1-03-831396-6 (eBook)

1. FICTION, CRIME

Distributed to the trade by The Ingram Book Company

Although *Putin's Assassin* is a work of fiction, Matt Kozar's reports on the atrocities committed by Russian soldiers in the Ukrainian city of Bucha are based on actual documented events.

DEDICATION

For my beautiful granddaughter, Mika.

THE IPHONE MIRACLE

I was dead. My heart had stopped. I had no pulse, no vital signs.

The last thing I remember was the shooter: a cold-blooded Russian hitman pointing a Glock at my chest. We were in the office of a prominent US senator involved in a sinister plot to steal international aid shipments of wheat intended for the Horn of Africa. I really didn't think he would pull the trigger.

Then everything went black.

I was told the DC Capitol cops ripped open my shirt and started performing CPR after they stormed the room. Several minutes later, they passed me over to the paramedics. I had no vitals. No heartbeat. The emergency medical technicians continued with CPR, keeping at it until they pulled up on the hospital emergency ramp and rolled me into the ER, where a trauma doctor zapped me with successive jolts of electricity. The third one kickstarted my heart.

For three days I lay in a coma, hooked up to an array of beeping machines. I could feel myself floating in some kind of alternate reality—one in which there was nothing, just a dark, quiet void. There was no white light and no stairway to heaven. There were no harp-strumming angels and no celestial trumpets blaring. And mercifully, there was no hot highway to hell.

As I regained consciousness, all I could feel was an excruciating pain in my chest. I opened my eyes a crack. I had no idea where I was. The room was totally white with long, fluorescent bulbs attached to the ceiling. Moving my head to the left, I realized I was on a bed, wired to a heart monitor and an IV drip. I turned my head to the right. On a chair near the window was Mei, my girlfriend, lost in a book she was reading.

In a hoarse whisper, I called out her name.

Mei leapt to her feet and rushed to my bedside. She grabbed my hand and began sobbing.

"What's going on? Why am I here?" I asked. My throat was dry and raspy.

"You're in the hospital. You were shot."

"What do you mean I was shot?" I asked.

I heard the heart monitor shift into overdrive. It was now beeping fast. Moments later, a doctor rushed into the room followed by two nurses pushing a crash cart filled with medical equipment.

One of the nurses touched Mei on the shoulder. "Miss, you have to leave," she instructed in a firm but calm voice.

Mei kissed me lightly on the forehead. "Matt, I'll be right outside in the corridor. When the doctor is finished, I'll come back and explain everything. I love you."

The doctor placed a stethoscope on my chest. "Mr. Kozar, I'm Dr. Santok Singh. I'm a cardiologist."

I could feel myself spiraling into panic mode. I couldn't catch my breath.

"Mr. Kozar, you must try to remain calm," the doctor said, placing his hand on my shoulder. "You have been in a coma for three days. I need to take some tests."

Dr. Singh's demeanor had a calming effect on me. He had a long, white beard and wore an orange turban. What I noticed most about him were his eyes: focused and caring. He began asking questions while reading a printout from the heart monitor. "How are you feeling, Mr. Kozar?"

"My chest hurts. What is this place?"

"You are in the trauma wing at the George Washington University Hospital in Washington, DC."

My mind was a scrambled mess. I could feel the panic welling up once again in my chest. And I could hear the beeping of the heart monitor picking up speed.

"Mr. Kozar, try to calm yourself. Tell me, what is the last thing you remember?"

"I don't know." I closed my eyes and desperately scoured my memory banks. A vision of an office with an American flag draped on the wall behind a large, antique desk came into focus. There was a man sitting behind it, his forehead lined with tension. Then it all came flooding back like a tidal wave.

The man was Samuel Caine, Republican senator from Kansas and chair of the US Subcommittee on International Aid. I had gone to Caine's office to confront him about his role in a multi-million-dollar fraud I had uncovered involving the shipment of American food aid to the starving population in the Horn of Africa. Sitting across from him were Reverend Lionel Powers, the charismatic evangelical leader of the Global Crusade, and Yuri Lukov, a hitman who worked for Ivan and Sergei Melekov, two unsavory oligarchs from Rostov-on-Don in Russia. With the backroom collaboration of Enrico Kamra, the chair of the United Nations International Food Fund, this corrupt cabal hatched a scheme to reroute millions of tons of top-grade American wheat and replace it with substandard Russian grain. The American wheat was then sold on the open market by the Russians and their chaff was fed to the hungry.

Dr. Singh snapped me back to reality. "Mr. Kozar, you have been shot. The bullet hit the left side of your chest. The impact stopped your heart. You suffered cardiac arrest."

"My heart stopped?"

"Yes. When the paramedics got to you, they performed CPR, and when you arrived at the hospital, we restarted your heart with a defibrillator."

"I was dead?"

"Technically, yes, Mr. Kozar. You are extremely fortunate to be alive. Your cell phone took the brunt of the gunshot. It saved your life."

Again, my thoughts drifted back to the day I was shot. I remembered that before entering the senator's office, I placed my iPhone in the breast pocket of my blazer with the video on, transmitting the entire confrontation in the senator's office to my editor back at the *Tribune* in New York. I couldn't believe my iPhone saved my life.

For the next several minutes, Dr. Singh peppered me with a series of questions to determine, as he explained it, if I had experienced "neurologic dysfunction, brain injury, and/or neurocognitive deficits." I had no idea what any of that meant.

He also had me wiggle my toes, touch my nose, and follow his finger with my eyes.

When he was done, I asked, "Did I pass?"

"Yes. It is truly somewhat of a miracle that you appear not to have suffered any brain damage or serious physical injury aside from three fractured ribs," he said.

"I want to see Mei. I need to see Mei."

"We'll call her in a moment. Tomorrow, you will be seen by our psychologist."

"Why?"

"She will be assessing your psychological wellbeing," Dr. Singh explained. "A trauma such as the one you have suffered often triggers what we refer to as PCAS, post-cardiac arrest syndrome, which can include severe bouts of anxiety, depression, and post-traumatic stress disorder. I realize all of this is a lot for you to take in, so, I ask you to try to remain calm. You must rest and avoid stress. I have prescribed a mild sedative. The nurse will bring it to you after you have had some solid food."

"I want to see Mei. Can she come back in?"

Dr. Singh nodded to the nurse. She left the room and returned with Mei.

"You may visit for a little while and then he needs to rest. At all costs, Mr. Kozar must avoid stress," the doctor instructed Mei.

"I understand."

After the doctor and nurses left, Mei calmly filled in the missing pieces.

"Matt, it was a miracle. Thank goodness for your phone," she said, her eyes filled with tears.

That was all I remembered of the conversation before I drifted off.

*

When I woke up the following morning, Mei was sitting by my bedside, gazing intently at my face and stroking my head. She smiled and kissed my cheek.

"How are you feeling, Sunshine?" she asked.

"Like I'm in this fog. I can't seem to shake it, and my chest feels like it's in a vice."

"I'm just glad you're okay," Mei said.

But I could tell from her glistening eyes she wasn't okay. "How are you holding up?"

"Matt, you gave me such a scare. When I first heard the news and it was reported you were dead, I broke down. I couldn't believe it. I wouldn't let myself believe it."

"I'm sorry."

"For what?" she asked.

"For putting you through this."

"You don't need to be sorry for anything. I'm just so happy you're alive."

"Mei, I need you to take me through this. The doctor said I was in a coma for three days."

"Yes. You were brought to the hospital four days ago."

"What happened to my stories? Did they make it into the paper?"

"Typical journalist," Mei said with a laugh. "Three days on the front page. Three days trending number one on social media. And you're on the front page again today."

"Why today?"

"The headline: *Tribune* Reporter Matthew Kozar Out of Coma."

"I hate being called Matthew."

I stared up at the ceiling, recalling all that had happened.

"I can't believe that Russian bastard shot me. What happened to him? Was he arrested?"

"No. Somehow, he managed to sneak out of the Senate building during all the commotion and make a mad dash for the Russian embassy. Word is he was on a private jet to Moscow that very evening."

"The cops didn't try to stop him?"

"Couldn't. The embassy invoked diplomatic immunity. They refused to surrender him to the police," Mei said.

"What about Powers and Senator Caine? What happened to them?"

"Both arrested. They're in jail. They have a bail hearing later today."

"What about the Trib?"

"Like I said, your stories have been splashed across the front pages for the past three days. They've triggered one hell of a firestorm in Washington, the UN, Moscow, and the evangelical movement in this country. Parts of the video you recorded on your iPhone in the senator's office are trending number one on social media. You've done good, Matt. Oh, and the UN has ordered a full investigation into the International Food Fund."

"Which like everything the UN does will go nowhere," I said.

"Well, one good thing has already come out of it. Enrico Kamra resigned the day after your feature on the Emperor of Food Aid hit the stands. He packed up and high-tailed it back to his family home in Lebanon."

Staring into Mei's eyes, I could still see the fear, the anguish, and the relief. "How long have you been here?"

"I took the week off. I wanted to be here when you woke up. Just in case."

"In case what?"

Mei fought back her emotions. "The doctors thought you might suffer brain damage as a result of being, you know, clinically dead."

"Do you know how long I was dead?"

"I was told you showed no vitals for eight minutes. If not for the Capitol police rushing into the senator's office and performing CPR literally seconds after you were shot, you probably would have suffered permanent brain damage."

There was a light rap on the door.

"May we come in?" It was Patrick Doyle, managing editor of the *Tribune*, and Heather James, the national editor and my direct boss. She was carrying a bouquet of red and white carnations.

"Welcome back to the land of the living," Doyle said with a warm smile. "Now, when are you going to quit loafing in bed and get back to work?"

We all laughed. I cut my laugh short when a sharp pain shot across my chest.

"Everyone at the office sends their best. They all wish you a speedy recovery," Heather said.

"We've received calls from journalists across the country requesting interviews with you once you're up and about," Doyle added.

"I really don't want to talk to anyone," I said.

"You don't have to if you don't want to. You just get better," Doyle said.

"By the way, we have something for you," Heather said, handing me a small package wrapped in a tear sheet of the *Tribune* and topped with a silver bow. Mei ripped off the wrapping and handed me the box.

"It's a new iPhone," Heather said with a smile.

"Thanks, I'll make sure to keep it close to my heart."

They all laughed.

"We'll be going," Doyle said. "Get well. We'll see you back at work when you're good and ready. Not before."

*

I remained in the hospital for another two weeks while the doctors monitored my return to normal. To keep me from going stir-crazy, Mei retrieved my laptop from my apartment. I read through my investigative pieces in the Trib and accounts of my exploits in a slew of newspapers, magazines, and online forums. It lifted my spirits and sent my ego soaring into the stratosphere. I was grateful to Mei for keeping my head earthbound.

The fallout from my investigation amazed me. To think it all began with the shooting death of a humble, low-level pastor connected to the Global Crusade, which was headquartered at Reverend Powers' Golden Temple complex in Cedar Springs, Arizona. The death of Pastor Harold Corbin was initially ruled a suicide by the local police chief and the coroner. But with the help of a gun-spatter expert Mei had called, it was unequivocally ruled that the pastor had been murdered.

*

When I was released from the hospital, Mei insisted I stay at her Manhattan apartment. I agreed, and for the next four months she hovered over me like a mother hen to the point where I was champing at the bit to return to my hovel in the Bronx.

Mei Liu Chen and I had been a couple for six years. I first saw her testifying as an expert witness in DNA analysis at a sexual assault trial in a New York City courthouse. Cupid fired an arrow, and I was smitten. I was blown away by her confidence and her looks, so I managed to bump into her on the courthouse steps. I introduced myself, told her I was a journalist, and asked if she had time for a coffee to discuss the use of DNA in criminal cases. Mei looked at me, smiled, and we headed off to a nearby Starbucks. The rest is history.

Mei is my rock. She owns my heart. I'm crazy in love with her. But from time to time, the woman, who is an internationally renowned forensics analyst, ticks me off big time: mostly when she decides to home in on my minor faults and idiosyncrasies. Well, actually, my major faults.

I stayed with her while I healed but her minimalist abode is not my style. Everything is neat, clean, and in its place. Journalists tend to swaddle in clutter with books scattered helter-skelter, stacks of newspapers and magazines on the floor, and piles of file folders stuffed with research perched precariously on top of a small desk. At least that's what my place is like. Mei calls it chaos. It isn't. I know exactly where everything is when I need it. Almost everything.

HERO'S WELCOME

My return to the Trib was a moment I prefer to forget. It was a Class A dud. There were no streamers or balloons. There was no Welcome Back Matt banner hanging over the main entrance to the newsroom, no marching band, and—what was truly unforgiveable—no cake. I must admit, I was disappointed. After all, I took a bullet for the paper.

Doyle dutifully summoned the newsroom staff to gather outside his office and called me to his side.

"As you all know, Matt has been away for the past several months recuperating from his injury. I'm happy to say he's back now and ready to take on the bad guys," Doyle intoned, and then he turned to me. "You know there's an old adage in journalism: 'You're only as good as your last story,' and in your case, Matt, your last story was a blockbuster. Let's see if you can match it or do one better. So, welcome back. Now, all of you get to work. We've got a paper to put out."

The entire festivity lasted less than two minutes.

As I headed to my cubicle, Doyle's resuscitation of the old adage echoed loudly in my ears. How in hell could I ever match my last story? My first day back and I was filled with angst. I needed to find a story, another front-page scoop. But getting back into the groove proved no easy task. For a little more than a year, I covered various assignments and whenever I could I'd hit the phone in hopes of reeling in a big fish, but all I ever managed to net were sardines. I was getting frustrated, and it was beginning to show. My mood was dark and my temper short.

Then on February 24, 2022, Russia invaded Ukraine and my entire world changed. I was stunned by the profound impact it had on me, which was as strange as it was confusing, because until that day I had no real connection—physical or emotional—to Ukraine, although the undiluted blood of my Ukrainian ancestors coursed through my veins.

I had always considered myself an American through and through. As Bruce Springsteen aptly put it, I was "born in the USA." As far back as I could remember, I proudly pledged allegiance to the Stars and Stripes with my right hand on my heart. And I ate apple pie.

I was aware of my Ukrainian heritage, but just barely. My great-grand-parents immigrated to the States from Ukraine in the early 1900s, ending up in Chicago. My grandparents and my parents were born in the Windy City. And over the many decades, the Kozar family connection to the Motherland faded into the mist.

I didn't speak a word of Ukrainian. I knew next to nothing about Ukraine's culture and even less about its history. Throughout my youth, I had nothing to do with the hyphenated Ukrainian-American community, its organizations, or its churches. I never even had a Ukrainian friend.

Yet for some reason, it took Russia's murderous war against Ukraine to ignite a long dormant spark in my soul and turn it into a raging inferno. From the day Russian president Vladimir Putin ordered his military to invade Ukraine, reports of the daily carnage of his barbaric war machine dominated my life. I spent hours scanning social media websites for news and updates about the war. My heart broke seeing the images of the immense suffering and the slaughter committed by Putin's killers. I couldn't think straight, and I couldn't find peace in sleep. My dreams were constantly haunted by the death of innocents.

My obsession with Russia's war on Ukraine began to worry Mei.

"You've got to find a balance," she counseled. "Look at you. You're a wreck. You're not eating well. You're not sleeping well. You toss and turn. You're always tense and stressed out."

"I don't get it," I said, trying to figure out why this was happening to me. "I mean, up until the Russians invaded Ukraine and started killing innocent civilians, Ukraine played no role in my life, and now it's center stage."

"Matt, you're American, but face it, the war has awakened your Ukrainian soul."

"And it's driving me crazy."

"Then do something about it."

"Like what? Go to Ukraine, join the army and fight?"

"No. Nothing that drastic. There are a lot of things you can do that are not that extreme," Mei said.

"Like what then?"

"Like joining the protest marches."

"What good is a protest march when bombs keep falling on innocent people?"

"It lets the people of Ukraine know the world stands for Ukraine. That you stand for Ukraine."

"I'm not one for demonstrations, waving placards, chanting slogans. It's never been my thing," I countered.

"Then get involved at the organizational level. There are dozens of Ukrainian-American groups that could use your expertise."

"What expertise?"

"You're a journalist. You know how the media works. You can help the organizations in getting the word out. From what little I've read, there are lots of groups and they're doing more than just protesting. They're raising millions of dollars to deliver humanitarian aid to Ukraine. You could help in that way. You can lend your voice, a calm and measured voice, to the debate."

"What voice? I'm a nobody in the Ukrainian community here."

"Matt, you're a well-known and respected correspondent. I'm sure the community would welcome you. I'm sure many people in leadership positions here are aware of what you did in exposing those Russian oligarchs who were stealing US food aid shipments."

"I don't know."

"Look, you're not working on anything major at the moment. You've got a lot of free time. Use it for something good. It will help you feel better about yourself and ease your mind," Mei suggested.

"Nothing will ease my mine until Vladimir Putin and his thugs are stopped," I said. "That bastard needs to be put into the ground."

"Like I said, a calm and measured voice," Mei noted in a reproving tone.

"May he meet his Maker, and may he rot in hell. Is that better?"

Mei rolled her eyes.

DICTATOR OF DEATH

US senator Bill Bradford sat quietly on the stage listening to a pack of pundits opine at an international forum on the Russian invasion of Ukraine. There were five noted speakers, each allotted twenty minutes to articulate their various insights. The massive main auditorium at Georgetown University in Washington, DC, was filled to capacity with participants, most clutching a small yellow and blue flag of Ukraine. Two large adjoining rooms held the overflow of attendees watching the discussion on giant flat-screen monitors.

I was sitting across from Heather in her office with my feet on her desk, sipping an Americano, black, no sugar. We were glued to the fifty-five-inch TV on her wall.

Not being a political junkie, I had only a vague idea who Bradford was, but a quick online search brought me up to speed.

Senator William David Bradford III—Bill to his friends and colleagues—was a highly respected Democrat from California and chair of the powerful Senate Appropriations Committee. He was also an outspoken critic of Russian president Vladimir Putin's invasion of Ukraine. Magazine and newspaper articles described the senator as a staunch defender of democracy who spoke his mind, pulled no punches, and stood up to bullies. An interesting offhand snippet noted the senator "didn't suffer fools gladly," which quickly became apparent as he listened to each speaker. Bradford's face was a moving tableau of winces and grimaces as they rambled on about the war and standing up for freedom.

With the fourth speaker retreating to her seat, the moderator approached the dais and the audience shifted in their seats. No more slouching. No more sneaking a peek at cell phone messages and missed calls. They sat erect in anticipation of what was to come.

"Our final speaker needs no introduction," the moderator announced, and he was right. Before he could say another word, Senator Bradford rose and approached the podium with determination and resolve etched into his face.

There was no thanking the sponsors of the event or the moderator. The senator simply launched into his speech. "Let me begin by setting the record straight in unequivocal terms: Vladimir Putin is a malignant, sadistic, treacherous, and delusional dictator."

The audience broke out in loud applause.

The senator continued: "Putin is a bully, a predator, and a murderous psychopath. He is also a sociopath incapable of empathy. He is a narcissist and a liar and does not possess an ounce of remorse or guilt.

"When Putin began his invasion of Ukraine on February 24, he thought he would roll into Kyiv in three days atop a tank, the triumphant and benevolent liberator, and be welcomed by hordes of people waving Russian flags and tossing rose petals on the boulevard. After all, Russia allegedly boasted one of the most powerful armies on the planet, and Putin was convinced the Ukrainian people would surrender trembling like aspens in a windstorm.

"But the vengeful dictator, this so-called brilliant tactician, got it seriously wrong. He grossly underestimated the strength, the resolve, and the tenacity of Ukraine's national resistance led by the country's brave president, Volodymyr Zelenskyy."

As I listened, my heart swelled with pride. I glanced over at Heather and smiled. "I gotta say I like this guy."

Heather nodded.

The senator continued his broadside. "Missing from Putin's assessment of Ukraine was one important gene in the make-up of Ukrainians. They hate bullies. They stand up to bullies. They don't wave white flags. They hold the blue and yellow flag of Ukraine high and proud, and they will fight to the death in defense of their beloved homeland.

"This barbaric invasion of Ukraine started in a brutal and unprovoked way," Bradford explained. "It is nothing short of a disastrous miscalculation, and mark my words, it will go down in history as one of the biggest geopolitical blunders of the modern era. For Putin and his henchmen, this is a war of aggression. It is a grotesque, imperialist land grab. For Ukraine, it is a war of defense. A war of survival."

My eyes were riveted to the screen. I could feel my chest tighten as the senator described the sheer level of brutality unleashed by the Russian military against Ukraine.

"The scenes of suffering tear at your heart. Every village, town, and city that this barbarous army has invaded is paved with a trail of horrific atrocities and unimaginable destruction. Putin's soldiers are committing untold war crimes. They are executing ordinary civilians. They are raping women and girls. They are abducting children and deporting them to the far reaches of eastern Russia to be brainwashed and turned into obedient Russian automatons and soldiers."

The senator touched on the relentless bombing of the Ukrainian city of Mariupol and the invasion of the Black Sea port city of Kherson. He cited the case of a young woman who was in a hospital to give birth when a Russian guided missile slammed into the building. She and her unborn baby were killed.

"And for what? Of what strategic importance was that hospital? Of what strategic importance are schools and children's playgrounds? Of what strategic importance are farming villages?" Bradford demanded, his voice booming across the auditorium. "The only reason they are being targeted is to terrorize the general population—the innocent men, women, and children of Ukraine who simply want to live in peace.

"Let me be clear about Russia's war against Ukraine. Putin's prime objective is to erase Ukraine from the map of the world; to expunge a nation; to extinguish its identity, its language, and its history; and to steal its rich culture. There is only one word to describe what the leader of Russia is committing in Ukraine: genocide.

"And one has to wonder why no one inside Russia's inner circle has the courage to stand up to this evil. Why this dictator of death is still in power baffles me. Vladimir Putin is a war criminal. He is directly responsible for the deaths of tens of thousands of Ukrainians."

What fascinated me was Bradford's description of Putin's method of dealing with Russians who dare to cross him, challenge him, or suggest that he is deranged.

"Putin is notorious for exacting revenge on anyone getting in his way," the senator noted, citing numerous incidents in which Russians in positions of power and influence met an untimely and gruesome end. Many had fallen to their deaths from windows and balconies in high-rise buildings or died in unlikely car crashes. Others were poisoned while sipping tea, while others managed to commit suicide by shooting themselves multiple times.

"All these deaths were recorded as suicides by local and state investigators," the senator pointed out, his words tinged with sarcasm.

Bradford paused to take a sip of water. "Putin's assassins can strike anywhere in the world. Two years ago, a Russian hitman struck on American soil. The incident involved the theft of US food aid by two notorious Russian oligarchs with direct links to Putin. These crooks, along with a US senator, an evangelical minister, and the head of the UN International Food Fund, put together a scheme to divert one and a half million tons of top-grade American wheat worth more than three hundred million dollars onto the open market—food aid earmarked to feed people in the famine-ravaged Horn of Africa. It was then surreptitiously swapped with worthless, substandard Russian grain you wouldn't feed to a pig."

I leapt to my feet. "He's citing my investigation."

"Well, there's an eagle feather in your cap," Heather said with a smile.

The senator continued. "The scheme began to unravel when the Russian hitman murdered an American pastor, a father of three children who was threatening to blow the whistle on the operation. The death, a single shot to the head, was initially ruled a suicide. That is when *New York Tribune* reporter Matt Kozar entered the picture and proved unequivocally that the pastor was executed in cold blood. In an unrelenting investigation, the reporter peeled back the layers of this corrupt scheme. As Kozar was closing in, Putin's henchman planted a bomb under the hood of his car in New York City. It detonated, killing a police officer, a tow truck operator, and an innocent bystander. The bomb was meant for the reporter.

"In a final attempt to silence Kozar, the hitman shot him at point-blank range in, of all places, Senator Caine's office right here in Washington, DC. Fortunately, the reporter survived."

The senator concluded his speech by saying Putin had to be stopped and announcing that he would be meeting with the US president to demand more lethal aid for Ukraine in its daunting fight for freedom. That aid, he pointed out, would include Bradley Fighting Vehicles, Abrams tanks, long-range missiles, and possibly F-16 fighter jets.

"We must give Ukraine the military means to defend itself. We must provide President Zelenskyy and his army with the military might to drive Russia out of all its occupied territories: Donetsk, Luhansk, and Crimea."

The senator also said he would ask the president to shut down the Russian embassy in Washington. "Every single Russian diplomat I have ever met or ever heard speak is a shameless, lying apologist for a murderous, criminal regime. It's time to yank the welcome mat and send them home.

"Lastly, I will be asking the president to designate Russia as a state sponsor of terrorism."

Bradford stared out at the audience. He took a deep breath and let it out slowly. "Vladimir Putin is a war criminal who should be dragged in chains to the International Criminal Court in The Hague to face charges of war crimes, crimes against humanity, and genocide. Thank you."

The senator folded his speaking notes and returned to his seat to a thunderous standing ovation.

For a guy who never met a politician he liked, I found myself in awe of Bradford. He didn't obfuscate. He didn't dance around the issue. He slam-dunked it. And I was riding high.

"That was one incredible speech," I said, turning to Heather. "A politician who is not afraid to call it like it is. He's definitely on my Christmas card list."

"You don't send Christmas cards," Heather noted.

"Well, I will this Christmas."

"Admit it, you like him because he cited your investigation and because you're Ukrainian," she noted with a wry smile.

"Heather, I am one hundred percent American," I countered. "You know that."

"Ah, but your DNA says otherwise."

"That may be so. But I was born here and that makes me a full-blooded American."

Heather shook her head. "Look, I'm not blind. I know what's happening in Ukraine is affecting you big time. I've noticed a change in you ever since the Russian invasion began. You're tense. You snap at people. You're distracted. You're always on social media poring over the latest news on the war."

"It's impossible to get away from it," I shot back in my defense.

"I get that," Heather said. "I'm not Ukrainian and I find myself consumed by the war. The images of the killings and the indiscriminate bombings are heart-wrenching."

"I can't believe how hard this has hit me," I confessed. "It's affected me in ways I can't begin to express. Ever since that Russian bastard invaded Ukraine, I've been having trouble thinking straight. I don't understand it. I mean, over the years I've read and watched news coverage of wars and disasters around the world, and while I was concerned, nothing has ever affected me like this."

"Face it, Matt. The war has awakened your Ukrainian spirit and brought it to the surface. Best thing for you to maintain your equilibrium is to step back from time to time to reset your brain, or this will drive you insane."

"That's what Mei told me."

"Good advice. Listen to her."

Listening to advice was one thing; following it was another. In my angst over the war, I had come up with a plan I knew would take a lot of subtle arm-twisting on my part.

Looking straight at Heather, I cleared my throat and made the pitch. "I've been giving some thought to something and before you say no, hear me out."

"What is it?"

"I want to be sent to Ukraine to cover the war."

"No! No way," Heather said. Have you not heard how many journalists have been killed or seriously wounded over there?"

"I could just as easily be killed here with all the random gun violence."

"You almost lost your life at the hands of a Russian hitman right here. There is no way I'm going to give you the green light to risk your life in Ukraine."

"Why not?" I challenged. "It's my life."

"For several reasons. You've never been to Ukraine. You don't speak the language. You've never covered a war, and this is one extremely dangerous war."

"Would your nose get out of joint if I ask Doyle to send me?"

Heather grimaced. "The proper channel to go through is Philip Nolan. You know that. He's the foreign editor."

"The jerk hates me."

"And you hate him. So, the two of you are even."

"Will you back me?"

Heather looked down at her desk. "I already gave you my answer."

I left her office and headed for Nolan's lair. I felt tension grip my chest. I absolutely loathed the ground Nolan walked on with his old-school, lace-up, black Oxford shoes. I mean, who the hell wears Oxford shoes except dickheads who went to expensive private schools?

What I really detested was his arrogance. He held two master's degrees: one in European history from Princeton and one in international relations from Yale, both encased in cheap black and gold frames and hung at eye level on the wall behind his desk.

It was beneath Nolan to speak to any reporters who didn't belong to his stable of foreign correspondents, all of whom possessed a university degree in either history, political science, economics, or international studies. He looked down his narrow beak at anyone with a degree in journalism, discarding them as unworldly and insignificant troglodytes. The definition of me.

Things had come to a head between us two years earlier when I asked him to dig into his foreign news budget and send me to Eritrea as part of my investigation into the international food aid scandal. Before I could even make my pitch, he cut me off and ordered me to leave his office.

I lost it, calling him a pompous jerk loudly enough for everyone in the newsroom to hear.

Heather had come to my rescue. She asked Doyle if she could take money out of her national budget and earmark it for a special project on the famine in the Horn of Africa. Doyle agreed, but the decision cost Heather no end of grief with Nolan.

This time around, Heather was not about to go to bat for me. I was on my own.

If there was one thing that grated on Nolan's nerves it was anyone other than Doyle walking into his office without knocking and waiting for permission to enter. I didn't knock or wait for permission to enter.

Nolan peered over his wire-rimmed reading glasses. He was a balding ferret of a man with a pencil mustache and beady eyes. When he saw me standing in front of his desk, a look of arrant disdain swept over his face.

"I'm busy," he barked. "Get out."

I held my ground. "I need to speak to you about something important."

"I doubt anything you have to say is important. So get out!"

"I want to go to Ukraine to cover the war."

Nolan laughed. It was a derisive laugh that made me want to walk over and slap the condescending sneer off his face.

"I want to cover the war from the front lines," I continued.

He kept on chuckling.

"I'm serious. I know I can do a good job."

Removing his glasses, he looked at me and asked, "What do you know about the war in Ukraine that would be of the slightest interest to this newspaper and its readers?"

"I've been following it closely ever since Putin invaded Ukraine."

"Pray tell, when was that?"

"February 24, 2022."

"Wrong. Vladimir Putin invaded Ukraine on February 20, 2014, when the Russian military seized Crimea. A month later, his troops invaded the Ukrainian regions of Donetsk and Luhansk. I suggest you do your homework before coming in here like a puffed-up baboon demanding to be sent to Ukraine as one of my foreign correspondents. Now, once again, get out of my office."

"I know I can do a way better job than the idiot you sent there."

"Maybe I should send you, and with luck, this time you *will* get killed," Nolan snapped.

"Philip!" Heather shouted, bursting into the office. She had been standing in earshot but out of Nolan's sightline. "I can't believe what you just said."

"You're fucking lucky I don't rearrange that smug look on your face," I shouted at Nolan.

Within seconds, a small crowd rushed into the corridor outside his office. A few moments later, it parted as Patrick Doyle pushed through.

"What is going on here?" he demanded.

"This arrogant know-nothing wouldn't leave my office when I asked him to," Nolan sputtered.

"Both of you in my office now. You too, Heather."

The three of us followed Doyle.

With the door shut, the managing editor first acknowledged Nolan, who was part of the management team.

"Philip, you were saying," Doyle said as he sat down at his desk.

"Kozar barged into my office demanding to be sent to Ukraine. I told him this was not going to happen, and he blew his top. He threatened me. Said I was lucky he didn't rearrange my face. His words, not mine. Heather was standing right there. I'm filing a complaint with human resources. No one threatens me. I want him fired."

I smiled and shook my head.

"Matt, is that correct?" Doyle asked.

"Let's just say Nolan's version of events clearly demonstrates a serious disconnect with reality. Either that, or he's a pathetic liar."

"I'm not going to stand for defamatory accusations. Matt, you owe Philip an apology," Doyle ordered.

"When hell freezes over."

Heather finally piped in. "Mr. Doyle, I think Philip is the one who owes Matt an apology. The way he spoke to Matt was insulting and demeaning. And what's far worse was his comment that if he decided to send Matt to Ukraine, and these are his words, 'with luck, this time you will get killed.' That's when I intervened to defuse the situation."

Doyle turned to the foreign editor. "Philip, is this a more accurate version of events?"

"More or less. But Kozar did threaten me."

"Only after what you said to him," Heather noted.

"Had you said that to me, I'd have threatened you," the managing editor said. "You owe Matt an apology and you'd better hope he doesn't file a complaint with human resources."

Nolan's face was ashen as he turned to me. "I apologize."

"Not accepted," I countered.

"Matt, cut the games," Doyle warned.

"Nolan's apology embodies all the sincerity of a vacuum cleaner salesman's pitch."

Doyle glared at Nolan. "Go back to your office. Matt, you stay."

Heather retreated to her office, and like an obedient puppy I remained standing.

Doyle stared at me for a long moment. I was beginning to feel uneasy, wondering if he was going to tear a strip off me. He didn't. His face softened. I knew he didn't play favorites with his reporters, but I also knew he liked me. He never said as much. But I just felt it. After all, he bought me a new cell phone.

Finally, he asked. "Now, what's this about you wanting to go to Ukraine? And sit down."

"I want to cover the war from the front lines," I said.

Doyle looked at me and slowly shook his head. "That is not going to happen. We already have a reporter on the ground."

"Tim Knox. The guy is nothing more than a glorified stenographer. He parks his butt in a posh hotel in Lviv and writes daily summaries of the war put out by the Ukrainian government. He watches government officials delivering speeches and updates on local television and reports on them like he's covering them live. The guy's too chickenshit to go to the front lines. If I go to Ukraine, I'll head straight for the battle and file from there."

"I cleared Tim for the assignment," Doyle pointed out.

"No doubt on the recommendation of his good pal Nolan."

"Philip Nolan is the foreign editor."

"And you know he would never okay my request."

"Neither will I."

"Why not?"

"For two reasons. One, I am not going to override Nolan's decision on who he sends on a foreign assignment. And two, which is the most important reason, I don't want to risk you getting killed."

"It's my life."

"And you work for the *Tribune*."

"Then what if I quit?"

"I wouldn't go there if I were you."

I got up. He pointed to the chair. I sat back down.

Doyle tried to calm the stubborn storm swirling in my head. "Matt, you know I think the world of you. You're an excellent reporter. If you're so hot to cover what's happening in Ukraine, why don't you ask Heather to assign you to stories on Ukraine from here. There's a lot going on, especially with the president's strong support for Ukraine. We're training Ukrainian troops on Patriot Missile systems. We're sending weapons and tanks to Ukraine. American-Ukrainian organizations throughout the country are raising tens of millions of dollars to fund humanitarian projects in Ukraine. There are demonstrations and protest marches. Tens of thousands of Ukrainian refugees are fleeing the war and coming here. There's a lot for you to report and I'm sure you'll do an outstanding job."

I nodded with the spent energy of a defeated boxer. I left the office and headed to Riff's, my favorite Manhattan blues bar and oasis, to brood.

*

As I walked into Mei's apartment that evening, she called out from the kitchen. "Did you watch the speech by Senator Bradford?"

"Yes, and I know you'll get upset, but it's time someone picked up a gun and put a hole in Putin's head."

Mei stomped into the living room. "Then what? Someone else will take his place."

"Hopefully someone else will say enough is enough, wave a white flag, and pull the Russian army out of Ukraine, and I mean all of Ukraine."

Always one to offer tempered, sage advice, Mei said, "Matt, I know you're upset, and you know you can vent to me, but you've got to be careful what you say, especially to your colleagues at the newspaper. Choose your words carefully. Don't go ballistic saying things like Putin should be assassinated."

I lost it. I slammed my hand on the dining room table. "Look at all the death and destruction he's causing in Ukraine. He's made it his personal killing field and you want me to choose my words carefully. He deserves to be put in front of a firing squad."

"Putin will be judged for what he has done."

"By whom? God?"

Mei shrugged. "With any luck, he'll be arrested one day soon and brought to the International Criminal Court in chains and convicted for crimes against humanity."

"And live out the rest of his life in a posh prison cell."

"Matt, I know how much this war is affecting you. You're always tense. You have to find a way not to let this war drag you down," Mei said.

"I want to do something. I want to go to Ukraine to cover the war."

"Matt, I don't want to spend my days and nights waiting for someone to call and tell me you've been killed. I went through that once. I can't go through that again."

"I have to figure things out for myself. I need to find a way to deal with this or I'll go crazy."

"Just don't go and do something stupid. Promise you won't do something stupid," Mei said.

I nodded, but I already had something she would define as stupid percolating in my brain.

PETRA'S QUEST

Petra Petrovich stood in front of the mirror in her washroom and swabbed the inside of her cheek. She put the saliva sample into a tube. Then she carefully inserted the tube into a pre-paid package and mailed it to a "state-of-the-art" lab for analysis. Her objective: to have her DNA placed in a database in the hope of finding a family member.

Stefan Holuk, her protective fiancé, warned her repeatedly not to do it. "The chances of you discovering a living relative are slim at best."

Petra wasn't listening. "We talked about this, Stefan. I need to do this. Ever since my mom died, I don't have anyone. She was a single mother, and she never said a word about having a living relative. I just need to do this."

Stefan wasn't giving up. "It hurts me when you say you don't have anyone. You have me. You have my mom and dad who absolutely love you. And my brother and his wife are crazy about you."

It wasn't enough to dissuade Petra. "I know that. I'm so lucky to be included in your family. I would just like there to be one person somewhere in the world who is connected to me."

That was at the heart of the matter. Petra never got to know her birth father. She had no idea who he was. Her mother told her he died before Petra was born, but she would say nothing more. And that bothered Petra immensely.

Stefan was aware of Petra's mother's steadfast refusal to reveal any details about the father. He sensed there was something dark at play, and that made him anxious about Petra's quest.

"I just want to find out if I have a relative out there somewhere. I have to try," Petra argued.

"What if this relative turns out to be a psycho or a drunk, or a drug addict or a convicted criminal?" Stefan asked.

"Why are you putting such a negative spin on this? I would think you of all people would understand," Petra shot back.

"I do understand. I see how you sometimes retreat into your own private world when you watch my brother and me joking with each other and with our parents. I see the longing and the sadness in your eyes. I just wish you would let yourself go and embrace my family as your own."

"You know I love them with all my heart," Petra said. "It's just that I have this feeling in my soul that there is someone out there. I feel it."

Stefan threw up his arms in defeat. "If nothing comes of your search, you have to stop all this brooding."

Petra shot a chilling glance at Stefan. "I don't brood."

"Sorry. Wrong choice of word."

"And what if I do find someone?" Petra asked.

Stefan bit his lip. He took a deep breath, and this time he chose his words carefully.

"I'd still be worried. I've read about people who've gone onto these DNA sites looking for long lost family members and it's ended in a pile of pain and suffering. I don't want you to be hit with an unpleasant surprise."

"I've read that a lot of searches have had very happy endings. Look, whatever happens will happen. I'm a strong woman. I'll deal with it. I just want your support, not your negative scenarios."

Beaten down, Stefan reluctantly offered his support, even though he didn't mean it.

HEINZ 57

After a sumptuous dinner, Mei and I retreated to the living room with our wine glasses and perched on her designer sofa. Perch was the only thing I could manage. While it cost Mei a small fortune, it was bloody hard and uncomfortable.

Mei took a sip of wine, placed her glass on the coffee table and stared intently into my face. I knew that look. In fact, I hated that look. It usually meant I was in for a Mei day.

With trepidation I asked, "Is something wrong?"

"I need to tell you something."

"Was it something I did?"

"Not you this time. It's what I did."

"Now I'm intrigued," I said.

"You might get upset."

"Did you cheat on me?" I asked, knowing the answer.

"No, you idiot. You know I would never cheat on you."

"Whoa ... You're not pregnant, are you?"

"Oh, and that would rate as something that would upset you?"

"Okay. So, what did you do?"

"Remember when I once asked you about your heritage?"

"Yeah," I said. "I think I said something about Ukrainians carrying a smattering of DNA from all the hordes that invaded the country over the centuries. What about it?"

Mei took another sip of wine. "I did something silly."

I was getting antsy. "Are you going to keep me in suspense or are you going to tell me?"

"I was curious to see what your DNA would reveal, so I sent a sample to a lab that determines an individual's ancestry."

I snapped. "You did what? Mei, that's a serious invasion of my privacy. I don't want, in fact I never want, my DNA out there in some data bank that can be accessed by some hacker or even worse, the government."

"That won't happen," she said, assuredly.

"How do you figure that?"

"I sent it in under a false name. I also set up a login with a protected password and an email address under that name."

That gave me no sense of relief. I had read numerous articles on the potential pitfalls of people sending off their DNA to companies offering to trace their ancestral roots and, as a bonus, possibly hook them up with long-lost relatives. I had all I needed to know about my roots, and I wasn't the least bit interested in finding a relative.

But what bothered me most about these ancestry sites was the huge cybersecurity implications of the genetic make-up of millions of people being stored in databases. These for-profit companies own that data and can sell it, without identifying the donors, to governments and pharmaceutical companies for use in studies and experiments. It's in the fine print.

Then there's the unintended consequence of revealing long-held family secrets, like those of a teenage girl who got pregnant and decided to give up her baby for adoption. Or those of an anonymous, benevolent sperm donor who suddenly has his door knocked on by a dozen of his offspring who want to meet their biological daddy.

I was starting to steam. "How did you get my DNA?" I asked. "I don't recall you ever asking to take a swab of my mouth."

"Matt, are you joking? Your DNA is all over my apartment. On cups, glasses, dishes, cutlery, and most of all on my bed sheets."

"I still can't get my head around you doing this without asking me."

"I wanted to surprise you with the results. But after I sent it in, I realized I shouldn't have done that without first getting your permission."

My mind began spinning about the possible implications. One in particular. I had my share of flings in my university years, and in a few not-so-sober encounters, I didn't wear protection.

"You're sure no one will ever find out it's my DNA?" I asked.

"I'm one hundred percent sure. In the computer vaults of the company that analyzed your DNA, you are Michael Kozak," Mei said.

Despite her assurances of my anonymity, I was still anxious about my genetic information floating around in the data banks of some DNA outfit. But truth be told, I was curious about what the search revealed about Michael Kozak.

"So, what did Kozak's DNA turn up?" I asked.

Mei rushed into her bedroom. A moment later, she returned with the results in her hand. She studied them, and then she announced, "You are most definitely a Heinz 57. You're eighty-two percent Ukrainian, with a smattering of Tatar, Turkish, Romanian, Austrian, Polish, Scandinavian, and even Mongolian DNA swishing through your gorgeous body."

I was fascinated and wanted to know more about the process. "So, how do you go about determining someone's ethnic background through DNA? Do I carry a Ukrainian gene in my chromosomes?"

Mei explained there is no way to tell someone's ethnicity through DNA. What these ancestry companies have done is amass the DNA of hundreds of thousands of people with known deep roots in geographic areas around the world. Because people possess genomic markers inherited from their ancestors, researchers can determine an individual's origins, both maternal and paternal.

I looked at Mei with one concern burning in my brain. "I need to know. Please, please, please tell me I don't have a drop of Russian sludge in my DNA."

"Not a drop."

Despite her apology and her assertion that my DNA was submitted under a pseudonym, I couldn't shake the anxious feeling that it was now stored in some random company computer. I was pissed off, and Mei could see the anger on my face.

GREAT IDEA

That night, I hardly slept. I tossed and turned. No matter how hard I tried to empty my cluttered mind, I couldn't. My angst had nothing to do with my DNA. It was triggered by my work. I kept going over Doyle's unequivocal refusal to let me go to Ukraine to cover the war.

I was also ticked at Heather for refusing to back me. She was my immediate boss, but she was also a good friend. We both joined the newspaper as rookie reporters, but unlike me, Heather was driven, and she had a five-year plan: landing a management position. At year four, she nailed a promotion to Metro assignment editor and with that, she became my immediate boss.

Then she met Mr. Right, an investment analyst on Wall Street. After a whirlwind romance, they tied the knot and moved into a sprawling four-bedroom townhouse in Brooklyn's posh Cobble Hill. They have two beautiful children: a boy and a girl. And in the fifth year of her plan, Heather was ushered into management. I liked working for Heather. She was calm and nurturing, always trying to get the best out of her team.

With Mei fast asleep, I crawled out of bed, tiptoed into the living room, and signed onto my laptop. An idea hit me. It was one I knew would land me in hot water. But then again, it was my life.

The next morning, after a quick breakfast of coffee and a bran muffin, Mei hesitantly approached, gave me a peck on the cheek, and headed off to work. No words were exchanged. I wanted her to stew. I retreated to my apartment to think. The idea was still percolating in my brain.

I pulled out my cell phone and messaged Heather.

"I need to chill. Nothing much going on. I'm going to take two weeks of my vacation time. Hope that's alright."

Always one to react instantly to the ding of her cell phone, she replied. "Great idea. Take the time to relax. See you in two weeks."

*

When Mei got back from work, I sat her down and gave her the news.

"I'm going to Ukraine to cover the war."

The look on her face said it all. She was shocked. "The Trib actually decided to let you go?"

"Not exactly."

"What exactly does not exactly mean?"

"The Trib isn't sending me."

Mei was confused. "Back up a minute. What am I not getting here?"

I cleared my throat. "I decided to take two weeks of my vacation time and go to Ukraine on my own."

"Matt, have you thought this through? I mean seriously thought this through?"

"Yes."

"When did you do that?"

"Last night while you were sleeping."

"And you didn't think to mention it while we were having coffee this morning?" she asked.

"I was kind of still working out the details in my head. Anyway, I was still pissed off about the DNA fiasco, and I thought you'd just shoot me down. I didn't want to hear another voice shooting me down."

"You'd be wrong about that," Mei said.

"About what?"

"That I would shoot you down."

That came as a surprise. I was sure Mei would join the chorus of naysayers.

"Look, Matt. If I had my way, I'd beg you not to go. And take it that I am begging you not to go. But that has everything to do with me. I love you, and I don't want to lose you. Once was bad enough. But this is about you. I've seen how this war has affected you. If you feel you have to do this, then I support you, even if it means you'll leave me in a puddle of tears."

Tears running down her cheeks, Mei put her arms around me. "Just be careful. I don't know what I would do if I lost you."

"I'll be careful. I promise."

Drying her eyes, Mei asked, "What did Heather say when you told her?"

"That's another thing. I haven't told her. She'd just charge into Doyle's office, tell him, and he'd blow a gasket. And I'm sure if Nolan got wind of my plan, he'd find a way to get the Ukrainian government to block my entry into the country. I sent Heather an email saying I'm taking two weeks of my vacation time, which I'm allowed to do, and she okayed it."

"What you're doing could get you fired," Mei warned.

"So, I'll find a job somewhere else. But I don't think Doyle will fire me. Under that gruff exterior, he likes me."

That evening, I parked myself at Mei's desk and scanned airlines landing closest to Ukraine. I booked an evening flight on LOT Airlines to Warsaw for the next day. I figured from there I would hire a driver to take me to the nearest border crossing where I would walk over to the Ukrainian side. Once I cleared customs, I would hitch a ride to Lviv and head for the train station, grabbing the overnight to Kyiv.

My biggest hurdle was finding a fixer: someone who spoke English and could translate for me. Someone who could steer me through the maze of government red tape I was certain I'd encounter. Most importantly, I needed someone who could get me close to the front line. I scanned a dozen Ukrainian websites that publish articles and opinion pieces on the war in English. Not one pontificator stood out. They were all writers without action. My next deep dive was on Twitter, where it didn't take long to find exactly what and who I was looking for.

Marko, whose call sign was "The Leopard" after the famed German main battle tank, was my kind of journalist—a tried and tested war correspondent who risked his life venturing to the front lines to get a story firsthand.

His reporting was riveting and gut-wrenching. He interviewed young recruits heading into battle. He saw the fear in their eyes and felt the bravery of their spirit. He spoke to soldiers in the trenches holding the line against overwhelming odds. He interviewed the wounded: young men and women who had lost their limbs or their eyesight, and he knelt whenever ambulances drove past carrying the bodies of dead warriors and civilians to their final resting place.

I sent Marko a message through Twitter, asking if I could hire him to help me out; I needed him to take me into a war zone, translate for me, and maybe set up an interview with a top military official who could talk about the situation on the ground.

By way of introduction, I suggested he check me out on Google. There were hundreds of news stories on my food aid investigation, and the two deadly attempts on my life.

The following morning, I received a reply. Marko said he was in Kyiv for some much-needed downtime to recoup and regroup after weeks in the embattled Donetsk region in eastern Ukraine. He sent me his cell number and asked me to call him. I grabbed my phone.

"I am very impressed with your investigative stories," he began. "I cannot believe that Russian pig shot you and you were brought back to life. You must be a hero in America."

"So, are you saying you'll help me?" I asked.

"Yes. But you must understand I cannot guarantee to get you to the front. The situation is fluid. It is always changing and can blow up at any moment."

"As long as you try. That's all I ask."

I felt I had made a connection and knew in my gut I had chosen well.

"How long do you intend to be in Ukraine?" Marko asked.

"Unfortunately, my assignment is only for two weeks."

He laughed. "You ask for such a tall order in such a short space of time. I will see what I can do. But I make no promises."

"I'm flying LOT to Warsaw tomorrow and then taking a taxi to the border."

"A tip for when you cross the border," Marko advised. "It will be very busy. The line of cars and trucks can be backed up for several kilometers. I suggest you walk to Ukrainian Customs. Inform the officer you are an American journalist. You should not have a problem getting clearance to enter."

Next, Marko told me about the fleet of private cars in Ukraine that could transport me to Lviv, some ninety minutes away.

"Have the driver take you to the train station. Then buy a ticket for the overnight to Kyiv. Book a sleeper car. No doubt you will be tired after the flight. Call me the minute you get to Kyiv, and I will pick you up at the train station."

"Will do. By the way, how will I recognize you?" I asked.

"Not to worry. I know what you look like from your photos on Google. Have a safe flight."

*

Mei put on a brave face, but I could see she was scared as we stood outside my apartment building waiting for an Uber to take me to JFK International Airport.

"What if your office calls looking for you? What should I tell them?" she asked.

"I doubt they will. As far as Heather is concerned, I've taken two weeks off for R & R."

"Promise me you won't do anything crazy."

"I won't. I'll be careful. I swear."

"You know I love you," she said, hugging me as my ride pulled up.

We kissed.

"And you know I love you," I said.

As I got into the cab, I waved to Mei. She was wiping tears from her eyes.

THE BRIEFING

Marko was thirty-eight but looked ten years older. His long, brown hair was tied in a ponytail, and he sported a drooping Kozak mustache. His eyes were hard and focused. His face was weathered and marked with scars. He wore camouflage army fatigues with a Ukrainian flag patch on the right shoulder of his jacket.

We shook hands, his powerful grip crushing my knuckles. I fought not to wince in pain. When we released, I made a mental note never to shake hands with him again. I'd go in for a bear hug instead.

My first full day on the ground was an in-depth orientation on the first two months of the invasion. Marko knew his stuff. We sat at a café not far from the building of the *Verkhovna Rada*, the Ukrainian parliament, sipping coffee. While we talked, it seemed his phone never stopped buzzing. He'd look at the caller ID and most times would not answer.

Marko asked if he should set up interviews with various government officials. "I have many contacts in the Ministry of Defense and in Foreign Affairs."

"If you don't mind, I leave that kind of stuff to the sheep."

"Sheep?"

"Reporters who follow each other in packs, content with covering press conferences and briefings."

"I know precisely what you mean," Marko said.

"I'm here to get to the front line."

Marko reminded me that was not a given. "What you are hoping for is very difficult and very dangerous. I am working on it. Please, do not be disappointed if it does not happen. You are only here, as you informed me, for twelve days. But every day brings another horror. I am sure we will find something for you to write."

*

I had been in Kyiv for eight days and was feeling edgy and discouraged. I was parked in neutral in my hotel room waiting for Marko's call, but he seemed to have disappeared. I called his phone at least a half-dozen times each day and he never picked up. I got the feeling that maybe he couldn't deliver and was now avoiding me.

That evening, I called Mei. She picked up on the first ring.

"Matt, I've been worried sick about you. You can't just leave and then wait a week to call."

"I'm sorry. I'm just so frustrated, and I was in no mood to talk. Nothing is happening. I mean, I hear the air raid sirens and we all make our way into the depths of the subway stations. I hear missiles slam into buildings. But I can't seem to get out of the city and up to the front lines."

"I hope you're being careful," Mei said.

"I am. Anyway, it looks like I'll be heading back to Warsaw and then home in another few days. The trip's been a colossal dud. The guy who was supposed to help me has vanished. He's not returning my calls or my texts. I think he's ghosted me."

"Did you at least get to talk to some people about the war?"

"Every reporter here has done that story a hundred times over."

"I feel bad for you, but at least you gave it a try."

After I hung up, I sat on the edge of the bed contemplating my next move. I was disillusioned and seriously pissed off at Marko for ignoring my calls. I was done with him. There was nothing to do but check out in the morning and make my way back home.

BIG FOOT

Homicide Captain Detective Ron Spencer was a man who enjoyed seeing his name in newspaper headlines and his mug on TV screens. The walls of his office at Washington, DC, headquarters were adorned with dozens of framed newspaper cuttings featuring the tall, strapping detective arriving or leaving the scene of a gruesome murder or standing at a bank of microphones waxing on about hunting down the killer and bringing him to justice. No stone would be left unturned, he'd intone. He would bring closure to the victim's family because he was a cop on a mission.

The pool of homicide detectives who worked under the captain's dominion weren't the least bit conned by the performance of the man they called Big Foot behind his back—a reference to his habit of "big footing" his way into any investigation that offered even a whiff of media attention. He'd simply pull up at a murder scene in his unmarked GMC Suburban and pull rank. After all, he was the boss. And if the lower dicks didn't like it, there was always traffic detail.

Despite his many local flashes of fame, there was one goal that eluded Spencer, and that was to see himself on national television as lead detective in a high-profile murder case. Over the past decade, all he ever managed to front were gangbanger murders and domestic homicides. But all that was about to change. And big time.

Spencer had no idea of the political storm that was about to unfold. He was sitting in his SUV outside the Dunkin' shop on Massachusetts Avenue sipping his double cream, double sugar coffee and chomping on a cruller when he heard the chatter crackle on his portable police radio. He tossed the wrapper and coffee container into a nearby trash bin, placed a blue flasher on the roof of his vehicle, and sped off, siren wailing. As he pulled up in front of a nondescript, six-story apartment complex, Spencer was greeted by four uniformed police officers. He was escorted down a dimly lit corridor on the first floor and into apartment 119.

Detective Jake Wells looked up and turned to his partner, Detective Alyssa Lamont. "Big Foot has arrived."

"Surprise, surprise," she whispered bitterly.

"So, Captain, what brings you out here on this cold and mournful day?" Wells asked.

"Here to lend a helping hand if needed."

"Nothing we can't handle," Lamont offered.

"What have we got here?" Spencer asked, edging his way past the duo toward the bedroom.

Lying naked on a queen-size bed, eyes bulging wide open in horror, was a young woman who appeared to be in her mid-twenties. She had long, auburn hair and a milk-white complexion.

Spencer approached the victim for a closer look. "From the marks on her neck it's obvious the cause of death was manual strangulation."

"Appears she was also sexually assaulted," Lamont noted.

Spencer nodded. "What else have you found?"

Detective Lamont shook her head. She realized right then that she and Jake would be sidelined or shunted off to another case once they handed their boss the critical piece of evidence they had discovered at the scene.

Gritting his teeth, Wells retrieved a plastic evidence bag from his jacket pocket, opened it, and pulled out a US government-issue employee identification card. He handed it to the captain.

Spencer's eyes popped. "Holy Mother of God! This is going to set off some serious alarm bells."

"Imagine what'll happen when the media gets wind of this," Lamont added with a wry smirk.

"Other than you two, who else knows about this?" Spencer asked.

"Just me and Alyssa," Wells said.

"This has to be kept under wraps until I speak to the chief and we determine how to handle this. Got it?"

"We've got it, Captain," Wells said.

"Where are the CSI guys? I want this apartment sealed tighter than Fort Knox and gone over with a fine-tooth comb. This is big," Spencer said. He could feel his pulse racing.

"They're on their way. Should be here in about five minutes," Wells replied.

There was a light rap on the front door.

"Sir, the medical examiner is here," a police officer announced. "Send him in," Spencer said.

Dr. Raymond Whitmore, a portly man in his early sixties, fit the Hollywood image of a man who cut up bodies for a living. He was bald and dour. His face was pale. He had bags under his eyes and a swollen, reddish-purple nose, the tell-tale sign of a serious boozer.

"What do we have here?" he asked, as he stepped into the bedroom.

"Homicide. Appears the vic was sexually assaulted," Spencer stated.

The ME examined the victim's neck. "Her trachea has been crushed. Based on rigor mortis setting in, I'd say she's been dead anywhere from ten to twelve hours. I'll have a more definitive time of death once I've completed the autopsy."

The ME carefully lifted the bedsheet covering the victim's feet.

"Well, look what we have here," he said.

"Looks like the perp got sloppy," Spencer said. "Or he was just plain stupid. Rule number one: Never leave your fingerprints at a crime scene if you don't want to get caught. In this case, a used condom. That's one hell of a fingerprint to leave behind."

"Most sexual predators are driven by their perverted desires. Leaving behind a spotless crime scene is often not high on their to-do list," Dr. Whitmore said.

"When do you think you can perform the autopsy?" Spencer asked.

"Might get round to it in a couple of days."

The detective winced. "No. This is priority one. I need your findings no later than tomorrow morning."

"Spence, my office is swamped with stiffs. She goes on ice. Anyway, we know the cause of death and the approximate time. Why the hurry?"

Spencer discreetly flashed the woman's government ID pass.

Whitmore nervously cleared his throat. "Whoa. This is going to cause quite the stir. I'll make room on the table."

"Today?"

"This evening. After I've had dinner." Without saying another word, the ME left.

Turning his attention to his homicide team, Spencer asked, "Who called this in?"

"Neighbor across the hall," Wells said, reading from his notebook. "The call came in at eight sixteen a.m. The neighbor was leaving her apartment on her way to work when she noticed the vic's door was ajar. She called out the vic's name. When she got no reply, she pushed the door open, walked in, and found the body."

"Did she see or hear anything?" Spencer asked.

"No idea. She's in no condition to talk," Lamont said.

"She couldn't give you anything? She lives right across the hall."

"Captain, the woman is an emotional wreck," Lamont continued. "She'll be having nightmares for a long time. I called victim services. They sent a grief counselor. She's with her right now."

A police officer waved at Spencer. "CSI just pulled up, sir. And there are a bunch of reporters gathering outside. They want to know if you'll be making a statement."

Spencer's eyes lit up. Lamont and Wells suppressed a knowing smile.

"I'll talk to the reporters in a minute. In the meantime, I want you and the other officers to start canvassing the building. I want to know if anyone saw or heard anything suspicious last evening or early this morning."

"Yes, sir."

Spencer's cell phone chirped. He darted out of the room and returned seconds later.

"When it rains, it pours," he announced. "We've got another homicide at a condo on 11th Street. You two roll on it. I'll handle this one. I'll see you both back at the office."

As Spencer left the apartment, he looked for a security camera and found one on the ceiling in the lobby with its lens aimed at the entrance. He looked around and saw a balding, middle-aged Hispanic man lurking in a nearby alcove, wearing a blue, one-piece coverall. He was holding a damp cloth and a small tin of paint thinner. Up against the wall was a twelve-foot aluminum stepladder.

Approaching the man, Spencer asked, "And you are?"

"The super," he responded nervously.

"The security camera. I presume it records the comings and goings 24/7?"

"Yes. But it is out of order. For two days now."

Spencer clenched his jaw. "And when you noticed it was out of order two days ago, you didn't feel the need to get it repaired immediately so the tenants could remain safe and secure?"

"I was about to fix it this morning when all this happened," he said, pointing to the police officers outside.

"Too bad you didn't do your job two days ago," Spencer said.

The detective shook his head in disgust and headed out to meet the press.

A dozen or so reporters and camera operators were parked beyond the yellow police tape strung across the front lawn of the apartment building.

"Detective, can you tell us what happened here?" a young journalist shouted as Spencer came out the door.

"We have what appears to be a homicide," Spencer replied in his made-for-broadcast tone. "It's early stages in the investigation, so there's not much I can add at this time."

"Anything you can tell us about the victim?"

"Not at this time. We have yet to make a positive ID and inform the next of kin. That's all I have to say. Once I get more information, I will make certain to pass it on."

He headed for his vehicle, the next move weighing heavily on his mind.

THE ESCORT

A uniformed police officer was standing outside an apartment door on the fourth floor of a twelve-storey condo when detectives Lamont and Wells arrived at the second crime scene.

"What have we got here?" Wells asked the officer.

"Woman. Deceased. Lying on the sofa. Fully clothed. Something off about the way she's lying there."

"Anyone other than you enter the apartment?"

"Just me."

"Where's your partner?" Lamont asked.

"Went to the car to get a roll of crime scene tape."

Lamont and Wells entered the apartment.

"Looks like the woman and another person were having a celebration of sorts," Lamont said, pointing to an empty bottle of Moët and two Champagne flutes on a teak coffee table.

The detective bent down to examine the victim. "Bruising on her neck. She's been strangled."

"I'll call the ME and CSI," Wells said. "Why don't you canvass the floor and see if anyone heard or saw anything suspicious?"

"Will do," Lamont said, pulling a notebook from the inside pocket of her burgundy blazer.

"Who called this in?" she asked the uniform.

"Guy across the hall. Said he went out to drop some trash down the garbage chute, and when he was heading back, he noticed the door wasn't shut. He pushed it open and saw the woman lying on the sofa. He called out her name several times and when she didn't answer, he figured something was wrong and called 911."

The elevator dinged, the door opened, and Dr. Whitmore stepped into the corridor.

"Two in one day," he grumbled.

It took only a moment for the medical examiner to determine the cause of death.

"Strangulation. Her trachea is completely crushed. Dead approximately twelve, maybe fourteen, hours. I'll know more when I perform the post-mortem."

Detective Wells walked over to the bedroom.

"The bed's unmade," he said, entering the room.

On the dresser was an open purse. The detective put on a pair of latex gloves, retrieved the wallet, and pulled out a driver's licence.

"Janet Walker. Age twenty-four. She's a real looker. One thousand dollars in crisp, one-hundred-dollar bills in her purse. At least we know robbery wasn't the motive."

"From the violent manner in which she was killed, I would tend to agree," Dr. Whitmore noted. "This was personal and deliberate."

Lamont rushed into the apartment. "You won't believe this. I talked to a couple of tenants on the floor. The woman was a high-end escort. She had a lot of well-heeled male visitors."

"That explains the grand in her wallet," Wells said.

"And there's more. Did you notice the security camera when we rode up the elevator?" Lamont asked.

"Yeah. I hope the thing is operational. I'm fed up with all these places that have security cameras that are either non-functional or dummies just for show."

"I talked to the super. He said it's functional. He's getting me copies of all the comings and goings over the past week," Lamont said.

"That oughta keep you busy," Wells said with a laugh.

"And what are you going to be doing?"

"Finding out if she worked for an escort service or a pimp, or if she was freelance. And if she had a client list. You know, basic detective stuff. Did you get to everyone on this floor?"

"No. I have a few more. I got distracted by the superintendent."

"I'll finish up," Wells said.

His first stop was apartment 412. He knocked on the door and waited a full minute. He knocked louder and shouted, "DC police! Detective Jake Wells."

There was no response. Assuming no one was home, he took out his business card, wrote a note asking the occupant to call him, and slipped it under the door.

THE ROAD OF DEATH

At 5:10 a.m. my cell phone rang, waking me from a restless sleep. It was Marko. I could tell from his voice he was extremely tense and excited.

"Meet me outside the hotel in twenty minutes. I will be in a jeep. I have a flak jacket and a combat helmet for you. We are on our way to Bucha."

I had no idea where Bucha was or what was happening there. But from an incredible low, I was suddenly riding high on a rush of adrenaline. I raced through the lobby and jumped into the back of the military jeep flying the Ukrainian flag from a tall radio antenna.

"What's happening?" I asked, as I pulled on the flak jacket.

"Our heroes have driven the Russians out of Bucha. The orcs have retreated," he explained in a hushed whisper. "My friend, we will be the first journalists to enter the city. I must warn you. I am told the situation in Bucha is one of great horror and destruction. You must be prepared for what you will witness. You have your cell phone with you?"

"Yes, right here," I said, pulling it from my jacket pocket.

"Fully charged?"

"Yes."

"There will be many photographs and videos to take."

I was nervous, but it was a good nervous.

"Tell me about Bucha. Where is it? What's going on there?"

As we drove to the city eighteen miles northwest of Kyiv, Marko explained that the Russian forces had captured Bucha after ferocious fighting a few days after the invasion began on February 24.

"This was Putin's road to Kyiv. It is where our heroes stopped the Russian advance in its tracks. And yesterday evening, the orcs were suddenly ordered to pull back," Marko said.

*

It was a cold, damp morning. The sky was a heavy, ominous gray as we lurched into the outskirts of Bucha behind a winding convoy of armored personnel carriers flying Ukrainian flags. The column came to a grinding standstill as the commanding officer stepped out onto the road and surveyed the area through a pair of powerful binoculars. A few minutes later, he gave the order and scores of soldiers, with their Ukrainian-made M4-WAC-47 assault rifles primed, leapt out of the trucks. With precision, they weaved their way into the city, eyes peeled for Russian snipers and booby traps.

As the soldiers wound their way deeper into the city, shell-shocked residents slowly emerged from their basements and bomb shelters. There was no celebration or flag waving, just fear and desperation on their haggard faces.

Marko and I hung back to wait for the all clear. It came ninety minutes later. We started walking down Yablunska Street, the main road into the center of the city. The over-powering stench of death hung in the air.

This once quiet, tree-lined suburb was a shattered mess. The roads were filled with craters and the outside wall of virtually every building was riddled with bullet holes and shards of shrapnel. But most shocking of all, Yablunska Street was strewn with the bodies of dozens of civilians—men, women, and children. They lay where they died, shot by Russian soldiers, their corpses left in the open for more than a month. No one had dared venture out to claim them for a proper funeral and burial.

I reeled at the sight of a man lying face down in the street beside his bicycle, a bag of rotting potatoes by his side. He had been shot in the back. I watched in tense silence as a soldier prodded the man's body with a stick to check for an explosive device placed under him by the retreating Russians.

Nearby, several cars raked by bullets littered the street. I walked over to one, its windshield shattered. I froze at the horror inside. A woman, turned and facing the back seats, was dead. She was shot in the back while trying to shield her children from gunfire. A baby girl dressed in a pink snowsuit and a toddler wearing a blue parka were slumped over, still strapped in their car seats. They had been attempting to flee to safety.

I couldn't move. My hands started to shake uncontrollably. My heart was pounding in my chest, and I couldn't catch my breath. Tears began streaming down my face.

Marko put his arm around my shoulder. "Take deep breaths. Breathe in and out slowly."

Wiping my tears on my sleeve, I felt a wave of incredible sadness surge through my body. "Why would anyone do this? I don't … I can't understand this."

"The Russians are here to kill us. All of us. I am sorry to say we will see much more of this murder by the Russian military. If you wish, we can return to the Jeep and go back to Kyiv."

"No. It's important I document this."

"Then we must keep moving."

But I couldn't move. My feet felt like they were welded to the asphalt.

Marko grabbed my arm and pulled me away. "We have to go."

And we did, straight into one horrifying nightmare after another.

In front of 144 Yablunska, a sprawling, four-story office complex the invaders used as their headquarters, the bloated bodies of thirty-two men, many with their hands tied behind their backs, lay scattered along the street. They had been executed, many with a single bullet to the back of the head.

The sight shook me to my core. I stared at the corpses, unable to fathom the human slaughter I was witnessing.

"Are you okay?" Marko asked.

I didn't answer. I was in shock. I couldn't control my breathing.

Marko grabbed me by the arms and shook me. "You must snap out of it. I know this is difficult. It is difficult for all of us. But you must focus."

"I can't believe this. I can't understand this," I said.

"None of us can. But this is war. This is what Putin has ordered. It is what he wants. He wants to terrorize the people of Ukraine into submission."

"Women and children murdered? Innocent men …? What did these poor souls do to deserve this?" I asked.

"They were born Ukrainian. Putin hates Ukrainians. He wants to erase Ukraine and to succeed he kills Ukrainians. That is his objective," Marko explained. "Take out your cell phone and photograph the war crimes that have been committed by Putin and his army. Take videos of the brutality of Putin's killers and show them to the people of the United States."

I took dozens of photos. I wasn't interested in framing. I kept clicking. I switched to video mode and did a slow pan of the bodies.

A Ukrainian soldier standing guard at the entrance to 144 Yablunska waved us over.

"This was the headquarters, the command center of the Russian soldiers in Bucha," he told Marko. "It is here that hundreds of people from the city were brought for filtration. They were interrogated, tortured, and in many cases executed. There are bodies in the basement. All bear the marks of torture before they were shot."

Marko made his way to the stairwell. He stopped and turned to me.

"Are you coming?" he asked.

"I can't," I said. My feet wouldn't let me move. I was feeling nauseous from the smell of death.

When Marko returned, his face was pale. He was shaking. "There are more than a dozen bodies of women, men, and some children. They have been brutally tortured. Many are unrecognizable. Their faces have been beaten to a pulp. Some had their ears cut off," he said, his voice breaking.

When we stepped back outside, we ran into one of the Ukrainian army commanders. His head was shaved. He had the build of a tank. There was no fear in his dark eyes, just the scowl of intense hatred for the enemy.

"This is Bohdan. You are not to use his name," Marko instructed. "I will translate."

I nodded.

"What has happened in Bucha is genocide," the commander said. "One old man who lives across from this place told me he heard Russian soldiers talking about *zachistka*."

"What is that?" I asked.

"Cleansing. The victims lying dead on Yablunska did not die in the cross-fire between Russian and Ukrainian forces. They are the intentional victims of the systematic targeting of Ukrainians for extermination."

The commander continued. "On this day, we have found forty bodies along Yablunska alone, and from what I have been able to determine in my talks with local people, Russian forces murdered more than four hundred and fifty civilians in and around Bucha. We are sure to find many, many more bodies in the coming hours."

The commander stared at the bodies lying on the pavement. He closed his eyes as if in a moment of prayer. "We will never forgive what has happened here," he vowed. "We will hunt down and punish everyone involved in this massacre."

Marko and I headed down a side street and reeled at the sight of nine men lying dead in the courtyard behind 144 Yablunska. Their tee-shirts and sweaters were pulled over their heads. All had been shot. Most had their hands tied behind their back.

As we passed another building, we stumbled across the body of a young man near a dumpster, a tablecloth covering his head. A woman who was searching for a relative walked over to the body and lifted the cloth. She closed her eyes, crossed herself, and whispered a prayer.

Marko asked if she knew the man.

"He is Dima. Dmytro Chaplyhin. He was a store clerk. A good man. His grandmother has not seen him since he was taken away from her home a month ago. Her heart will break when she learns of his fate."

A little farther into the area, we came across a woman kneeling on a mud-filled grave topped with a crude wooden cross in her front yard. She was weeping. Her name was Natalia Vlasenko.

Marko offered his condolences and asked who was buried in the yard.

"My husband. He went out to find food and was shot by a sniper. For a month, he lay dead in my yard. I could not go out to bury him. After the Russians left last night, I dug the grave myself and buried him," the woman recounted.

"My fear now is what has happened to my grandson, Dima. On March 4, the soldiers came to my house and demanded Dima hand over his cell phone. They found photos of Russian tanks on it and took him away. I fell to my knees and begged the soldiers not to hurt him. Dima told me not to worry. He would be back. He never came back. I have asked people to look for him."

Marko and I looked at each other and said nothing.

"I will inform the commander about the identity of the body, and ask that he inform the woman," Marko said as we continued deeper into the city.

As we passed a cottage, a matronly woman who was cleaning debris from her front yard called out to us. In her hand she was holding a half-dozen small metal darts she had raked up from her front yard.

"What are they?" I asked Marko.

"Fléchettes," he said. "They are packed into artillery shells and when they explode, the darts burst out in a conical pattern covering an area the size of three football fields."

The woman pointed to the outside wall of her house and to vehicles parked on the street. They were pockmarked by hundreds of fléchettes. She told us a dozen people were out for a walk when a shell detonated. They were all killed when the darts slammed into their heads and chests.

"They are buried in the cemetery," she said, adding that many more victims were seriously wounded by the deadly darts.

For several hours, we walked through the city talking to locals, listening to gut-wrenching accounts of torture and summary executions and the rape of women and girls by Russian soldiers. The locals recounted how gangs of soldiers raided their homes and stole whatever they could get their hands on: jewelry, electronics, appliances, food, liquor, and even toilets.

As we approached a church yard, we noticed a massive, mud-covered mound in a far corner of the cemetery. The local priest came out to greet us.

"There are about seventy bodies here," the priest said, pointing to the mound. "The Russian soldiers dug a large pit and dumped the bodies like they are garbage. There was no funeral. Nothing. There are many pits like this throughout Bucha."

At the far end of town, a middle-aged woman was staring at a sprawling one-story brick building that looked like a school. A boy who appeared to be about thirteen years old and a girl who was around ten stood beside her holding hands.

The woman identified herself as Maria. The place, she explained, was an *internat*, an institution for orphaned children. She was the director.

"I had sixty-four children under my care," Maria recounted, her voice trembling as Marko translated. "Several days ago, a Russian commander with four soldiers arrived in a bus and took the children. In the confusion, Danylo and Yulia managed to escape from the back door."

Maria continued. "One of the caretakers who worked for me begged them not to take the children. The commander told her the children will be safe in Russia, that they will be adopted by Russian families. It is a lie."

"What will happen to them?" I asked.

Maria pulled Marko and me away from the children and whispered, "My fear is the boys will be sent to farms to be used as slaves. The girls will suffer a much worse fate. They will be groomed for the sex trade. Many will be trafficked to Moscow and abroad," she said, desperation etched on her face. "I have to find a way to rescue the children."

We went inside the building. Both the girls' and boys' dormitories looked like a mini tornado had blown through. The beds and bureaus were overturned. The floors were littered with stuffed animals, running shoes, sandals, slippers, and piles of clothing.

"The Russian soldiers kept yelling at us to take only what we are wearing and a jacket. They said they were taking us to safety because when the Ukrainian soldiers come, they will torture us," Danylo recounted, as Marko translated.

"Did you believe that?" I asked.

Danylo looked at me defiantly. "No. I am Ukrainian. I am proud to be Ukrainian, *Slava Ukraini!*"

Maria, Yulia, and Marko responded, "*Heroyam Slava!*"

Maria led us up into her office. It had been ransacked. The computer was gone, as was the phone, the television, and the radio. Files were scattered on the floor.

On the wall was a framed color photograph of the children.

Maria began to weep. "It was taken at Christmas. Look at their beautiful, smiling faces. They are my children. My heart breaks every day since they were taken away."

Marko and I had been in Bucha for only six hours, but my mind was starting to shut down. All the death, all the suffering, and the sadness tore at my soul. I thought about the children who were abducted and could only imagine their fear. I wondered if they would ever find their way home or if they would ever be rescued.

Marko took one look at my face and suggested it was time to head back to Kyiv. We didn't say a word during the two-hour drive. It was 4:35 p.m. when we pulled up outside my hotel.

"We will speak tomorrow. I cannot say have a good night. It will surely not be possible," Marko said. "I will leave you to write your story."

*

I went straight to my room, pulled out my laptop, and started typing like a madman on fire. The main story detailed the horrors of Bucha—a bloody, macabre trail of mass murder. My mind was racing. I wrote about the bloated bodies left to rot on Yablunska Street. About men dragged from their homes, hands tied behind their backs, shirts pulled over their heads, forced to kneel and shot at point-blank range in the back of the head.

I wrote about the distraught wife who stood vigil over her murdered husband after she buried him in their front yard.

I wrote about a man who was shot by a Russian sniper positioned high up on a construction crane. The victim was on his bicycle heading home with a bag of potatoes.

I wrote about sixty-eight-year-old Volodymyr Borovchenko, who was walking along Yablunska on his way to a home for special-needs children where he worked. He was shot by a Russian sniper perched on the roof of a nine-story building.

I wrote about the bodies of a young mother and her two children still in their bullet-riddled car; and seeing the body of a naked woman who had been gang-raped by Russian soldiers, left to rot on the side of the road.

I wrote about the torture chambers in the basements of buildings along Yablunska Street, and the rivers of tears shed by those whose family members and neighbors were shot by Russian soldiers for no reason other than they were Ukrainian.

I ended with the solemn visit to the huge, muddy mound in a corner of the church yard.

My second story, a sidebar, dealt with the fléchettes, the small dart-like, lethal projectiles packed in tank and artillery shells. I wrote another sidebar about the children stolen from the orphanage.

It was 9:45 p.m. when I finished writing. Bleary-eyed, I reread the stories twice. Then I scanned the dozens of photographs I had taken and selected eight. I edited my video footage into two thirty-second clips for the Trib's online page.

On my Gmail site, I typed Heather's *Tribune* email address, wrote "Bucha Massacre" in the subject slot, and composed a short message.

"Got into Bucha with the Ukrainian soldiers early this morning after the retreat of Russian troops last night. Main story and two sidebars, eight photos, and two video clips attached. I am the first foreign journalist to enter the town with the Ukrainian military."

I checked my watch. It was now 11:20 p.m., making it 4:20 p.m. in New York, more than enough time for my stories to make the morning paper. My hands were shaking as I pressed send. I knew what was about to hit the fan.

NEWSROOM MAYHEM

Exactly fourteen minutes later, my phone rang. The caller ID showed it was Heather. I didn't answer. She left a voice message. I could tell she was in freak-out mode.

"Matt, call me now. I can't believe you went to Ukraine against Mr. Doyle's orders. You don't know the trouble you're in. Call me."

The message ticked me right off. She didn't mention my stories, and it was obvious to me she hadn't bothered to read them. She was just angry that I had gone to Ukraine. I didn't call her back.

Twenty-three minutes later, Mei called.

"Matt, Heather called me. She's going crazy. She wants to know if you really are in Ukraine. I told her you left ten days ago. She told me to tell you to call her ASAP."

I could feel my ears steaming. I had written about a horrific massacre in Bucha and Heather was preoccupied with my presence in Ukraine.

"Call her back and tell her to read the damn stories. Tell her I'll call in an hour. That should give her and Doyle enough time to go through my stuff and decide whether to run it."

Mei was quiet, sensing something was wrong. "Matt, are you okay? Your voice sounds strange."

The gentleness of her voice brought me back to reality.

"I'm not okay. I mean, I'm not hurt or anything like that. I'm just seriously messed up. I've just come back from a town where hundreds of women and children and men have been massacred. There were so many bodies lying in the streets. I'm trying to keep myself from completely losing it. I can't believe what I've witnessed. I can't believe the depth of this inhumanity."

My voice was starting to break. I was forcing myself not to cry, and I was completely exhausted.

"Matt, you need to keep it together. I know it's going to be hard trying to keep the images from entering your thoughts and your dreams. You have to stay strong."

But the images of the victims kept swirling through my mind. It was like a horror movie.

"I can't believe this. I'm sitting on my bed, and all of a sudden, I start thinking about my father. The things he must have seen fighting in Vietnam. I'm sure that's what messed him up."

I broke down and started to cry. Mei heard my sobs.

"Matt, please come home. You need to come home," she pleaded.

I couldn't speak. I hung up on her and raided the liquor bar in my room.

*

Heather walked into Doyle's office looking totally frazzled.

Seeing her face, Doyle asked: "Something wrong?"

"I'm going to send you a news pack I received from one of our reporters. Please go through it. I'll be back in a few minutes. I need to clear my head."

Heather hit forward on her email and left the office. She wasn't four steps down the corridor when she heard Doyle yell, "What in hell is that little SOB doing in Ukraine?"

She kept walking, making a beeline to the safety of the women's washroom. Locked in a cubicle, she pulled out her phone.

"Mei, did you manage to get in touch with Matt? I really need to speak with him."

"I did."

"What did he say?"

"He'll call you in an hour after you've had time to read his stories."

*

It took me a little longer to pull myself together. I called the newsroom ninety minutes later and didn't even get a chance to say hello.

"What are you doing in Ukraine?" Heather yelled into the phone.

"In case you might be worried, I'm fine," I said. My tone was curt.

"What are you doing in Ukraine?"

"Have you read my stories?"

"Yes. Now answer my question."

"I came here on vacation and walked into a massacre. I figured I'd write it up and send it in."

Heather wasn't buying it. "Cut the bullshit, Matt! You deliberately disobeyed Doyle."

I stood by my claim. "I did no such thing. I took two weeks off and decided to go to Ukraine. There is no law against that. And I just happened to land on a huge story. So, rather than attacking me for being here, I'd think your focus should be on the story. The question for me is whether the Trib will print it."

Heather was quiet for a moment. Perhaps my words finally resonated.

"I don't know. Doyle's in his office right now reading your report," she said.

"Has your buddy Nolan seen them?"

"First, he's not my buddy, and second, there's absolutely no doubt in my mind that he's going to blow his top once this hits his desk," Heather shot back. "Don't go anywhere. I'm getting a call from Doyle."

Not ten seconds later, Heather was back. "He wants me to conference him in."

Patrick Doyle didn't give me a chance to utter a word.

"Matt, you conniving, little snake. I told you we would not send you to Ukraine," Doyle shouted. "When you get back, I want to see you in my office first thing. You understand me?"

"With all respect, sir, you didn't send me. I took two weeks of my vacation time. I flew here on a ticket I bought with my own money. And I happened to be in the right place at the right time and was offered a ride to Bucha. What I want to know is are you going to run my article?"

"You know we're going to run it."

"On front?"

Doyle hung up.

I could almost hear Heather's anxiety level zap into the stratosphere. "Oh, crap," she cursed. "I just saw Nolan storm into Doyle's office. He looks like he's about to have a coronary."

"He's probably hoping I get shot."

"Don't joke. The mood he's in, I'd bet if he had a gun he'd shoot you himself."

"Screw him." I hung up and collapsed onto my bed.

*

"I want Kozar fired," Nolan demanded. "I want that prick out of here."

"On what grounds?" Doyle asked calmly.

"He deliberately ignored my decision he not be sent to Ukraine. He disobeyed me and he disobeyed you. That's grounds for immediate dismissal."

"Matt went to Ukraine on his own dime and on his own time," Doyle pointed out.

"I don't care. He is not going to make a fool out of me."

"I don't think that was his intention."

"Yes, it was. And what am I supposed to tell Tim Knox? He's our correspondent in Ukraine. If this runs in the Trib, it's going to be a huge embarrassment for him, especially in front of his colleagues here and in Ukraine."

"Tell him Matt went to Ukraine on his own and filed a story."

"We should refuse to run his stories," the foreign editor said.

"That is not going to happen," Doyle countered.

"Why not?"

"Philip, have you bothered to read what Matt wrote?"

"I wouldn't waste my time."

"I suggest you go back to your office, cool down, and read the articles. Then come back in here and tell me what I should do with them," Doyle said in a firm voice.

Nolan almost rammed Heather into a wall as he charged past her.

She rapped on Doyle's door and entered.

"I'm sorry about all this," Heather began.

"About all what? The fact that you can't manage a hothead?"

"You know he marches to a different drummer."

"I've gone through this," Doyle said, pointing to his computer screen. "It's outstanding, top-notch reporting."

"I know. Have you seen the photos? All those poor people lying dead in the streets. It's all so evil. And the woman shot in her car while trying to protect her babies. I started to cry."

"The photos are too graphic," Doyle said. "We have to be careful choosing the ones we use. But at the same time, we can't turn away from the horrors of war and the heinous war crimes committed by these invaders."

Nolan knocked on the door.

"Have you read Kozar's stories?" Doyle asked.

"Yes."

"And?"

"We have to run them on front."

"Good decision. I'll let you take it from here. And Philip, one other thing. I want Matt Kozar to be identified as a war correspondent. Run a thumb-size photo of him beside his byline."

Nolan nodded and left without saying another word.

"I guess that seals Matt's fate with Nolan," Heather said.

"When Matt gets back, I'm going to seal his fate. No one sidesteps me. I'm not buying this vacation crap. What he did was deliberate."

"About that."

"What now?"

"I got a text from Matt. He says he wants to stay in Kyiv to get President Zelenskyy's reaction to the massacre in Bucha," Heather said.

"That's not going to happen. Get him on the phone," Doyle said.

*

It was 1:55 a.m. when the incessant beeping of my phone woke me up. Caller ID indicated it was Patrick Doyle. I figured he wanted to check a fact or two on my stories. I answered.

Doyle was direct. "When are you flying back?"

"I figured I'd stick around to cover Zelenskyy's press conference. It's scheduled for eleven tomorrow morning."

"No need. You can head back home."

"You don't want me to cover Zelenskyy's reaction on the Bucha massacre?"

"Tim Knox will be covering the press conference. He's the *Tribune*'s correspondent in Ukraine. In fact, he's on his way to Kyiv from Lviv," Doyle said.

I could feel my stress level rising. Doyle was punishing me.

"It's my story," I argued.

"No. Your story is on front. You know—the one you just happened on while on vacation in Ukraine. The Zelenskyy press conference falls under the foreign desk and Knox will be covering it."

I didn't respond. I figured if I did, I'd be fired.

"Matt, are you still there?" Doyle asked.

"Yes."

"Do not forget, I want to see you in my office the moment you get back from your vacation."

The line went dead.

I felt like smashing my cell phone against the wall. I knew exactly what Doyle was doing and I was bloody certain Nolan was behind it. My nerves were fried. I couldn't get back to sleep. I stared at the ceiling cursing Nolan under my breath and wondering what Doyle had in store for me.

THE AUTOPSY

Detective Spencer walked into the medical examiner's lab, the overpowering scent of corpses and formaldehyde knocking him a step backward. No matter how many times he'd entered the place, he could never adjust to the smell. He covered his mouth and nose with a handkerchief and approached the table. It was a little after 8 p.m. Dr. Whitmore had just completed his examination of the murder victim and was in the process of stitching her together.

The detective glanced at the young woman's face and shook his head. "I'm not going to rest until I get my hands on the bastard who did this," he swore.

Whitmore looked up and nodded.

"What did you find?" Spencer asked.

"As I suspected when I first saw her, death by asphyxiation. Her larynx was manually crushed."

"It appeared she may have been sexually assaulted, given the used condom on her bedside and what looked like semen on her abdomen," the detective added.

The medical examiner paused, a look of consternation on his face. "There's something odd about that. The victim was never penetrated. There are no signs of vaginal penetration."

Spencer didn't miss a beat. "I guess the killer got over-excited and ejaculated before he could complete the deed. In anger, he strangled her, removed his condom, and smeared her body with his semen."

The medical examiner shrugged. "I guess that's one way of looking at it."

"Time of death?"

"Sometime between midnight and two in the morning."

"When can I expect your report?"

"On your desk no later than noon tomorrow."

DNA SWABS

Senator Bradford arrived at his office to find Detective Spencer and a female police officer in uniform waiting in the reception area. The detective flashed his credentials.

"What is this about?" the senator asked.

"Sir, can we speak to you privately?" Spencer asked.

Bradford led them into his office.

"Now, Detective, what is this about?" Bradford repeated.

"Do you know Gail Peterson?"

"Yes. She's one of my political interns. Is something wrong? Would you like me to call her in here?"

"When was the last time you saw her?" Spencer continued.

"Yesterday afternoon. I thanked her for proofreading a speech I'm delivering later this week."

"Did you speak to her last evening?"

The senator was starting to get agitated. "No. Again, what is this all about, Detective?"

"No contact whatsoever?"

"What is this about? Has something happened to her?"

"Senator, I regret to inform you that Gail Peterson was found earlier this morning in her apartment. She was murdered," Spencer said.

"Murdered? No," Bradford said, slumping in his chair. "Who would do this to Gail? She's such a wonderful young woman. Everyone here thinks the world of her."

Keeping his eyes rivetted on the senator, Spencer did not respond.

"Do you have any idea who did this?" Bradford asked.

"We're working on a couple of leads. That's all I can say right now."

"I understand."

"Senator, I hope you don't take this the wrong way, but I have to ask. Where were you yesterday evening, particularly between the hours of nine and two a.m.?"

Spencer kept his eyes fixed on the senator for the slightest reaction, and he caught it: a hard, nervous swallow.

"I was at home," Bradford said.

"Can anyone verify this?"

"No. I was alone."

Spencer jotted down the senator's response in his notebook.

"I also need to ask if you would be willing to submit to a DNA test."

"Detective, am I a suspect?"

"No. What I need to do is eliminate you as a possible suspect. It's standard procedure in cases like this," the detective explained.

"I see no problem with that."

"Another question. How many males work for you in this office?"

"Four."

"I'd like to speak to each of them. I'll also ask them to provide a DNA sample."

"What I'm getting from this is that Gail may have been the victim of a sexual assault."

"Why would you say that?" the detective asked, his radar flashing amber.

"Why else would you ask the men on my staff to give a DNA sample?"

"I'm not at liberty to discuss the circumstances surrounding Ms. Peterson's death. It's still very early in my investigation, and I'm waiting for the coroner's autopsy report."

"Of course."

The officer accompanying the detective removed a DNA test kit from her brief case and swabbed the senator's mouth.

Bradford then buzzed his receptionist on the intercom and asked her to gather the entire staff in the boardroom.

As the grim-faced senator and the detective entered, the room fell silent.

Bradford cleared his throat and began in a solemn tone. "I have tragic news. Gail Peterson has been murdered. She was found in her apartment this morning."

A female staff member gasped and began sobbing. The four male staffers stood frozen, shock registering on their faces.

"Detective Spencer is a homicide investigator with the DC police. He wants to speak to each one of you individually. After which, if anyone wishes to take the rest of the day off to deal with this, please do," the senator said.

Spencer turned to the women on Bradford's staff. "You two are excused."

The women stared, bewildered.

"Detective, I have to get back to my office. Please stop by before you leave," the senator said as he left the boardroom.

Spencer looked at each man in the room, studying them for clues, and it had its desired effect. The men began shifting nervously.

"I would like to ask each of you to allow the officer to take a DNA swab from the back of your mouth. It's standard procedure in a case like this," he began.

With hands in his pockets, Jamal Hudson, the senator's chief political analyst, asked, "Why do you need to take DNA?"

"As I said, it's pretty much standard. It's to rule out each of you as a potential suspect."

"I'm not going to submit to a DNA swab," Hudson said flatly.

"Can I ask why?" Spencer asked, eyeing the young Black man with suspicion.

"I don't want to. I don't have to. You want my DNA, get a warrant."

"I can do that."

"Not without probable cause." Hudson pointed out.

"Can I ask where you were last night between six and midnight?"

"You can ask but I'm not answering any of your questions without my lawyer present."

"Well, maybe I could make your day by bringing you in and questioning you at the station."

Hudson glared defiantly at the detective. "That sounds a lot like coercion with the heavy hand of racial profiling,"

"And you sound a lot like someone who has something to hide," Spencer countered.

"Actually, I don't. I simply don't trust cops. If you bring me in simply because I won't submit to a DNA test or answer any of your questions because I don't want to without a lawyer present, then I'll immediately file a harassment complaint against you and your department. I don't need any of your strong-arm detective intimidation."

Spencer tried to stare down Jamal. It didn't work. The staffer stood his ground.

The other three men, all white, offered up their saliva without hesitation and provided alibis for the previous evening.

When Spencer returned to the senator's office, Bradford was sitting quietly at his desk. He looked shaken and sad.

"I hope everyone was cooperative, Detective." he said in a subdued voice.

"All but one. Tell me about this Jamal Hudson character," Spencer said.

"Good man. Lots of positive energy. Wants to get things done. I see him being elected to Congress one day."

"Did he have an interest or a special relationship with Ms. Peterson?"

"Not that I'm aware of. Why do you ask?"

"For a guy who you say has lots of positive energy, he sure showed a lot of negative attitude when I asked if he would take the DNA test. He refused, and he also refused to say where he was last night without his lawyer present."

"Well, that is his right, Detective. But I can vouch for Jamal. He is an upstanding young man. There is no way he would ever hurt Gail."

"Upstanding citizens don't refuse to cooperate with police investigating a violent homicide."

"Detective, Jamal's refusal to cooperate is rooted in his deep distrust of police. Given what African Americans have suffered at the hands of law enforcement across this country, I can't say I blame him."

Bradford's executive assistant tiptoed into the office.

"Sir, your meeting with the president is in twenty minutes. Your car is waiting outside."

"Detective, I have an important engagement to get to. I would appreciate you keeping me abreast of any developments in your investigation."

"I'll do that, Senator."

"One other thing. Have Gail's parents been informed?"

"Yes, I spoke to them by phone this morning. We made certain a grief counselor was at their home in Montclair, New Jersey. They identified the body via video link. Understandably, they were devastated. Mr. Peterson fainted."

"It's a terrible tragedy. I'll phone Gail's parents from my car. I hope you catch the person who did this."

"I will. Mark my words, Senator, I'll catch the person who did this," Spencer swore. "You have my word on that."

On their way out of the building, the uniformed officer, who had not said a word the entire time she was in the office, turned to the detective. "That Jamal character is one piece of work. Got some serious attitude issues."

"You got that right, and he just made himself my prime suspect. By the time I get through investigating him, he'll need a lawyer," Spencer said.

"Are you going to get a warrant?" she asked.

"Won't need a warrant. I'll put a plainclothes officer on him. At some point he'll spit out his gum on the street or toss a paper coffee cup in the trash or blow his nose into a tissue. We'll pick it up and bingo, we'll have his DNA. Then we've got that smug, little punk."

TONE IT DOWN

"Bill, great to see you," the president said as Bradford entered the Oval Office.

"Right back at you, sir."

The two men shook hands warmly.

"Terrible news about your intern being murdered," the president said.

"News travels fast," Bradford noted.

"I'm the president, Bill. I hear everything that happens in DC. And as the president, I have to ask you. Is there anything for me to be concerned about?"

"What do you mean?"

"Did the woman have anything going with someone at your office?"

"Not that I'm aware of. But you can rest assured no one on my staff would ever hurt her. They all thought the world of Gail," Bradford said.

"Has her family been informed?" the president asked.

"I called Gail's parents from the car on the way over. Understandably, they're shattered. She was their only child."

"Better be prepared for the vultures. They're going to descend like flies on shit," the president warned.

"My press secretary is preparing a news release as we speak. Beyond that, I am not holding a press conference. I don't want this to become a circus," Bradford said.

The reason I asked to see you is to urge you to tone down your attacks on President Putin. We've received a formal complaint from the Russian ambassador."

"Then I'm doing precisely what I set out to do. Putin is a murderer and a war criminal. He's committing genocide against Ukraine."

"I get all that, Bill. Just do me this one favor. Tone down the rhetoric," the president demanded.

"With all due respect, Mr. President, I don't bend over for war criminals and terrorists."

"I'm not asking you to shut it down. Just tone it down."

"How many more innocent people does that psychopath have to murder before someone has the balls to do something? Did you read what his soldiers did in Bucha?"

"Yes, and I called in the Russian ambassador and denounced the Russian military."

"What happened in Bucha is a war crime. It's genocide."

The president was getting frustrated with his rogue senator. The tension was heavily creased on his face. He took a deep breath.

"One other thing, Bill. I didn't appreciate the shot you took at my expense about not expelling the ambassador and shutting down the Russian embassy, and especially about not declaring Russia a state sponsor of terrorism. Need I remind you we're on the same team?"

Bradford gritted his teeth and kept his mouth clamped shut.

"Nice seeing you," the president said curtly.

With those three words, the meeting was over.

*

As the senator's limo pulled up to the Dirksen Senate Office Building, he noticed a large pack of journalists camped outside the main entrance. For a moment, he wondered why they were there. That was until he exited the vehicle.

"Vultures," he muttered under his breath as they charged with microphones and cameras zooming in on his face.

A CNN reporter fired off the first question. "Senator Bradford, could you comment on the murder of your intern, Gail Peterson?"

The senator closed his eyes, gathering his thoughts.

"I was informed this morning that Gail had been murdered. I was devastated, as was my entire staff. Gail was an amazing young woman with so many dreams. It's all so senseless."

"In your conversation with the homicide detective, did he tell you what had happened to Ms. Peterson?" a CNN reporter asked.

"The detective informed me of her passing, that she had been the victim of a homicide, and that the investigation is ongoing."

A Fox hound cut in. "My sources tell me the woman had been sexually assaulted."

Senator Bradford shot the reporter an icy stare. "I am not aware of the details of Ms. Peterson's death. I have nothing more to say," he stated before retreating to his office.

THE WAR CORRESPONDENT RETURNS

Heather was lying in wait as I walked into the newsroom.

"I don't know if I should say welcome home or punch you," she said.

I wasn't worried one bit about her reaction. "Is Doyle still ticked off?" I asked.

"You'll find out soon enough. He told me the minute you get in here, you're to go directly to this office."

"How's that jerk Nolan?"

"How do you think he is?"

"Well, he got revenge getting me taken off the Zelenskyy press conference on the Bucha massacre. That was my story."

"Knox got his nose so far out of joint when he saw the paper that Nolan had to calm him down. Knox said he was ridiculed by a lot of the correspondents covering Ukraine. I mean, think about it. He's been there since the start of the war and all he's filed are stories on briefings by the Ukrainian military and the endless parade of world leaders going to Kyiv to meet with Zelenskyy. Then you head to Ukraine on your bullshit vacation and a week later you break the biggest story since the invasion began."

"Knox should try breathing the air closer to the front line instead of camping out in his hotel room in Lviv," I suggested, and then switched the topic to a news item I came across on airline Wi-Fi.

"On the flight back, I read an online report in the *Washington Post* that Senator Bradford's intern was murdered."

"It's horrible. The poor woman was raped and strangled to death," Heather said.

"Did the cops catch the killer?"

"No. They're still investigating," Heather said. "We can talk about that later. I'm glad you made it home safely. But now it's time to face the maestro."

"Am I going to be suspended?"

"I have no idea. Doyle has said nothing to me, other than he was going to deal with you the moment you got back. Good luck."

I felt like a grade school kid being sent to the principal's office by my teacher for disrupting the class. My pulse started to pound as I lightly rapped on the managing editor's door. Doyle was typing on his computer. He looked up and the expression on his face turned to ice. I knew I was in big trouble.

"Get in here and close the door behind you," he ordered.

I walked in and sat down in a chair facing his desk.

"I didn't tell you to sit."

"Sorry, sir." I stood right up.

"You disobeyed my orders. I don't take kindly to hotheads who disobey my orders."

I said nothing.

"Are you just going to stand there like a meathead?" Doyle asked.

"Mr. Doyle, in my defense, I didn't disobey you. I took two weeks of my vacation time and decided to go to Ukraine to see first-hand what was going on."

"If you know what's good for you, I strongly suggest you cut the bullshit. You knew precisely what you were doing. I said you couldn't go, and you went anyway."

"And I landed on a huge story. What was I supposed to do? Ignore it?"

"You're not getting paid a penny for working on your vacation," Doyle said.

"I didn't expect to, and I'm not asking to get paid."

Then he threw me an unexpected curve ball. "I want a full accounting of what you spent. Airfare, taxis, hotel, meals, incidentals. Everything."

"What for? I went on my own dime."

"Despite the fact that I'm angry as hell at you for disobeying my orders, you did an incredible job. The least the paper can do is pay your expenses. And Matt, you're to tell no one, I mean no one, including Heather, that the *Tribune* is covering your expenses. You got that?"

"Yes, sir."

Doyle's eyes narrowed. "One last thing. You ever pull a stunt like that again, you'll be packing up your desk. Now get out of my office."

"What do I tell Heather?"

"You're on a tight leash. You're on probation. You step out of line one more time, I will fire you."

"Got it. And I'd just like to say one thing."

"What is it?" Doyle snapped.

"I take offense at you calling me a meathead." With that, I rushed out of his office before he could think of a more appropriate name.

CASE REVIEWS

When Detectives Lamont and Wells got back to headquarters, they made a beeline for the captain's office. Two homicides in one day. Two young women. Both had been strangled. One worked as a political assistant to a powerful senator. The other, according to a surly neighbor across the hall, worked in the sex trade.

"What do you have?" Spencer asked as they came in.

"Dead hooker. Strangled," Wells said.

"Any leads?"

"We got a bit of luck. The building has a working security camera in the elevator. We've got an entire week of people coming and going. Alyssa is going to zero in on the past two days. With luck, we'll catch a shot of the perp," Wells said.

"Security camera at the Peterson apartment building was out of order. The dumbass super was getting around to fixing it this morning," Spencer interjected. "Fortunately, we've got the perp's DNA. Fingers crossed he's in the system."

"CSI is still processing the hooker's apartment. The lead tech called a few minutes ago. They lifted fingerprints off two glasses and a Champagne bottle, and they've got DNA off the bedsheets," Lamont said.

"Run the prints as soon as they come in. I was told the lab is swamped but with any luck you should get the DNA results in a week," Spencer said.

"Prints are being run as we speak," Wells said.

"Who called it in?" Spencer asked.

"Guy living across the hall. He noticed the door was ajar, so he pushed it open and saw the victim laying on the floor. He called 911. Said he never entered the apartment," Lamont said.

"He see or hear anything?"

"Nada. Guy's a loner. Bit of an oddball. I didn't get a good vibe from him. Says he minds his own business."

Spencer pursed his lips. "Did he give up anything on the vic?"

Lamont nodded. "Referred to her as a paid whore. His exact words. A lot of bitterness in his tone."

"Did you get around to asking him to submit to a DNA test, maybe give us his fingerprints?" Spencer asked.

"Yeah. Told me to suck air," Lamont said.

"Got him on your suspect list?"

"Right now, he's our number one," Wells said.

"The canvass of the condo turn up any clues?" Spencer continued.

Wells said he and Lamont canvassed the entire fourth floor. "Guys in uniform did the rest of the building. No one saw or heard a thing," he added.

"Great world we live in. No one ever seems to see or hear a thing when someone is murdered," Spencer spat.

"Most everyone we talked to on the fourth floor knew the vic was some kind of high-class escort. They said she never caused any trouble, and they never had a problem with any of her clients," Lamont recounted.

Wells chimed in. "I'm checking if she worked for an escort service, or whether she was freelance or under the control of a pimp. She had a grand in her purse. Ten crisp one-hundred-dollar bills."

"Keep me up to date," Spencer ordered.

"How's your case going, Captain?" Wells asked.

"Not much to go on just yet. I put a rush on the DNA. I went to Senator Bradford's office earlier this afternoon. He was visibly shaken when I told him Peterson had been murdered. He called his entire staff into the boardroom and broke the news."

"Anyone offer up a clue as to who could have done this?" Wells asked.

"No. They all said Peterson was a hard worker and everyone loved her. Said work was her life. She had her sights set on becoming a representative. No boyfriend. No real social life."

"Did you get to question the senator?" Wells continued.

"Yeah. I asked him where he was last night. Said he was home alone the entire evening."

"No witnesses to back up his alibi?" Lamont asked.

"Nope. But my gut says it wasn't him. His reaction to the news of his intern's death shook him hard. Anyway, I asked if he'd be willing to give us a DNA sample. He agreed. No hesitation. He also let me use the boardroom to talk to his staff individually. I asked each of the male members if they would agree to submit to a DNA test. One guy refused. Said he knew his rights and told me if I wanted his DNA, I'd need to get a warrant. The jerk was putting on a show in front of the staff."

"I guess that puts him at the top of your prime suspect list," Lamont said.

"The thing is we can't get a warrant to force him to submit his DNA. No probable cause. We don't have a shred of evidence linking him to the vic," Spencer noted.

"What's with these jerks refusing to give their DNA if they're innocent?" Wells asked.

"It's their right under the law. Anyway, I've got one of our guys tailing this character. He so much as blows snot into a tissue, we retrieve it, test it, and bingo. I'll cuff him," Spencer said. "I got a strong feeling this is our guy. My radar gun is on him."

*

Alyssa Lamont loaded the security tape into her computer and zeroed in on the timeline provided by the medical examiner in Janet Walker's death. She started at the 7 p.m. mark. At 9:02 p.m., she hit the pause button and called out to her partner.

"Jake, come look at this guy. He's wearing a black baseball cap with the visor pulled down so you can't see his face."

Wells studied the lone man in the elevator. The cap had LA embroidered in white above the brim. "That's an LA Dodgers baseball cap. And I'll bet the bag he's carrying has a Champagne bottle in it."

Alyssa hit play. They watched the man push a button and then get off on the fourth floor.

Lamont fast-forwarded the tape to 10:12 p.m. "Now watch as the same guy gets into the elevator on the fourth floor. Like he did earlier, he keeps his head down and the visor on his baseball cap pulled down. When the elevator gets to the lobby, he scoots out the door."

"Too bad we don't have a clear shot of the guy's face. But I'll bet it's him," Wells said, adding, "I ran the fingerprints CSI took off the glasses and the Champagne bottle through the National Fingerprint Data Base. One of the glasses had the hooker's prints on it. The prints on the other glass and the Champagne bottle are from the same person, but we didn't get a hit. I'm hoping we'll get a positive ID when the DNA results come in. I was told we should get them in a few days at best. Maybe a week. The lab is backlogged."

"A dead prostitute doesn't rate a priority tag on her toe," Lamont noted caustically.

UNIVERSITY CONFESSIONS

Petra's eyes filled with tears when she clicked on the database link and found a match to her DNA. The result left her gasping for air. She could feel her heart fluttering in her chest. All she could focus on were two words: half brother.

Her hands were shaking as she clicked open a message window. For more than an hour she sat frozen in front of the screen, wondering what to write. She understood she had to be careful. A wrong turn of phrase could ruin any chance of a reply. She decided to keep her message perfunctory. "I found a DNA connection to you in the match link. I have been searching for a biological family connection. I would like it if we could connect."

Hesitantly, she pressed send, then grabbed her purse and raced over to Stefan's apartment to break the news. Her fiancé smiled but kept his concerns bottled up. All he could hope for now was that her DNA match would refuse any contact.

Six days later, Petra, who hadn't been able to get a solid night's sleep since she sent the message, received a reply. With her hands shaking, she took a deep breath and opened it.

It read: "This comes as a surprise. Tell me a little about yourself."

Petra immediately called Stefan with the update. Although he told her he was happy for her, he wasn't. Red lights were flashing in his head. He'd read about biological matches that ended in disaster, and he ignored those that resulted in fulfilling connections. All he cared about was Petra's safety and happiness. He didn't want to be left picking up the pieces.

*

The moment I walked into Mei's apartment I knew something was up. She was circling the living room like a bee high on honey.

"Would you like a drink?" Mei asked as I sat down on the sofa.

I found the offer puzzling since I never drink on a weekday. Well, occasionally I down a cold bottle of Grolsch at Riff's after work. But the hard stuff I leave for special occasions, and as far as I could determine, this was not a special occasion.

"Not right now," I said.

"I think you should have a drink."

"I'm not thirsty."

"Just a sip to steady your nerves."

Mei walked over to the fridge. She pulled a bottle of vodka from the freezer and poured an ounce into a shot glass. I knew something was up.

I looked up at her and did not reach for the glass.

"I said I don't want a drink. What's with you? You're not pregnant, are you?"

"No," she shot back in a huff. "And what if I were?"

Again, one dumb question and she nails me with a left hook.

"Just asking. You thinking of dumping me?"

"Will you please put a sock in it? I have something I need to tell you and I have a feeling once I do, you're going to be super mad at me," Mei confessed.

I grabbed the shot glass and downed the cold contents in one gulp. "Okay, I'm ready. My nerves are now made of reinforced concrete. Talk to me."

"You remember the DNA I sent to determine your ancestry?"

My stomach clenched. "What about it?"

"Well, it got a hit."

"What do you mean, a hit?"

"An inquiry. From someone who may be connected to you."

"I don't get it. What do you mean by connected?"

"Someone whose DNA is a very close match to your DNA."

I could feel my blood pressure start to climb. "Could you get to the point?"

"A young woman is trying to get in touch with you."

"And she thinks I'm her father?"

"What? Why would you think that?"

Hesitantly, I said, "I had a few flings in university. Maybe I slipped up, and maybe it's coming back to haunt me."

Mei pursed her lips. Not a good sign. "What would you have done if you'd gotten someone pregnant?"

"What my father did, I guess."

"I don't understand."

"I would have done the honorable thing. I would have said 'I do' and you and I would never have met. Or at best, we would have passed each other on a street and wondered 'what if?'"

"What does this have to do with what your father did?"

"My father met my mother at a Ukrainian New Year's Eve dance. They dated and she got pregnant. I found their marriage certificate online. I was born two months later."

"So, you're saying your dad felt he had to marry your mother."

"I guess."

"Why do you guess?"

"Well, for one thing, I don't think they loved each other. Maybe there was something at the start, but I can't recall them ever having a meaningful moment together. They were distant. No hugs, no kisses, no conversation, nothing. As far back as I can remember, I always felt my birth trapped my parents in a loveless marriage."

"Well, that explains a lot."

"Here we go again. The shrink is back in the house."

"Oh, stop it! What are you going to do about this woman who wants to contact you?"

I felt myself reaching my wits' end. "Geez, Mei. I don't need complications right now. Why did you have to go and stick your nose in my life?"

Once the words came out of my mouth, I knew I was in trouble.

Mei's eyes narrowed. "Stick my nose in your life? I've been the major part of your life for the past six years. I stuck by you through thick and thin. I spent three horrible days at your bedside in the hospital after you got shot."

"I'm sorry."

In a desperate attempt to shift the conversation back to the matter at hand, I asked, "What exactly did the woman say in her email?"

"That there's a close DNA match and she wants to know if she can contact you."

"Well, that's easy. No."

"What do you mean, no?" Mei snapped.

"What part of no do you not get?"

"Aren't you the least bit curious? I mean, you are a journalist. Isn't having a healthy dose of curiosity one of the major prerequisites?"

"Yes. But in this case, I'm not the least bit curious."

"What if she is your daughter? Or your cousin?"

"Better I leave this alone."

"You really frustrate me sometimes. If it were me, I would want to know who this person is and what she's all about."

"Unlike you, I don't watch all those syrupy Hallmark shows."

"Watch it," Mei warned.

"Let me put it another way. My life is not a soap opera and it sure as hell isn't about to become one."

"You are such a jerk."

"Well, this jerk is going to his apartment to sleep it off." I grabbed my blazer and left.

*

Petra was ecstatic when she received another email from Michael Kozak, unaware that Mei had sent it. There wasn't much detail. It said he lived in New York City and was interested in learning more about her. When Petra showed the email to Stefan, he grabbed his laptop and typed the man's name into Google, LinkedIn, Facebook, Twitter, and Instagram. There were at least five Michael Kozaks living in New York City.

"I don't have a good feeling about this," he told Petra.

"There you go again with your negative spin," she said. "I'm going to write him, tell him a bit about myself."

"What if this guy's a sex offender or a trafficker?" Stefan asked.

"What is wrong with you?" Petra shot back angrily.

"Nothing is wrong with me. What's wrong with wanting to protect the woman I love, the woman I'm engaged to marry in a couple of months?"

"I'm twenty-eight years old. I'm a nurse who works in the trauma unit at Chicago General where we get dozens of shooting victims every week. I know how to handle myself. Quit treating me like some kind of helpless child. I don't appreciate it."

Stefan ran his hands roughly over his scalp. "So, what's your next step?" he asked, trying hard not to lose his cool.

"I told you already. I'm going to write back and see what he has to say. Are you okay with that?"

Stefan wasn't okay with that, but he nodded anyway.

YOU ARE NOT THE FATHER

The following evening Mei showed up at my apartment with a large black Americano coffee and a blueberry bran muffin. She always brought me bran muffins after a tiff. I once joked she did it to keep me regular. Or maybe it was her way of telling me something else.

"Still upset with me, my little pierogi?" Mei asked with a pout.

I took a sip of coffee and left the muffin in the bag.

"Oh, the infamous Kozar silent treatment. I tremble where I stand," she teased.

I didn't bite.

"I need to tell you something."

That captured my attention. I couldn't hold off. "What now? Another surprise?"

"Kind of. I have good news," she said.

"Yeah? What?"

"You are not the father."

"What are you talking about?"

"The woman who is trying to get in touch with you is not your long-lost love child."

"Well, that's a relief," I said. I felt a heavy weight lift off my shoulders, and then I caught that look in Mei's eyes. Something was up.

"How do you know that?" I asked.

"I got an email from her last night."

Once again, my stomach clenched. "What do you mean *you* got an email?"

"Well, actually, Michael Kozak wrote to her, and she replied."

I couldn't believe it. But it was just like Mei to chase a mystery to its conclusion. She loathed unresolved issues.

Now I was totally pissed off. "I don't believe this. You just can't leave well enough alone, can you? I never gave you permission to do any of this, and yet you just keep on chugging."

"All she wants is some information about …"

"I want nothing to do with her," I said, my voice rising to an angry pitch. "And now, I'd bet a million bucks you've got another bloody curveball in your bag to throw at me."

"What do you mean by curveball?"

In my rational, deductive mind, there was only one other reason this woman wanted to connect with me, and there was no way I was going to open that door.

"I can't believe my so-called birth mother had another kid. The girl must be one messed up fruitcake having that woman as her mother," I said.

Before Mei could get in another word, I stormed out of my apartment and headed for my refuge. The moment I walked into Riff's, Robin pulled a cold bottle of Grolsch from the cooler and placed it in front of me. She nodded and left me alone. Robin was the quintessential bartender. She knew when to console and, more importantly, when to back off. She could see I was in no mood to talk. I was brooding and my brain was in a tailspin.

I was very much in love with Mei, but from time to time she really got under my skin, and it almost always had something to do with my childhood. Over the years, she managed to pry out bits and pieces, but only after determined prodding, and Mei could be relentless.

I remember once getting so fed up with her poking that I blurted out that my father had shot himself in a stupid game of Russian roulette that went terribly wrong. I told her I was just seven years old and a few weeks after the funeral my mother abandoned me. She took off, as she put it, "to find herself," and she never came back. I figured she got lost. I was placed in foster care. Case closed.

Mei burst into tears and spent the entire evening hugging me.

But Mei wasn't one to leave the matter closed. She continued to poke and prod, trying to get me to open up. Most times, I'd shut down or simply walk out. She had this theory spinning in her head that my cool detachment from people took root way back in the day. She believed I was repressing my past, which, as she expounded, was the cause of my attachment issues, my unease in social situations, my sleep disturbances, my bouts of anxiety and depression, and probably everything else that ailed me.

I preferred to leave my roots undisturbed. For me, the past was just that: the past. I couldn't change it, so there was no point in dwelling on it or revisiting it. Now, Mei had gone and unlocked a door, and I had absolutely no interest in finding out what was on the other side. In this case, a half sibling. I figured after my father shot himself and my mother took off on her quest to find herself, she met some guy and got pregnant.

A few years back, Mei got into my head about my mother and urged me to try and find her. She said it would resolve a lot of my issues. The only issue I had was Mei ragging on me, so to placate her, I ignored my instinct and went looking for my mother. It was the biggest, most painful mistake I've ever made.

I hadn't seen or heard from the woman since she took off, but it wasn't difficult to track her down. I found her on Facebook, under her maiden name. From her mundane bantering with her virtual friends, I learned she was working as a server at a greasy spoon in the south side of the Bronx. I found that somewhat freaky because my apartment was in the Bronx not five blocks away from the restaurant.

Against my better judgment, I showed up late one evening at the all-night diner. I sat down at the counter and looked right at my mother as she poured me a cup of coffee. She didn't recognize me. Not that I expected her to. After the longest half hour of my life, she came over and asked in a detached tone if I wanted a refill or the bill. I looked up from my empty mug, stared into her face, and told her my name. She froze, her eyes turning to ice. It was definitely not a Hallmark greeting card moment. She didn't rush over to give me a hug or burst into tears and beg for my forgiveness. All I got was a splash of stone-cold indifference. The conversation, if you can call it that, was stilted.

"Why did you come here?" she asked.

"I was curious."

"Now that your curiosity has been satisfied, you can leave," she snapped, waving her right hand toward the door.

That was it. After two decades, I didn't merit an explanation about why she abandoned me. Before I walked out, I turned and asked, "Did you ever find yourself?"

Without uttering another word, Mary Leschuk retreated into the kitchen.

I learned an important lesson that day. Leave well enough alone. Nothing good can come from digging up the past.

Now, this half sibling—no doubt the offspring of my so-called mother—spelled trouble, and there was no way in hell I was ever going to meet her.

THE RIGHT TO REMAIN SILENT

When Detective Spencer read the results of the DNA swabs in the Gail Peterson case, his jaw dropped. He was stunned. He couldn't believe he got it so wrong. He had been dead certain the man was innocent. Now, the man was guilty as sin. The indisputable DNA evidence showed him to be a rapist and a cold-blooded killer. The detective immediately called the chief of police and was firmly instructed to play it by the book. No grandstanding. A low-key arrest. No media circus.

That was what the chief wanted. But not Spencer. This arrest was his ticket to fame. He was going to snag a big fish, and it was going to make the national news and international headlines. Like hell he was going to follow the chief's orders. As he drove his SUV, accompanied by two cops in a police cruiser, he speed-dialed a close media relations contact.

"Do me a favor. Call all the major TV news networks. Tell them to be outside the Dirksen Senate Office Building. ASAP."

"What do I tell them?" the contact asked.

"Just tell them something huge is about to go down, and I mean huge," Spencer said. "It will be the story of the year."

At the entrance to the senate building, the detective flashed his badge, informed security he was on official police business, and barreled through the metal detector, setting off the alarm. He was followed by the two officers. As the trio headed for the elevator, three Capitol cops hurried down the corridor and joined them.

When the posse reached their destination, Spencer instructed the Capitol cops to remain in the corridor.

As he entered the reception area, he asked the administrative assistant if Senator Bradford was in his office. "I need to speak to him. It's urgent."

The assistant buzzed her boss on the office line. "Senator, Detective Spencer is here. He says it's urgent he speak to you."

"Send him in," Bradford responded.

The homicide detective entered the office with the two uniforms.

The senator rose from behind his desk, shook Spencer's hand and sat back down.

"Do you have a lead on Gail's murder?" he asked.

"We do," Spencer said.

"Well, I hope it leads you to the person who did it."

"It has," the detective said flatly.

The senator looked at all three men. From their expressions, he was suddenly aware something wasn't quite right.

"How can I help you, Detective?" he asked hesitantly.

"I need to clarify a couple of things," Spencer began. "When we first spoke, I asked where you were on the night Gail Peterson was murdered."

"Yes, and I told you I was at home."

"Alone."

"That's correct."

"You also told me you have no one who can verify that," he noted.

"What are you driving at, Detective?"

"It's a simple statement, Senator."

"Pretty hard for anyone, as you put it, to verify he was home alone when he was alone."

Spencer stared coldly at the senator.

"I'm asking you again, Detective. What's going on here?" Bradford demanded.

"Senator, would you please stand?" Spencer instructed in a firm tone.

"Why?"

"Please stand."

Bradford remained seated.

"I need to read you your rights. Senator Bradford, you have the right to remain silent. Anything you say can and will be used against you in a court of law. You have the ..."

"Are you out of your mind? Do you know who you're talking to?" Bradford charged.

"Senator, please let me finish. You have the right to an attorney. If you cannot afford an attorney, one will be appointed to you."

Reaching for his cell phone, Bradford said, "I'm calling my attorney."

Spencer lunged over the desk and forcefully yanked the phone out of the senator's hand. "You can call your attorney from the police station. You are under arrest for the sexual assault and murder of Gail Peterson. Now, please stand and put your hands behind your back. Officers, cuff him."

As the senator was being escorted out of his office, he called out to his executive assistant. "George, call Brian Tate. Tell him I've been arrested for murder. I need him to get to the police station right away."

A horde of journalists was lying in wait outside the building.

"You bastard. You rigged this media frenzy," the senator snarled, turning to Spencer. "I'll have your badge for this."

The detective didn't respond.

A CNN reporter shouted, "Senator, why are you being arrested?"

Bradford did not respond.

"Does this have anything to do with the murder of Gail Peterson?" an NBC journalist called out.

The senator said nothing.

"Senator, did you murder Gail Peterson?" a Fox stringer barked.

Again, nothing.

The reporters then turned their attention to the detective.

"Detective Spencer, why is Senator Bradford in handcuffs? Why has he been arrested?" an ABC reporter asked. "Does this have anything to do with the murder of his intern?"

"I can't comment at the moment," Spencer replied. "However, there will be a news conference later this afternoon at which time I will explain the reason for the senator's arrest."

In the few minutes it took to get to DC police headquarters, "breaking news" banners were flashing across local and national newscasts throughout the United States:

Senator William Bradford arrested for sexual assault and murder of 26-year-old intern.

Standing in front of cameras, television journalists filed virtually identical reports:

> *Gail Peterson was found in her apartment last week. She had been sexually assaulted and then strangled to death.*
>
> *Senator Bradford, chair of the powerful US Senate Appropriations Committee, did not respond to reporters' questions as he was led out of the Dirksen Senate Office Building in handcuffs.*
>
> *Homicide detective Ron Spencer remained tight-lipped about the arrest. We have been informed the DC police will be holding a news conference in four hours.*

*

Heather and I were sitting in her office when the *Tribune*'s Washington correspondent sent a terse text on iMessage. "Turn on CNN."

We did, and then we watched the media spectacle unfold in stunned silence.

"I thought he was one of the good guys," I said at last.

"Why? Because he's the voice for Ukraine in the Senate?"

"Yeah, and now he's muzzled."

"By his own hand," Heather pointed out.

HOME ALONE

At police headquarters, the senator was fingerprinted and had his mugshot taken, after which he was escorted to an interview room and informed that his attorney was on his way. Throughout the entire process, as humiliating as it was, Bradford remained unshaken and defiant. He knew the cops had the wrong man, and he knew once released, he would sue the DC police for millions along with a non-negotiable demand that Detective Ron Spencer turn in his badge.

An hour later, Brian Tate, one of the top criminal defense attorneys in the country, strode into the station. Before he was led to an interrogation room, he cornered Spencer and issued a stern warning.

"There is to be no eavesdropping or filming while I'm in there with my client. Is that understood?"

"Got it," the detective acknowledged.

"I'm serious. If I find out that anyone was even lurking behind that one-way mirror, I will have their badge," the attorney threatened.

"I said I got it," Spencer repeated.

As Tate entered the interrogation room, Bradford leapt to his feet. "Brian, you've got to get me out of here."

"Bill, given the severity of the charges, that's going to be extremely difficult. The DA will fight any motion to grant you bail."

"But I didn't kill Gail. I don't know why I've been arrested."

"I'm going to find out why. You just have to remain calm," Tate counseled.

"How can I stay calm? I heard one of the police officers say they're going to send me to the DC jail and lock me up in isolation for my own protection. Protection from what?"

"Bill, you've been charged with sexual assault and first-degree murder of a young woman. Inmates are known not to take kindly to rapists."

"But I didn't rape anyone," Bradford repeated.

"The one important piece of advice I'm going to give you is this: Keep your mouth shut. Do not talk to any prisoners. Do not let them engage you in conversation. If anyone asks why you're in there, say nothing. Stay away from anyone trying to be your friend. He could well be a plant or a snitch wanting to make a deal by feeding information to the DA."

"What information?"

"That in a moment of mental distress, you confessed to raping and killing Gail Peterson."

"Why would I do something as stupid as that when I didn't kill her?"

There was a rap on the door. Detective Spencer walked in.

"Time's up. We're taking the prisoner to the Central Detention Facility," he pronounced.

"He is Senator Bradford," Tate admonished.

"Sorry. I'm taking Senator Bradford to the Central Detention Facility," Spencer mocked.

At the DC Jail, the accused faced further humiliation. He was ordered to strip naked in front of three guards, and then he was issued an orange prison jumpsuit. His clothes, cell phone, gold neck chain and cross pendant, wedding ring, and solid gold Rolex watch were placed in a bin and stored in the property cage.

*

Detective Ron Spencer strutted into the homicide squad room. The three-ring media circus was in full swing, and he was the lion-tamer in the center ring.

Alyssa Lamont was the first to spot him. "Big Foot is on his way in," she whispered to her partner. "Got one big toothy grin on his smug mug."

Jake Wells looked up. "How did it go, Captain?" he asked.

"Slam dunk. The news hounds are on this like hungry hyenas on a bone. I'm having to dodge them at every turn."

"I bet you are," Lamont muttered under her breath.

Wells interjected: "You think the reporters have gone wild? I was watching Fox News. The Republicans are having a field day slicing and dicing the Democrats on this. Bradford was their knight in shining armor. Now he's gone to rust."

"How was your face to face with the senator?" Lamont asked.

"Typical politician. Maintain the lie at all costs and hope the fools out there will swallow it hook, line, and sinker. The guy is adamant he didn't kill the Peterson woman. Swears on the bible. Swears on his mother's life. Swears on the lives of his kids. He just keeps swearing. Says he never ever set foot in Peterson's apartment. Maintains he's being framed. Swears to God he's innocent," Spencer recounted in a derisive tone.

He then turned to Wells and asked, "Anything on the dead hooker?"

"We're waiting for the results on the DNA we found on her bed. The prints on the Champagne bottle and one of the glasses belong to the same individual, but we didn't get a hit," Wells said.

"What about the video from the security camera on the elevator?" Spencer asked.

"I'm working on it," Lamont answered. "I'm sure we've got the killer, but the guy in the elevator was wearing an LA baseball cap with the visor pulled down to obscure his face. I'm going to go back over the timeline frame by frame in case I missed anything."

Spencer continued with his questions. "Do you know if the vic worked for an escort service or for a pimp?"

"I put a call into vice and asked them to run the woman through their database. They should get back to me later today," Wells said.

"What about the guy who found the vic?"

"I've already got plainclothes on him," Wells said, "just waiting to pick up the first coffee cup he tosses."

ENGERGIZER BUNNY

"You hear the news about Senator Bradford?" I called out as I entered Mei's apartment. "He just got charged with murdering his intern."

Mei was in the kitchen stir-frying some vegetables and didn't respond.

"Did you hear me?" I asked.

"What? Yes. The senator got charged. I saw him on CNN being led out of his office to a police car."

"I can't believe he killed his intern," I said.

Again, Mei didn't respond. She seemed distracted, not really listening to me. Instantly, I got an anxious feeling that something was wrong.

"Is something bothering you?" I asked. "You don't seem yourself."

"I just want to say I'm sorry about what I did with your DNA," she began.

"It's over, so let's forget it."

"Now don't fly off the handle, but I tried to fix it."

I closed my eyes, shook my head, and dared to ask. "Fix what?"

"I checked further into this and ..."

"What? Oh, here we go. What did you do now?"

"The person who shares your DNA ..."

"You just can't leave it alone, can you? You're like the Energizer Bunny pounding on a drum."

"Look, Matt. I know ever since we got the information ..."

"You got the information, not we."

"Whatever. I know it's been bothering you. You can't say it hasn't."

"Well, at the very least I don't have a kid out there somewhere. That's a relief."

"I'm glad for you on that point. Now take a deep breath."

"Oh, crap. You're not going to let up."

"I found out what the DNA connection is. Your sister is …"

"My half sister," I interjected.

Undaunted, Mei forged ahead and hit me with both barrels. "What I found out is that your half sister and you have different mothers but the same father."

It took my mind a few long seconds to process what she had revealed.

"That's not possible."

"It more than possible. It's a fact. DNA doesn't lie."

I felt my stomach knotting up and my blood pressure rising. "What you're saying is my father was screwing around while he was married and got some woman pregnant."

"Don't put words in my mouth. I never said that. But yes, it looks that way."

I took a deep breath, held it for a few seconds, and exhaled slowly.

"She wants to meet you," Mei said.

"Who?"

"Who? Your sister. That's who."

"Half sister, and for the record, it's never gonna happen."

"Why not?"

"Because I'm not interested in meeting her. Like I've repeatedly told you, I don't need complications in my life."

"I think you should meet her."

I was starting to get pissed off. "I think you should mind your own business. I'm not meeting with her."

"What would it hurt?"

"It's not gonna happen. Let it be."

"Matt, I think …"

I finally snapped. "Mei, I said let it be. You shouldn't have started this in the first place."

Mei pulled back and began pacing around the room like a possessed bedlamite. She did that when she was primed to explode, and this time, like most times, I lit the fuse. After a half-dozen spins, she came to a sudden stop and shouted inches from my face.

"What is wrong with you?"

That would take hours, even days, to explain, and then I'd only scratch the surface. So I kept my mouth shut.

"You frustrate the heck out of me. Do you know that?"

Again, my mouth remained clamped.

"You can be such an insensitive jerk at times."

I did not dare interrupt her rant.

"I'm going to read what she wrote to you in an email."

Now my fuse was lit. Nonetheless, Mei ignored my beet-red face and continued unabated.

"Just sit there and listen," she commanded, opening her cell phone and calling up Michael Kozak's email account. "Here's what she wrote. *'My name is Petra Petrovich.'*"

I stared down at the floor.

"*'I'm twenty-eight years old. I want to start off by saying I don't want anything from you, and I will understand if you don't want to meet me. It's just, imagine my surprise at finding out I have a brother. I'm sure it probably comes as a shock that you have a sister. What is vitally important to me is finding out about my father. It would be nice if you could help me with a few missing pieces of the puzzle that make up my life. If you can find it in your heart, I would really like to meet you. I'm sending you a photo of me in the attachment.'*"

Mei placed her phone with Petra's photo visible on the table.

My eyes remained glued to the floor.

"Petra. That's such a beautiful name," Mei said, desperate for a reaction.

She didn't get one.

"Matt, talk to me. What are you going to do?"

Mei picked up her cell and stared at the photo. "It's incredible. She looks so much like you. She has the same dark eyes, the same dimple in her chin, the same thick, wavy, brown hair, and the same brooding expression."

She finally got a rise out of me.

"I don't brood."

"Sure, you never brood. The issue right now is what are you going to do?"

Hesitantly, I glanced at the photo and refused to acknowledge any resemblance. "Look Mei, it's better I stay out of her life, and that she stays out of mine."

"Why?"

"What am I supposed to tell her? That my father blew his head off in a moronic game of Russian roulette with a few of his ex-Marine buddies. What good will it do when I tell her that?"

That drew a harsh response. "When you put it that way, it will do no good. It's just plain cold-hearted and cruel."

"Oh, give me a break, Mei. It was my reality."

"Well, it doesn't have to be her reality."

"So, what do you suggest? I tell her my father died a war hero?"

"Don't be glib."

I'd had enough. "You started all this by sending my DNA without my permission ..."

"I've apologized for it. It's time to move on. We're in a different space now."

"Easy for you to say now that you've saddled me with a ton of baggage I don't need in my life."

"Oh, please. This hardly rates as a ton of baggage."

I looked up at a modern art painting on the wall. I had glanced at it over the years and still didn't get what it was supposed to mean. Mei said it was a representation of the artist's view on life. To me, it looked like someone spilled a bowl of spaghetti Bolognese on a kitchen floor and slapped a canvas on it.

Staring at Petra's photograph, Mei said, "Your sister is very beautiful."

"She's not my sister," I said emphatically.

"Biologically she is your half sister. You share DNA."

"I don't need this."

Mei gave me a look that could ignite asbestos. "When you stop brooding—oh sorry, you don't brood. When you stop doing whatever you call what you do, maybe you could give some thought to what it would mean to Petra to meet her brother."

I remained bound to the sofa, arms crossed tightly across my chest like a petulant five-year-old. I was definitely brooding.

TRUST NO ONE

Brian Tate was perched on the edge of a metal chair that was bolted to the floor in the interview room at the DC Jail. He was staring blankly at the charge sheet while waiting for his client to appear. The room was stark, the walls painted a drab industrial gray. He bore the look of defeat.

The attorney jumped to his feet when a buzzer pierced the silence. He shoved the document into a file folder and placed it in his briefcase. Next came the clanging of an electronic prison door opening from the main cell block. A moment later, a muscle-bound guard led Senator Bradford into the room.

"Knock on the door when you're done, and an officer will come and let you out," the guard instructed Tate.

"Thank you. I know the drill," Tate noted, as he retrieved a large yellow writing pad from his briefcase. He looked up at the senator, who was fidgeting with the sleeve of his prison-issue jumpsuit.

"How are you holding up, Bill?" the attorney asked.

"How the fuck do you think I'm holding up?" Bradford cursed. "I've been charged with a murder and a rape I did not commit. And I'm stuck in this rat hole with a bunch of hardcore criminals."

"I hear what you're saying, but we've got literally nothing to prove your innocence. So you've got to help me out here. I've got the DNA report from the DA. Your semen was found on the woman. They even found a used condom on the floor beside the victim's bed with your semen in it."

"What are you saying? This is insane. I've never been to Gail's apartment," Bradford shouted.

"Then how did your DNA end up on the victim?"

"I swear to you I have no idea how it got there. As I told you, I've never ever been to Gail's apartment."

Tate glanced down at the blank yellow pad. His demeanor said it all.

"Good lord, Brian. You don't believe me. You think I'm guilty."

"I never said that," Tate countered.

"The look on your face says it all. Maybe I should get another attorney."

"Bill, I am going to defend you to the best of my ability," Tate said.

"But?"

"Right now, I have to confess it doesn't look good."

"So, what are you going to do? Roll over and accept the DA's bullshit evidence?" Bradford asked.

"The evidence *is* their case and it's damning. DNA does not lie."

"Well, someone is lying. I didn't kill Gail."

"Where were you the night Gail Peterson was killed?" Tate asked.

"I told the detective I was at home the whole night."

Tate was momentarily stunned. "Wait. What? You never told me that. When did you speak to the detective?"

"When he first came to my office to inform me that Gail was murdered. He had her Senate employee pass in his hand."

"And he asked you where you were the night of the intern's murder?" the attorney interjected.

"Yes."

"Damn it, Bill. You're a lawyer. Why didn't you simply refuse and tell the detective you wanted your attorney present before you said anything?"

"Because I had just been informed Gail was dead, that she had been murdered, and I had nothing to hide," Bradford said in his defense.

Tate closed his eyes and rubbed his temples. "Tell me someone was home with you to support your alibi."

"I told the detective I was home alone."

Tate shook his head in disbelief. "Did the detective ask you anything more that I should know about?"

"He asked me to provide a DNA sample. In fact, he asked all the men in my office to provide one."

"Let me guess," said Tate. "You provided one, which is precisely how the detective placed you at the victim's apartment."

"Like I told you, I have nothing to hide."

"I wish you hadn't done that," Tate said.

"Brian, do you honestly think I would willingly offer my DNA if I was in any way involved in Gail's death?"

Tate didn't respond. All that was running through his mind was the deep hole his client had dug for himself.

"Again, I want to know what you're going to do."

"I'm trying to figure that out," the attorney said.

"I'm paying you a thousand dollars an hour to do just that. So get on it."

"I'm working on it. I've asked a couple of private detectives if they'd take on the case. I'm waiting for an answer."

Bradford rolled his eyes. "They'll take the money and do nothing."

"We don't know that."

"Look, Brian. All I know is I've been set up. Someone is framing me."

"Bill, you've got to help me out here. Who is setting you up?"

"I've been driving myself crazy trying to figure that out. I've made a lot of enemies over the years."

"No doubt about that," Tate muttered.

The senator continued. "I have a few ideas. They came to me while I was pacing in my cell last night and I've been mulling them over in my head ever since. So, hear me out. I need a tough, thorough investigator. Someone who won't just sniff around, roll over, and collect a hefty paycheck."

"It sounds like you have someone in mind."

"I do. The investigative journalist from the *New York Tribune*, the one who reported on the massacre in Ukraine. He's the same reporter who broke that international food aid scandal a couple of years ago. Matt Kozar."

Tate sputtered. "Are you insane? I can't condone this. You're leaving your fate in the hands of a reporter? Come on, Bill. Remember he took down Senator Caine. The man is in prison doing fifteen years and Reverend Powers is doing twenty years to life as an accessory to murder."

"I know what Kozar did. That is precisely why I want him. He's a digger. He's unrelenting."

"I hate journalists. They're bottom feeders," Tate confessed.

"And they hate politicians and lawyers," the senator countered. "They see us as bottom feeders. So, we're all treading water in the same shark-infested pond, destined to spend an eternity burning in hell."

"What if Matt Kozar digs around and finds you're guilty?" Tate asked.

"He won't because I'm not guilty. Can you get that through your thick skull? I am not guilty."

"You have to calm down and think this through logically," Tate counseled.

"Believe me, I have."

"Look, this entire idea of yours may all be moot. I don't think Kozar will take on an investigation on your behalf. He's a reporter, not a PI."

"He's better than a PI and I'll pay him whatever he wants."

"Kozar can't be bought. That is one thing I know about the guy," Tate said.

"Everyone has a price. Ask him to come and see me."

"Bill, I want it on the record that I'm totally against this. I don't want it to come back and bite me on the ass later in a possible appeal."

"Write up your objection and I'll sign it. You'll be off the hook. I want to speak to Kozar."

Tate nodded, reluctantly.

"In the meantime, you've got to work on getting me out on bail. I've got to get out of here before I go crazy. The lights in my cell are on all day and night, and there's a camera on me at all times. I can't even use the toilet without someone watching me."

"You're on a suicide watch," Tate explained.

"What? I'm not going to kill myself. Why would I kill myself? I'm innocent."

The lawyer nodded.

Bradford wasn't finished. "The place has no air conditioning. It's bloody hot in my cell. The entire cell block smells of urine and body odor. I'm only allowed out for one hour twice a day to walk in the yard. I got a boiled egg and a slice of dry toast for breakfast with lukewarm, brown water I was told was coffee. At lunch, I got a baloney and cheese sandwich. How can they treat people like this?"

"Maybe when you get out, you can do something about it," Tate responded.

"Don't play the smartass with me. I'm paying you to represent me. I don't need your sarcasm."

"I didn't mean it that way."

"Yeah, you did."

Tate rapped his pen nervously on his notepad. "I have one more matter to discuss," he began, with hesitation in his voice. "Your wife phoned me. She wants you to put her on your visitors list."

"I can't face her right now."

"She has asked to see you. My advice is you should talk to her."

"Why?"

"Either that or you'll see her on Oprah yapping about your infidelity."

Bradford winced and caved. "Fine."

"And a warning. The prison visits are not face to face. They're done by video. Your wife will be at the visitation center in the building adjacent to the jail. You'll be in a cubicle down the corridor on this floor. I can't stress this enough. Be very careful about what you say. The video visits are monitored and recorded, and prosecutors have been known to listen to recordings in the hope an inmate will say something incriminating."

"That won't happen because I'm innocent."

"And I want you to know I believe you. Now, you are going to be arraigned tomorrow."

"I can't go to court looking like this, dressed like an orangutan in this orange jumpsuit. I look like a criminal."

"There's nothing I can do about that," Tate said flatly. "And Bill, please do not say a word in court other than when you're asked how you plead."

The senator nodded.

"I'm serious. Not a word!"

IT'S SENATOR BRADFORD!

Courtroom C-10 of the Superior Court of the District of Columbia was overflowing with the who's who of Washington's political elite. Several senators and senior members of Congress from both sides of the aisle used their influence to circumvent the long, winding queue of curious citizens outside the courthouse. Once they filed in, there was enough seating for only a handful of journalists at the very back.

Brian Tate was standing at the defense table shuffling papers as he waited for his client to appear. His assistant, a studious attorney wearing a navy-blue dress and red-framed glasses, appeared unfazed by the political power in the room.

Across the aisle, exuding an air of invincibility, Assistant US Attorney David Di Adamo, the lead prosecutor on the case, stood at his table chatting amiably with five junior attorneys from his office. The courtroom was his stage, and he couldn't have asked for a better script. Di Adamo had landed the leading role, and he was primed to play it as far as it could take him.

In the public gallery, directly behind the prosecution's battle station, a middle-aged couple sat in silence. They were Gail Peterson's parents. Wearing a black dress and clenching a tissue in her hand, Rachel Peterson looked like she hadn't slept in days. Her eyes were bloodshot, her face etched with grief. Richard Peterson, dressed in a black suit, white shirt, and black tie, showed no emotion. His expression was blank. He appeared catatonic, a lost soul adrift in a dark void. Sitting to Peterson's left, with his arms folded across his chest, was Detective Ron Spencer. He too imagined himself in the starring role of this script: the hard-nosed cop diligently working the case of a brutally raped and murdered young woman. In his mind, this was his investigation, and he would be known forever as the man who brought down a powerful US senator. He sat wondering who would play him in the inevitable Hollywood blockbuster: Leonardo DiCaprio, Ben Affleck, or his favorite actor, Matt Damon.

Suddenly, the courtroom fell silent as the side door leading to the holding cells opened.

Dressed in a crisp, freshly laundered prison jumpsuit, Senator Bradford was led into the courtroom in handcuffs and leg irons by two beefy deputy sheriffs. All eyes were rivetted on the accused. The senator avoided making eye contact with anyone, especially his colleagues. He held his head high, a look of determination on his face. The restraints removed, he shook hands with his lawyer and sat down.

"Did you contact Matt Kozar?" Bradford asked.

"I haven't had time. I was preparing a filing to obtain all materials and evidence on this case from the DA's office."

The senator snapped. "I told you to get Kozar. Do it."

"I'll get to it." Tate said.

"Today," Bradford said, firmly.

An aging bailiff shuffled to the front of the courtroom and shouted, "All rise," as the judge, dressed in black robes, entered through a door behind the bench.

"The court is now in session. Judge Harrison Hunter Hamilton III presiding," the bailiff announced.

"Oh, crap," Tate whispered under his breath.

"What is it?" the senator asked.

"Triple H."

"What?"

"Judge Harrison Hunter Hamilton III. He has a reputation of being the toughest judge on the DC circuit. No nonsense. All business."

Sporting a grizzly scowl, the judge sat down and scanned the courtroom with an intimidating stare.

The first to introduce himself was lead prosecutor David Di Adamo.

"I see you're accompanied by a retinue of lawyers. Is this case too difficult for you to handle on your own, Counselor?" the judge asked.

There was muted laughter in the courtroom.

"One more outburst and I will clear the room," Hamilton boomed. He then turned his attention to the defense table.

Tate stood. "Your Honor, Brian Tate for the defense."

The judge nodded at the court clerk. She rose and read out the charges against the senator. One count of murder in the first degree in the death of Gail Peterson and one count of sexual assault.

"Mr. Bradford, how do you plead?" the judge asked.

The accused rose to his feet and pronounced, "Your Honor, it's Senator Bradford."

"What was that?" the judge asked.

"Senator Bradford."

"Oh, fuck," Tate murmured under his breath.

"I will ask you one more time. How do you plead, Mr. Bradford?"

"Your Honor, I have been charged with a crime I did not commit. Under law, I am presumed innocent until proven guilty in a court of law. Your deliberate referral to me as Mr. Bradford rather than Senator Bradford is disrespectful and, some might suggest, tainted with bias."

The two bulls had locked horns. Brian Tate was sweating. David Di Adamo looked both stunned and amused.

The judge stared down at the accused, his lips pursed, his eyes firing guided missiles. He inhaled deeply and exhaled slowly. "Senator Bradford, how do you plead?"

Tate leaned over and hissed, "If you have any hope of getting bail, knock off the attitude and enter a plea."

"Your Honor, I plead not guilty to all charges on the grounds that I've been framed. I did not kill Gail Peterson."

"Senator Bradford, the court simply requires a plea. You will have ample opportunity to present your case at trial," the judge advised.

"Now, Mr. Tate, I gather you have a motion," Judge Hamilton continued.

"Your Honor, I would request that Senator Bradford be granted bail."

The prosecutor leapt to his feet. "Your Honor, we strongly request you deny bail. Given the gravity of the crime, the people request that Senator Bradford be held in custody."

"Sit down, Mr. Di Adamo. You will have your turn. Right now, I want to hear from the defense."

Tate continued. "Your Honor, as you are aware, Senator Bradford is a respected member of the community and a family man with three children. He poses no threat to the community."

Several people in the courtroom groaned. A few laughed.

"Mr. Di Adamo, I gather you have an objection," the judge said.

"Yes, Your Honor, I certainly do. The charge is first-degree murder. There are no conditions the court can order that can reasonably assure safety to the community."

Tate was back on his feet. "Your Honor, I beg to differ ..."

"Let me stop you there, Counselor. I suggest you save your breath and the court's time. The charges clearly demonstrate your client poses a danger to the community, and the public is entitled to demand the highest protection that can be afforded. Therefore, I am denying bail. The accused is to remain in custody. I can set the trial date for late next year unless you opt for a speedy trial as is your client's right under the law."

The senator whispered "speedy trial" in Tate's direction.

"Are you out of your mind? I need time to prepare," Tate whispered frantically.

"I'm not going to sit in prison for a year while you prepare. Do it," the senator ordered.

"Your Honor, my client has advised me that he wants a speedy trial."

"In that case, my calendar is open next month. We will meet here on the sixteenth for jury selection. This court is adjourned."

The deputies surrounded the senator to apply the handcuffs and leg irons, and then they ushered him out of the courtroom.

Di Adamo sauntered over to Tate. "I want you to know, I will not accept any plea deal."

"Just make certain you courier the documentation to me, and I mean all the evidence gathered by the police and the crime scene investigators, no later than tomorrow morning," Tate instructed.

"No problem. I'll have it sent to your office first thing this afternoon. No doubt, you'll find it a compelling read, particularly the DNA evidence."

Brian Tate grabbed his briefcase, marched out of the courtroom, and ran smack into a pack of reporters. He kept going, refusing to answer the questions tossed his way.

COLD CALL

I was sitting in my cubicle in the newsroom when I got a call from a man who began the conversation with four terse words: "This is Brian Tate." I sat bolt upright. I knew the famed criminal lawyer from watching CNN. He was a frequent legal commentator on high-profile murder trials. And I knew he was representing Bradford.

"Senator Bradford has asked to see you," Tate muttered.

His comment threw me for a loop. "Why?" I asked.

"He wants to talk with you."

"I kind of got that. About what, the murder of his intern?"

"The senator wants you to look into it."

"Why?"

"Because he swears he's innocent. He maintains he's being framed, and for some reason, he thinks you're the investigator he needs."

The last statement raised my hackles. "From the tone of your voice, I get the feeling you don't like me."

"What you hear in my voice is my general distrust of journalists."

"And I have little use for lawyers. So we're even," I shot back.

"Are you willing to entertain the senator and hear what he has to say?"

"First off, I don't entertain. Second, I'll have to discuss this with my boss. I'll get back to you in an hour. When does the senator want to meet with me?"

"Tomorrow afternoon. And Kozar, everything will be off the record."

"Then shove the meeting. I don't do off the record."

The lawyer relented. "Alright. But I manage the meeting, and there will be ground rules."

"If I go, it will be to listen to the senator, not his legal mouthpiece, and to ask questions. Those are my ground rules, and if you intend to interrupt the flow every time you think he might say something prejudicial, then I will walk."

Tate gritted his teeth. "I need your decision ASAP. I have to get clearance from the jail administration for your visit. I'll be putting you down as part of my investigative team."

"Whoa. I have a serious issue with that."

"It's the only way I can get you in."

"I work for one team. The *Tribune*."

"I'll give you a letter stating you're meeting the senator strictly as an investigative journalist for your newspaper. You have nothing to worry about."

"I'm okay with that. I'll call within the hour. However, don't hold your breath. I'm not sure my boss will green-light this."

"Then he'll make my day."

"She."

"What?"

"She. My boss is a woman."

I hung up the phone and made a beeline for Heather's office. "I need to talk to you and Mr. Doyle. It's urgent."

"What's it about?" Heather asked.

"You won't believe the call I just got."

We headed for the managing editor's office. Heather rapped on Dick Doyle's open door. He glanced up and waved us in.

"Matt says he has something urgent he needs to discuss."

"It had better not be a request to go to Ukraine," Doyle said.

"It's not that," I countered.

"What is it?"

"I just received a phone call from Brian Tate."

"Senator Bradford's lawyer?" Doyle asked.

"One and the same," I said.

I now had everyone's attention.

"What did he want?" Doyle asked.

"Tate said the senator asked to see me. He wants to meet me at the DC jail tomorrow afternoon."

"Any idea why?" Doyle asked.

"Something about the senator swearing he's innocent and that he's been framed for the murder. I have no idea what he's going to say, but I think I should hear him out."

"Have you heard what the prosecution has on Bradford? The word I got from our Washington bureau chief is that the senator's DNA is on the victim," Heather noted.

"And the senator maintains he didn't do it," I offered.

"Every moron in prison utters the same mantra. 'I didn't do it,' even when the evidence against them is rock solid."

"There have been dozens of cases where the so-called rock-solid evidence crumbled into a heap of dust when the case went to trial," I pointed out.

"Sure. When sleazy lawyers turn the proceeding into a three-ring circus and get their guilty clients off on a technicality," Heather shot back.

"Are you two done trading barbs?" Doyle interjected.

Heather and I nodded.

"Fine. Matt, I think you should go and hear what the senator has to say," Doyle ruled. "But make it crystal clear nothing he says is off the record. You got that?"

"You know me. I don't take anything off the record."

Heather didn't say another word, but I could tell from the look on her face she was ticked off. She didn't appreciate being overruled. As I headed back to my cubicle, she grabbed my arm and pulled me aside.

"I can't believe you're going to waste our time on that piece of slime."

"Heather, what the hell is with you? I'm not going there to figure out a way to get him off. If he killed the woman, then he's done. I'll slice, dice, and fry him."

"Just don't get duped."

I snapped. "Heather, don't ever insult me like that again or we'll be done as friends and as colleagues."

She apologized reluctantly. "It came out wrong. I didn't mean it that way."

"Like hell you didn't."

Heather turned and walked away.

*

Mei was incredulous. "The senator asked to speak to you?"

"Yes."

"What do you think he wants?"

"I don't know. Maybe he wants to get his side of the story out. I mean, the guy is getting roasted by the news media and on social media."

"Deservedly so. All you have to do is look at the evidence. It's indisputable."

"Have you seen the evidence?"

"I know one of the technicians who analyzed the DNA collected at the crime scene for the prosecution. He said the semen found on the woman's body is a hundred percent match to the DNA sample provided by the senator," Mei said.

"Why would he share this information with you?"

"He's a friend from my university days."

"Well, I'm left wondering why the senator would readily provide a DNA sample to the cops knowing that even a speck of his DNA at the crime scene would nail his sorry ass to the wall."

"Desperate men do stupid things."

"That's all you got?"

"Just be careful. The senator is a seasoned politician. He knows how to manipulate," Mei warned.

"And I'm a seasoned investigative reporter who knows how to cut through the political bullshit."

JAILHOUSE RULES

Entering the DC jail was like running the security gauntlet at an international airport. I was asked to produce two pieces of identification. My name was checked against an official visitor's list attached to a clipboard. Once cleared, I was ordered to empty my pockets, take off my belt, and pass through a metal detector. My cell phone was taken and placed in a secure box.

"You'll get it back when you leave," the guard advised, handing back my wallet and belt. "For your security and the security of the jail, I am obliged to inform you that the interview room is monitored at all times by a security camera. Sound is not recorded. There is to be no physical contact with the inmate. No handshakes. No hugs. If you attempt to pass any contraband to the inmate, you will be arrested and charged. Is that understood?"

"Yup. No contraband. No hugs," I said.

Brian Tate was already in the room when I was led in by a guard. He didn't get up, didn't bother with a handshake or even a polite greeting. I took a seat on his side of the table and waited for the accused.

When Senator Bradford shuffled through the door, he did not look at all like the cocksure politician I had seen during his frequent appearances on CNN and MSNBC. He was wearing a prison jumpsuit that looked like he'd slept in it. His face was drained of energy and there were thick, puffy bags under his eyes. His hair was greasy, and the stubble on his face was grizzled.

"Mr. Kozar, I'm grateful you could make it," the senator said. "I want to start off by saying I read your reports from Bucha. They were stellar. Powerful and heartbreaking."

I learned early on never to respond to platitudes uttered by politicians. Not that I get many.

"Kozar. I take it that you're Ukrainian?" the senator continued.

Again, I didn't respond.

Tate cleared his throat. "Here's the deal. I want this entire meeting to be off the record."

I cut in. "Here's my deal. Shove your deal. I informed you when you called, I don't do off-the-record interviews."

Turning to the senator, I continued. "Is that okay with you?"

"Yes."

"One more thing I want to make perfectly clear. If I find any evidence that proves your claim you've been framed, I run with it."

"No, you don't. You give it to me. I represent the senator," Tate interjected.

"And then what?" I asked.

"I present it to the judge in court."

"So, I dig and find evidence that may exonerate your client. You present it in court and all the freakin' news media hounds get to run with the results of my investigation at the same time?"

"That's your issue. My priority is the senator," Tate said.

"My priority is not seeing my work on CNN or MSNBC, or in the *Washington Post* or the *New York Times* before the *Tribune* gets to run it. And let me tell you flat out, that just isn't gonna happen. Absolutely no freakin' way."

"You heard my instructions," the lawyer said.

"Hey! I'm not your client, and I don't work for you."

"Then there is no deal," Tate said.

"What deal? You don't get to control me."

"Like I said, the senator is my priority," Tate said.

"Then I'm outta here," I said, getting up to leave.

Slamming his fist on the metal table, Bradford shouted, "Everyone cool down."

His breathing was labored. His eyes reflected desperation. "Mr. Kozar, I need your help. You find anything that proves my innocence, you run with it."

"Senator, as your lawyer I strongly advise you to rethink this," Tate interrupted.

"And Senator, if I find evidence that you're a sexual predator and a murderer, I will run with it," I countered.

The senator nodded his agreement.

With the niceties out of the way, I got down to the matter at hand. "Word is you alleged in court that you've been framed."

"I asked you to come because I need someone with an open mind to look into the charges that have been leveled at me."

"That you murdered your intern after sexually assaulting her," I said.

"Which I swear I did not do. Mr. Kozar, I was never in her apartment. I've never even been to her apartment. Gail was a sweet young woman with a promising political career ahead of her. I did not kill her. You've got to believe me."

"Senator, my job is to report the facts. Right now, the way things look, I have to confess I have a hard time believing you."

"You just said your job is to investigate the facts. All I'm asking is that you investigate the charges against me and then report the facts."

"At this time, the facts don't weigh in your favor. Not in the slightest."

"Because the so-called facts were ascertained by the police," the senator charged.

"That's their job when they show up at a murder scene. Ascertain the facts," I said.

"As far as the lead detective is concerned, the case has been solved. He's not looking at any other possibilities. He's clamped on a pair of horse blinders," Bradford insisted.

"Senator, for me to investigate this, I need a lead. Something I can chase, like a clue. You say you've been framed. By whom?" I asked.

"Where do I start? The Proud Boys, the Oath Keepers. I wouldn't even be surprised if Vladimir Putin is behind this."

"Seriously? You think Putin is behind the rape and murder of your intern?"

The senator did not respond.

"Let's get down to the facts that are in the possession of the DA. How did your semen get on the victim?"

"I have absolutely no idea. I told you I wasn't with her. I would never have touched Gail. I was never sexually involved with her. I always tread carefully with the women on my staff, what with all the allegations of sexual impropriety that have been leveled by staffers against senators and House representatives," he explained.

"Where were you on the night Peterson was murdered?"

Tate jumped in. "Don't answer that."

"Oh, give me a break. He's not on the witness stand," I shot back.

"I was home alone," Bradford said.

"Can anyone verify this?"

"I said I was home alone."

"Maybe someone called you at home?"

"No one called."

"Not even your wife to ask how your day went or to say goodnight?" I asked.

"No," the senator snapped, a look of exasperation on his face. "Look, I'm willing to pay you for your time."

"That's not even a starter. I work for the *Tribune* and I make it a point not to take bribes or any other form of payment from people I'm investigating."

"It's not a bribe," the senator insisted. "I could make a sizable donation to your favorite charity if you'd like."

"I'm not going there."

"Mr. Kozar, I know from your reputation you are a dogged investigative reporter. All I'm asking is that you to step back and take a hard look into this. I am being framed. I know it. I did not kill Gail Peterson," Bradford pleaded.

Looking into his eyes for the first time, I felt a twinge in my gut that maybe this guy was telling the truth. My brain spoke louder, warning me that based on the DNA evidence collected at the murder scene, this guy was stone cold guilty.

I deferred to my gut.

"Look, I'll dig around, but if I find out you're lying, I'll write it up, including this meeting, and you can rot in prison for the rest of your life for all I care."

"That's all I ask. Nothing more."

I had one last point. "On the way here, I heard that eighteen senators from your own caucus are calling on you to resign for the sake of the public's faith in the US Senate."

Bradford's eyes narrowed into angry slits. "I am innocent. I deserve the presumption of innocence. Resigning would be tantamount to admitting guilt."

"So, you're not going to step down?"

"No, and you can quote me."

Tate quickly interjected. "No quoting anybody."

I got up. Tate remained seated. He stayed behind to practice law, and I left the prison with absolutely no idea where to start digging.

GOLD ROLEX

Detective Alyssa Lamont was on her third frame-by-frame review of the elevator security tape. Her eyes were heavy and her brain half poached when something snagged her attention. She froze the frame.

"Jake, come over here and take a look at this," she called out.

Jake Wells stood behind his partner's desk and watched the video in slo-mo.

"This is when the perp gets back on the elevator at the fourth floor after his romantic interlude. Again, he's got his cap pulled down over his face, and see that? Right there, he's checking his watch."

Lamont hit freeze-frame and zoomed in on the man's left wrist. "It's a gold Rolex."

"That is one expensive time piece," her partner noted with a whistle. "The guy's got to be loaded."

Jake's cell phone dinged. It was Spencer requesting an update on the Janet Walker murder.

Lamont grimaced. "You go. I can't stand being in the same room as that jackass."

Detective Captain Spencer was drumming his fingers on his desk when Wells entered. The captain seemed in an upbeat mood. "Any progress on your investigation?"

"Our undercover tailed the neighbor who lived across from the hooker's apartment and recovered a coffee cup he tossed into the trash at a Starbucks. We got a clean set of fingerprints and compared them to the prints taken at the victim's apartment. It came up negative. We're back to square one. We're still waiting for the DNA results."

"Too bad on that. Anything more on the security camera on the elevator?"

"We think we've got the perp. The guy had to be really well off. When he got back on the elevator, Alyssa noticed he looked at his watch. It was a gold Rolex."

Spencer nodded. "What's your next step?"

"Vice came back. Told me the vic worked for an upscale escort service called Discreet Encounters. I'm trying to reach the manager but all I get is an answering machine. I left a message. Hopefully, someone will get back to me and maybe shed some light on who the woman was seeing the night she was killed."

"Keep me in the loop," Spencer instructed.

"Will do, Captain," Wells said.

MOTIVE TO COMMIT MURDER

I was mystified as I thought about my meeting with Senator Bradford. He had pointed the finger at two possible culprits he believed had the motive and the means to frame him. But the idea of someone killing his intern as some kind of payback was almost too far-fetched for me to swallow. I didn't buy into the senator's claim for a second. Still, I decided to give it a shot. I cold called a member of the Proud Boys and a top honcho with the Oath Keepers, and I was somewhat surprised when they agreed to be interviewed.

I met my first subject in a quiet corner of the Main Street Park in Brooklyn. He was wiry, about five-foot seven, clean shaven, and he sported a buzz cut. His face was covered in ink. Tattoos ran from both shoulders to the tips of his fingers. There was one he was most proud to display: two bold, capital letters, PB, encircled by a wreath on the right side of his neck. The letters stood for Proud Boys. He wore a jean jacket with cut-off sleeves and a PB crest on the back identifying him as a member of the far-right, neo-fascist, and exclusively male organization hell-bent on promoting political violence in America.

From the moment I laid eyes on him, I knew the interview would go south in a heartbeat. He refused to shake hands and refused to give his real name. Instead, he offered up his street tag, Spider, which I assumed had to do with the tattooed web on his right cheek. He also refused my invitation to sit on a nearby bench, preferring to remain standing and in my face.

Throughout our short time together, virtually every comment spewed from Spider's mouth was peppered with F-bombs. "You should know I hate fuckin' journalists. All fuckin' liars. Nothing but fuckin' purveyors of fake news," he began.

I figured no good would come from pretending to be the least bit interested in what he had to offer, so I cut to the chase.

"What are your thoughts on Senator William Bradford?"

"The fuckin' guy who killed the chick who worked for him?"

"Yes, that Senator Bradford."

"Why should I fuckin' care a rat's ass about him?"

"The Senator thinks one of the right-wing, neo-Nazi organizations like the Proud Boys or the Oath Keepers may have committed the murder in order to frame him."

Spider burst out laughing and kept on laughing for a good ten seconds, his face turning red. "The guy's a dumb fuck. Fucker rapes a chick, kills her, and fingers us? Absolutely fuckin' whack. I love it."

"The senator has been your most vocal critic in the Senate, at public speaking events, and on talk shows. In one of his appearances on CNN, he called the Proud Boys pathetic and dangerous."

"Like I give a fuck what he says about us. I know what we stand for, and that's all I care about."

"What is that?"

"What is what?"

"What you stand for."

"White people, Christians, Western civilization, and men."

"Doesn't it piss you off when the senator calls you pathetic? Maybe make you want to shut him down?"

"And go out and kill this chick? Get fuckin' serious. That what you're gonna print in your fuckin' rag?"

"I'm just asking a question."

"Well, here's my response. Fuck you and the donkey you rode in on. I'm done here." Spider shoved his middle finger inches from my face and walked away.

"Well, that was a moment in sports," I said to myself.

*

My next interview with a senior member of the Oath Keepers went a tad better. He was a burly, beer-bellied, bearded man who called himself Bull. His only tattoo was on the upper part of his left arm. It was a stylized keyblade—a special weapon wielded by the main characters in the popular video game *Kingdom Hearts*. We met at a hole-in-the-wall bar in downtown Jersey City.

"What'll you boys have?" a fifty-something female server asked, feigning a welcoming smile.

"You want a beer?" I asked.

"You buying?"

"Yes."

"I'll have a Coors and a double shot of Bourbon neat. You got Wild Turkey?" Bull asked.

"Yes. And you?" she asked, turning to me.

"Do you carry Grolsch?"

"When you're with me you drink American beer, not this foreign piss," Bull bellowed.

I changed my order. "Coors."

Bull looked around the bar taking in all the American kitsch. "My kind of bar. I like this place."

"Yeah, it's kinda cool in its own way. I like it."

"I don't like these minimalist bars where you sit on these skinny stools and pay like twenty dollars for a foreign beer that tastes like goat urine."

"It's a matter of taste," I suggested.

The server showed up with our drinks. Bull lifted his glass of Bourbon, sniffed the contents, held up his glass, and shouted, "America, the land of the free."

We clinked. He downed his double shot in one gulp.

"Now that's good Kentucky Bourbon. Another double," he called out to the server.

"So, what do you want to know?" he asked, taking a swig of beer.

I decided to ease into the interview and tossed out a softball question. "Tell me about the Oath Keepers. What does your organization stand for?"

"Our job is to defend the Constitution of the United States against all enemies, foreign and domestic."

No argument from me with that. "How many members does the Oath Keepers have?"

"Last count, thirty-eight thousand, and they're from all walks of life. We got police, military, veterans, elected politicians, religious leaders, teachers, government employees. Hell, we even got a big-name undertaker."

"Do you need one?"

"One what?"

"Undertaker."

Bull laughed. "You're a funny guy. What else you want to know?"

"Why do you feel the need for an organization like the Oath Keepers?"

"We believe the federal government is out to strip American citizens of their civil liberties, and let me tell you, we're not going to let that happen."

"The Oath Keepers have been described as a violent, extremist organization."

"Left-wing politicians paint us that way and portray themselves as defenders against tyranny," Bull countered.

"Is Senator William Bradford one of those defenders against tyranny?"

"Bradford is a piece of rat shit. Last I read he raped and murdered his intern."

"The senator maintains he didn't kill her. He maintains he's being framed."

"Sure, he's being framed. Who's framing him?"

"He suggested that your organization may have had something to do with it."

Bull grimaced and shook his head. "What a dumb motherfucker. He's trying to pawn off his dirty deed on us? The man's got a serious short circuit in his brain."

"You wouldn't want to see him publicly humiliated, convicted, and sent to prison for life? It would shut him down," I suggested.

"He don't need no help from us. He humiliates himself every time he opens his trap."

"So, the Oath Keepers wouldn't think of setting the senator up for a crime he says he didn't commit?"

"Why would we? Look, every time Bradford blathers on about us, we get a ton of new members. He's like a mega recruitment magnet for us. Why would we want to do away with our best PR agent? And we don't have to pay him a penny."

"I never thought of it that way."

"One of the objectives in our playbook is to gain access to the mainstream media, good or bad, 'cause every time our name gets dragged through the mud, you journalists cream in your drawers and run the bullshit. And we end up getting loads of new recruits banging on our door."

The server placed a double shot of Wild Turkey in front of Bull. He closed his eyes, sniffed the glass, and downed the amber brew. I signaled for the bill.

"So, what are you gonna write in your rag?" the Oath Keeper asked, his eyes locked on my face. "You gonna imply we had something to do with the murder of that woman? Let an unsubstantiated, hair-brained comment dangle out there blowing crap in the wind?"

"No. I don't report stuff I can't prove, and from where I sit there's no proof whatsoever that your organization was involved in the murder of Gail Peterson."

"All you got is the ramblings of a sleazebag politician who'll say anything to turn the attention on someone else for something everyone knows he did," Bull offered.

The server handed me the bill. I paid cash, thanked her, shook hands with Bull, and left. I was no further ahead in my investigation and had absolutely no idea where to turn next.

GAIL'S MOM

There was one more interview I knew would be difficult to get and, if I got it, would rile Brian Tate and upset Senator Bradford. A quick search on Google located the phone number and address. I called and was somewhat surprised when Rachel Peterson, Gail's mom, agreed albeit guardedly to a face-to-face interview. She refused to talk over the phone.

The Petersons lived in an elegant, three-bedroom, red-brick bungalow on a bucolic, tree-lined street in Montclair, New Jersey, about twelve miles west of Manhattan. Heading up the cobblestone walkway, I got a sick feeling in my stomach. It was like a dark shroud hung over the house. The shades were drawn tight. The mailbox was stuffed with dozens of cards, no doubt condolences from family, friends, and acquaintances. Flyers and leaflets were strewn over the porch. I rang the bell and waited. Two minutes passed and not a sound. I wondered if Mrs. Peterson had changed her mind. This time, I knocked loudly on the wooden door. A minute later, I heard the rattle of the lock on the other side. The door opened a crack and in a barely audible voice a woman asked, "Who is it?"

"Mrs. Peterson, my name is Matt Kozar. We spoke briefly on the phone yesterday. You said I should come over."

Rachel Peterson pulled the door open just enough to allow me to squeeze through. I was shocked when I saw her. She looked haggard in the black dress that hung loosely on her frail body. Her face was ashen and dotted with tiny, pink blotches. Thick, dark bags hung under her eyes. Her gray hair was a dry, tangled mess. The woman was an emotional and physical wreck.

Without speaking, she led me into the dimly lit living room. Not a sliver of light escaped the curtains covering the window. Sitting on a weathered, leather reclining sofa was Richard Peterson, Rachel's husband of thirty-four

years. He didn't look up when I approached and held out my hand to introduce myself. He looked totally detached, staring blankly into space.

I turned to Mrs. Peterson. "I am sorry for your loss."

She didn't respond.

I was starting to feel extremely uneasy. I had no business being there; I
was an interloper in their time of immense sorrow. I sat at one end of a floral
sofa and looked around the room. I was stunned when my eyes focused on
a shrine to their daughter on the right side of the fireplace. Scores of photos
were pasted on the wall: Gail's baby pictures; a smiling father teaching the
seven-year-old love of his life to ride a bike; mother and daughter doing arts
and crafts on the dining room table; a happy Christmas with the three of
them posing in front of a decorated tree; a portrait of their proud daughter
in cap and gown, graduating from Yale University. It all seemed so perfect.

As I scanned each photo, I was struck by one in particular. I was certain
it was taken in the US Senate. Half of it had been torn away. I wondered if
Senator Bradford was on the discarded half.

"Mrs. Peterson," I began in a respectful whisper. "I want to thank you for
agreeing to see me. I know this is extremely difficult for you."

There was no reply.

"Can you tell me about Gail?"

Rachel Peterson said nothing for a long moment and then began, her eyes
never leaving the shrine.

"Gail was our life. She was our little girl, always happy, always wanting to
do good. She was filled with dreams, and now she's gone."

The room was heavy with sadness. I felt almost suffocated by it.

Mrs. Peterson dabbed her eyes with a tissue and continued. "Why did
he do it? Why? I've been asking myself that question every day since she
was taken away from us. Gail had so much respect for that man. She was so
excited when he took her on as his intern. She admired him so much and
loved working for him. After her internship she was going to get her master's
degree," she said, her voice trailing off.

Her husband did not say a word. There was no reaction. He didn't move.
He just sat there alone in his nightmare.

"Gail worked so hard to prove herself, wanting him to see her worth. She
put in long hours and took her work home with her."

"Did Gail have someone special in her life?"

"Her life was her work. I urged her to find time for herself, but she was driven to succeed."

I searched for a polite way to ask the next question. It was the sole reason I came. I just hoped it wouldn't cause the woman more pain.

"I understand this is extremely difficult, but I need to ask. Did Gail ever tell you if Senator Bradford made an inappropriate advance on her?"

Mrs. Peterson turned sharply from the wall, her eyes a hate-filled glare. "The detective who came over here the other day asked the same question."

"Detective Spencer?"

"Yes. It felt more a statement than a question. It was like he was hiding something, that he knew the man had made advances towards Gail. Then he asked if I would testify that my daughter told me about it. I was shocked. I told the detective Gail never told me such a thing. Why are you asking me the same question? What do you know?" Mrs. Peterson asked, panic registering in her voice and on her face.

I was scrambling for a response. "I was just asking a question. I certainly don't have any knowledge of this ever happening, and I certainly didn't know Detective Spencer asked you about this."

Mrs. Peterson had endured enough. "I want you to leave this minute. Get out of my house."

"Mrs. Peterson, I'm sorry if I offended you in any way. I truly am."

"Get out! Leave us alone."

*

As I left the house, I closed my eyes and sucked in a lung-full of cool air. I was shaking. I felt dirty. I had invaded a family's privacy in their moment of mourning simply to follow up a lead for a man who, based solely on hard DNA evidence, had murdered their only child. I always loathed it when reporters were dispatched by their editors and producers to the scene of a tragedy and then, with a bogus look of caring, asked the bereaved family how they felt. Yet, here I was, doing the same thing. I now wished I had left the Peterson couple alone. But then, the trip had produced an interesting and disturbing piece of information: what I perceived as an attempt by Detective

Spencer to get Rachel Peterson to lie if called to the witness stand. Why, I wondered, would the detective even go there? The police had all the evidence they needed to convict Senator Bradford and send him to prison for life.

A HUNCH

Spencer had been up most of the night. Something was bothering him about the Walker investigation. As he drove to his office, he kept reviewing the briefing he'd had the day before with Wells. But the light didn't come on and it was making him edgy.

He was sitting at his desk sipping his third cup of coffee when it hit him like a bolt of lightning.

"Wells! Lamont! Get in here!" he yelled, sounding like he was in a panic.

"What is it, Captain?" Wells asked as he rushed into Spencer's office.

Lamont was right behind.

"The logo. What was the logo on the baseball cap?" the captain asked.

"LA Dodgers," Wells replied.

"And the Rolex?"

"I checked it out online. Turns out it's an eighteen-karat gold Yacht-Master. Sells for about forty-five grand," Lamont said.

Spencer waved his hand, dismissing the duo as he reached for the phone on his desk. His gut was pinging, his pulse racing as he punched in the extension number for the fingerprint unit. The phone was answered on the second ring.

"Mike. It's Spencer. Pull Senator Bradford's prints from the Peterson murder and compare them to the prints CSI lifted at the Walker murder scene. Let me know what you find, ASAP."

*

An hour later, Spencer summoned Wells and Lamont to his office. He bore the grin of a wily Cheshire cat.

"It's a match! It's a bloody match! I can't believe it," the captain roared.

"What's a match?" Wells asked.

"The fingerprints taken from the Walker woman's condo match the fingerprints we took when we booked Senator Bradford for the Peterson murder."

"You've got to be kidding," Wells interjected.

"Me thinks we've got a serial killer in our lock up," Spencer said gleefully.

"This is mind-blowing," Lamont said.

"Jake, I want you to put a priority rush on the DNA taken from the Walker crime scene and ask the techs to compare it to Bradford's DNA from the Peterson apartment."

"I'll get right on it," Wells said.

"Before you both go, I have to tell you I'll be taking over as lead detective on the Walker case now that it's connected to the Peterson murder."

When Lamont got to her desk, she kicked the waste bin clean across the squad room.

"Calm down," Wells counseled.

"He did it again. He big-footed us. Fucker is a glory hound."

"Alyssa, keep it down. Nothing we can do about it. He's the boss."

"I hope he steps in one huge pile of dog shit one day, and I pray the vultures will be there to record the event. That fuck-ass will deserve it," Lamont said.

Wells retreated to his cubicle and called the lab. A moment later, he was back in Spencer's office.

"The lab tech said no results until Monday. Everyone went home for the weekend."

"Did you tell them this is a top priority?"

"Look, Captain. The senator ain't going nowhere. We got him on the fingerprints, and we'll get the DNA results on Monday."

Spencer nodded.

"What was it that pointed you to Bradford on the Walker murder? Did you get a tip?" Wells asked.

"Two things. When I was in the senator's office I noticed a black LA Dodgers baseball cap on his credenza, and when we were taking his fingerprints, I noticed he was wearing a gold Rolex. I went down there to put one and one together, and then I rolled the dice."

"Amazing," Wells said.

Spencer's eyes narrowed. "Now, once Lamont gets over her tantrum, tell her to write up her report and get it to me before she checks out. I need to get it to the DA. Oh, and tell her if she doesn't like working here, there's a spot open on traffic detail."

THE BIG APPLE

Stefan was emphatic. "I don't want you to go."

Petra was more emphatic. "I'm going."

"What if he turns out to be some nutbar?" he stressed.

"My brother's girlfriend is picking me up at the airport, so I'm not worried. Anyway, I can take care of myself. You know that."

"You're already calling this stranger you've never laid eyes on your brother."

"Because he is."

Stefan was exasperated. "Let me go with you."

"I said no. I want to do this on my own."

"Then promise me you'll meet this Michael Kozak guy or whoever he is in a very public place like a café or restaurant, and you'll text me to let me know you're alright."

"Of course, I'll text you. I don't want you to worry, although I know you'll be worried the moment I get on the airplane."

Stefan stared down at his shoes. "You're wrong on that. I'm worried right now, and I'll stay that way until you come home."

"Remember, my other reason for going to New York is to take part in the demonstration in front of the UN to protest Russia's war on Ukraine. I'm meeting up with a bunch from the Chicago contingent of Ukies."

Stefan didn't buy it for one second. "Well, in that case, maybe I should join the contingent," he suggested.

"Again. No! Stop with the paranoia already. I'll be fine."

*

Mei was pacing when I entered her apartment. I knew something was up the instant she opened her mouth.

"Now, I don't want you to get angry," she began.

I could sense my Energizer Bunny getting ready to beat her drum.

"Which means I probably will, and I'm betting it has something to do with my so-called half sister."

I was right.

Mei stood behind her sofa. "I got an email from Petra this morning. She's coming to New York on Friday to take part in a march on Saturday from Times Square to the UN."

My mind began a slow sizzle. "Why are you still in touch with her? You know how I feel about this."

"Petra is not a *this*. She's your sister."

"Why is this so important to you?"

"Because you're so important to me. You should reconsider Matt. You should meet her. If not for your own peace of mind, for hers."

"You left out *your* peace of mind. I had peace of mind until you decided to rattle my cage."

"Will you at least agree to see her?" Mei asked, her eyes pleading.

I was tired, fed up, and worn down. This woman was not going to stop. I knew it. Grudgingly, I relented.

*

I rolled over on the bed and realized Mei wasn't there. I called out her name but there was no answer. On the night table next to me was a note.

Hope you slept well. I got up early. I'm on my way to pick up Petra from the airport. I'll pick up coffee and muffins. See you soon. And Matt, be good.

I took "be good" as a stern warning.

I got up and took a hot shower. Usually that helped settle any tension in my body. It didn't. I was wound up tight. My mind was reinforcing concrete walls on the dark side of my brain. Looking at myself in the mirror, I shook my head and asked, "What the hell did I let myself get into?"

*

When Petra came through the arrivals door at La Guardia, Mei waved and moved toward her. They did the European thing. They hugged and air kissed both cheeks.

"How was your flight?" Mei asked.

"It was okay. Kind of odd serving pretzels and Coke to passengers at ten a.m., but that's United."

"Whenever I have to fly, I grab a cup of coffee and a croissant at a café in the departures lounge. How are you feeling?"

"I can't tell you how nervous I am about meeting Michael," Petra said, as they got into a limo.

Mei knew it was time for her to come clean, and it made her anxious. "Yes. About that. I need to explain a few things. The first is his name isn't Michael Kozak."

Petra was taken aback. She thought for a moment she should have listened to Stefan. It was a set-up. Her defense mechanisms kicked in.

"His name is Matt Kozar."

"I don't understand. Why did you tell me his name was Michael Kozak?"

Mei took a deep breath. She knew her answer had to defuse a potentially nasty situation and not damage Matt's future relationship with his newfound sister.

"I was the one who put his DNA into the ancestry website. I wanted to see his ethnic makeup. I had no idea it would lead to this."

Petra tried to absorb Mei's confession. "I'm confused," she said.

"Matt didn't want his DNA out there. He was worried about his information being used or sold by some random outfit. He's a very private guy. Well, as private as he can be given who he is."

"Who he is? What do you mean?"

Mei laughed nervously. "Matt is an investigative journalist with the *New York Tribune*."

Petra's eyes popped wide open as she realized the implications of this new information. "Matt Kozar is my brother? I don't believe it. He's famous! He's the one who went to Bucha and wrote about the massacre."

"Yes."

"And he was shot by that Russian a couple of years ago in Washington. I remember the story. A few of my friends said he was Ukrainian and that he was originally from Chicago."

Mei was impressed with Petra's knowledge of her half brother. Even without knowing they were related, she had more than a basic understanding of the man she would soon meet.

"I think Matt should tell you about himself," Mei said, "or at least what he's willing to share with you."

Petra was beaming. This was better than she imagined. A well-respected investigative journalist was related to her. "I can't wait to meet him."

*

I was sitting on the sofa when the giddy duo arrived. Mei was gushing as she introduced Petra.

"Matt, this is your sister, Petra. Petra this is your brother, Matt."

Petra moved in for a hug. I stuck out my hand. She seemed to retreat a bit, but she recovered when Mei interrupted with food for the two of us. She was playing the role of Suzy Homemaker, which was getting on my nerves.

"I'll get some plates for the muffins. You two sit down and get to know each other," Mei said.

I did not appreciate the set-up and Mei's expectations that I would bond with this stranger and all would be good in the world. I could feel the tension twisting my shoulders into knots. I couldn't speak. It was Petra who broke the ice.

"I can't believe you're that journalist. Your reporting on Bucha was incredible. All my friends think you're a hero. I have been following your work. Your story on the stolen wheat a few years ago was riveting and then you get shot by the Russian and almost die. I'm so grateful you're okay."

Petra was gushing and I hated gush. All I wanted was for her to turn off her cheery faucet. I cut in.

"Mei told me you're in the city for a demonstration."

"I'm taking part in a march to the United Nations to protest Russia's war against Ukraine. It's going to be massive. We've got people coming in from all over the States and even Canada."

"How long are you here for?"

"I leave on Sunday. I have to be back at work on Monday morning."

"What do you do?" I asked, feeling like a disinterested reporter vapidly citing the Five Ws.

"I'm a nurse at Chicago General Hospital."

This small talk was annoying me. To my relief, Mei walking into the room. "I see you're getting to know each other."

I gave her a look that clearly showed I was not amused. Petra caught it and rose to her feet. She appeared tense.

"You know, I think this was a bad idea. I'm going to go to my hotel. I have some people I have to meet before the demonstration tomorrow to discuss a few things," she said, grabbing her purse and heading for the door.

Mei ran after her, turning quickly to fire a heated dart at me. If looks could kill, she would have been charged with manslaughter, and I knew I was in for a major broadside when she got back. But she didn't come back, at least not immediately.

*

When Mei caught up with Petra on the street, she could see the young woman's eyes were more than glistening with tears. She was weeping. Between sobs, Petra asked, "Is he always so detached?"

"Matt can be an insensitive ass sometimes," Mei confessed.

"What's his problem?"

"His past. It's locked up like Fort Knox in some bleak corner of his brain. He doesn't like discussing it or being reminded of it."

"And I remind him of this past?"

"Let's say you set off a lot of triggers in him."

"Maybe I should just stay away from him," Petra suggested, resigned to the realization that her search may not have been a good idea after all.

"I don't think that would be good for you or for Matt. Knowing Matt, he's probably wallowing in a vat of guilt over how he treated you. Underneath that gruff exterior he's a softy. It just takes him a bit of time to get there. Pissed off can quickly turn into pussy cat."

Petra muffled a laugh. "I don't want him to meet me out of guilt."

"Why don't you settle into your room. I'll see how he's feeling and call you in a couple of hours. Please, don't make any plans for dinner."

*

Mei's first words as she barreled into her apartment were "Matt, you're a grade A jerk!"

I remained glued to the sofa knowing full well what it felt like to be a grade A jerk.

"I can't believe the way you acted. What was that all about? You hurt Petra's feelings. She was so excited to meet you, and she left crying her eyes out."

I kept my eyes focused on the floor.

"Are you going to say anything?"

"What's there to say? So I'm a jerk. Tell me something I don't know."

"Why couldn't you just be polite?"

"Something inside me snapped. I just shut down."

"You have to make amends."

I was starting to get annoyed. "How do you propose I do that? Send her a text with a bunch of sad face emojis saying I'm sorry? Or should I buy a sword and fall on it?"

"Don't use that tone with me! I'm really upset with you."

"Where did the two of you go and what did you do? Talk about me?"

"Don't flatter yourself." Mei was still pissed off at me. I knew I had a lot of explaining to do but she didn't give me a chance. A stream of accusatory words about my behavior came fast and furious.

"I tried to convince her that you're not a cold, insensitive jerk, and believe me, that took a lot of doing."

"And I should thank you for that?"

"I want to invite her here for dinner tonight," she insisted.

I closed my eyes and rammed my fingers into my temples.

"Oh, quit being a drama queen. I'm not buying it."

"Fine. We'll do dinner. But you call her."

"And you'll be the gentleman I love."

"Yes, dear."

"You'd better be."

"I said I will, and I will."

ROUND TWO

Petra arrived promptly at 5:30 p.m. for cocktails before dinner. She brought Mei a bouquet of daisies. They hugged and air kissed. I hesitantly went in for a hug and got a cool handshake and a tepid smile. I was probably lucky to get even that. I could feel the frost in the air.

"Would you like a glass of white wine?" Mei asked as Petra sat down at the far end of the sofa. "It's a pinot grigio from Napa Valley."

"That would be nice. Thank you."

As Mei headed to the kitchen, I put in my request. "I'll have a glass of the J. Lohr cab."

"You know where the wine is kept," the love of my life replied in a clipped tone.

All three glasses filled, Mei raised hers and called for a toast. "To new friendships and polite conversations."

"Matt, do you have anything to add?" Mei asked.

What I wanted to add was, "Are you still my girlfriend and lover, or have you morphed into a nagging mother?" I wisely chose to walk on the safe side of the road.

I cleared my throat. "Petra, I want to apologize for my behavior. I got up on the wrong side of the bed to find there was no one on the other side. It discombobulated me."

"Apology accepted," she said with a reasonably warm but cautious smile.

After a dinner generously spiced with mindless banter, Mei ushered us into the living room.

"I'll leave you two alone. I'm sure you have a lot to talk about, now that Matt is aware of the rules of engagement and has re-read the chapter by Miss

Manners on good behavior," she said, smiling wickedly before disappearing into her bedroom.

I turned to Petra and gave her a big grin, knowing what was expected of me. "Round two," I said.

"I hope you don't knock me down a second time," she responded with a cautious smile.

"I promised Mei I would be a gentleman." Digging deep into the recesses of my mind, I came up with the most innocuous yet inquisitive request I could think of.

"So tell me a bit about yourself."

Petra said she worked at the Chicago General Hospital in the trauma unit. "I'm sure you're aware Chicago is known for gang violence. We deal with a lot of shootings, stabbings, and assaults. It's never-ending."

"It's got to get to you at times."

"Sure does. But never when I'm working. I have to stay focused. What happens afterwards is a different story. Sometimes I cry. I can never understand the level of hate and violence that has taken over the city."

"The entire country, for that matter," I noted.

I was moving into fully engaged reporter mode. "What led you to your online search for your father?"

"Since I was a little girl, I wondered who he was. My mom would never tell me anything about him. She never revealed his name. All she said was he died shortly before I was born, and that was it. She wanted to leave the past behind."

"She never told you how she met him? Nothing about the kind of man he was?"

"Mom told me there was no point. Yet I always had this feeling there was something she was keeping from me, and it troubled me."

"Does she know you sent your DNA to this company in hopes of finding someone connected to him?"

"My mom died of breast cancer two years ago. When she was dying, she still wouldn't tell me the name of my birth father. All she said was that he died in an accident. Is that true?"

"Yes," I said.

"What kind of accident?"

I looked for a tactful response. "He was cleaning his gun, and it went off. He forgot there was a bullet in the chamber."

"It must have been horrible for you."

I managed a slight nod.

"How old were you when he died?"

"Seven."

We sat in silence for a moment, wrapped in a heavy cloud of gloom. I was searching for a way to move on to another topic and found it after a quick hit at mental math.

"I was seven when my father was having a fling with your mother."

Petra's cheeks turned red with embarrassment. "It certainly appears that way."

"Funny how life has a way of throwing you a curve ball when you least expect it," I offered, trying to absorb the new information and the implications.

Petra got me back on track. "Tell me about my father. What kind of man was he?"

I could hear Mei's warning ringing in my ears. There was only so much I could tell this stranger about the man who helped create her. I threw out a softball. "Well, from what I remember, he was quite handsome."

"Do you look like him?"

"I have a lot of his features. You do as well. I mean, look at us. We look like brother and sister." It was the first time I admitted to myself there was a familial similarity. Up to this point I had been in denial, refusing to really look at the young woman sitting in front of me.

Petra smiled. "I have a feeling there's more to my father than the fact he was handsome."

I now felt myself being drawn into the uneasy zone. I could push forward or pull back. So I said, "Mei ordered me not to upset you."

"Matt, I'm a big girl. I'm a trauma nurse. I've seen and heard it all. Believe me."

I closed my eyes, took a deep breath, and exhaled slowly. A few minutes passed and then in a quiet whisper I told her about the fateful evening my father got together with a few of his Marine Corps buddies. "They were drunk and decided to play spin the barrel with a .45 Colt. He was first up and that was it."

"Russian roulette," Petra said, her hand over her mouth in shock.

"My father … I'm sorry I keep saying my father."

"It's okay. All I hear in my ears is my dad," Petra said.

"Our father joined the Marine Corps when he was eighteen. He fought in Vietnam and when he came back, he was basically a whack job. Unhinged."

"What do you mean by that?"

"He was an angry, violent man filled with demons clawing at his brain. He'd flip into a rage over the slightest things. He drank like a fish. Bourbon with a beer chaser. By midday he was drunk, and that's when it was best to stay out of his way. He could never seem to find peace or solace."

"It must have been horrible for you," Petra said.

"It was what it was."

I noticed Petra was no longer looking at me. She was staring at her hands, which were shaking.

"PTSD," she murmured.

"What?"

"He was suffering from post-traumatic stress disorder. At the hospital where I work, we deal with so many veterans returning from Iraq and Afghanistan suffering from PTSD. It's an extremely debilitating condition," Petra explained.

"Don't get me wrong. When my father was sober, he was the nicest guy you'd ever want to meet. The perfect dad. He'd take me to the park and toss a baseball. He bought me a bike on my sixth birthday and taught me how to ride. It was just this Jekyll and Hyde thing I found really scary. Deep down I always felt sad for him, and I guess in my own way I loved him. But like I said, a lot of times he scared the heck out of me."

I didn't know what else to say. I was done talking about him and desperately wanted to stop the torment pounding in my brain.

Petra could feel the tension but decided to press on. "Do you know where my father is buried?"

The question caught me completely off guard. I had absolutely no idea where he was pushing up daisies. I remember being in the back seat of a black limo and driving to a cemetery after the funeral in the church. It was the first and only time I had ever been there.

I shook my head.

"You never looked for his grave?" Petra asked.

"What for? If you believe the spirit lives on when it leaves your body after you die, then I very much doubt it would be hanging out in a cemetery."

Petra sat back, a look of hesitation in her eyes. I wondered where her mind was wandering. Seconds later, I got the answer, and it left my stomach tied in knots.

"I couldn't help but notice you've said nothing about your mother. Is she dead?"

"I don't want to go there."

"I'm sorry. I didn't mean to pry," Petra said.

Petra could see I was on the verge of breaking down, and she wanted to spare us both the awkwardness. She knew it was time to change the topic.

"Mei told me you're investigating the murder involving US Senator Bradford. I can't believe what he did to that poor woman."

The hair on the back of my neck bristled.

My response was terse. "I'm looking into it."

"The Ukrainian community is shaken by this. Bradford was our hero. Totally in our corner, and now he's gone and done this."

I was quick to admonish. "It's what he has been accused of doing. He hasn't had his day in court, so according to the law, he's innocent until proven guilty by a jury of his peers."

Petra stared at me in disbelief. "You don't believe he's guilty?" she asked, her tone incredulous.

I shrugged my shoulders.

"And you're trying to prove he didn't do it?"

"I'm trying to determine if he did or, as the senator swears, he didn't."

"Given all the evidence against him, how are you going to prove he didn't?"

"I'm still trying to figure that out."

The conversation had taken a turn I wasn't prepared to take. I didn't want to go there. I was talked out and needed a break. A moment later I was saved by the bell, or in this case, the opening of the bedroom door. Mei stuck her head out and peered into the living room. "Can I come in?" she asked hesitantly.

We both nodded. As she walked into the living room, Mei could sense the tension in the air. She sat beside Petra, reached for her hand, and smiled warmly. Typical Mei, she turned the topic away from uncomfortable issues to something unthreatening.

"I noticed you're wearing a diamond ring," Mei said.

"Yes! I'm engaged. His name is Stefan Holuk. He's thirthy-two, a civil engineer, and he's the man of my dreams. He's always there for me and makes me laugh. What else can a girl ask for?"

"Have you set a date?" Mei asked.

"We've booked the church and the hall for the second Saturday in July."

Mei had this way of lifting dark clouds when situations got tense. She looked over at me, smiled, and blew me a kiss. It was an ice breaker and a cue for me to get back into the conversation.

"What's this Stefan like?" I asked, and then blurted out, "After all, I need to know about the guy my little sister is about to marry."

Mei and Petra looked at each other in stunned silence and simultaneously burst into tears.

"What did I do?" I asked, wondering if I had yet again stuck my foot in my mouth.

Mei said, "Petra. You called Petra your little sister."

"Well, she kind of is," I said in my defense.

Petra leapt up and gave me a hug. The ice was broken.

Wiping her eyes with a napkin, Mei asked, "Anyone up for more cake and coffee?"

We all laughed. Mei believed food was the answer to what ailed you and she wasn't even a Jewish mother.

Suddenly and without hesitation, Petra blurted out, "I'd love for you and Mei to come to my wedding,"

Mei was the first to answer. "We wouldn't miss it."

I was a bit overwhelmed, which shocked me to the core. I couldn't answer right away, but I wasn't ready yet to share my emotions over what had just transpired. I was, after all, this incorrigible, tough investigative journalist. I dug deep and came up with a question I knew would keep a tear from spilling from my eye.

"What's Stefan's family like?" I blurted out.

"They're fantastic. Very close. His mom and dad are so caring and loving. I feel so blessed to have them in my life. Stefan's older brother, Andrej, is a dreamboat. He's a lawyer. Natalia, his wife, is a sweetheart. She's like a sister to me. And my life is even more special now that the two of you are in it."

"This is all so …" Mei began.

"Special?" I interjected jokingly. I had to lighten the mood for my own benefit. It's what I did in circumstances that made me uncomfortable and this was certainly one of them. I don't like people to see my sensitive side, as infrequently as it makes an appearance.

Petra looked right at me. "I thought I'd be walking down the aisle with absolutely no family in the church. I mean, I have a ton of friends. But that's different. Family is important."

We all stopped to reflect on what had happened over the past hour. Strangers becoming family. Several minutes passed quietly. It was Petra who broke the silence when she glanced at her watch and said, "It's getting late, and I meet the contingent from Chicago tomorrow morning to plan for the demo."

She stood up and hit me with a totally unexpected proposition.

"How do you feel about joining me at the protest march?"

"I'm a reporter. I don't take part in marches. If anything, I cover them," I said flatly.

"That's my man, always reporting on what's happening but never getting directly involved," Mei stated somewhat ironically.

"That's not fair. Reporting on important events is doing something," I countered.

"Well, you're not assigned to cover the demonstration for the newspaper," Mei pointed out, "so why don't you go in solidarity with your people?"

"Mei, don't pull my chain."

"Why don't you come?" Petra asked, looking beseechingly into my eyes.

"Truth is, I'd feel like a hypocrite. I don't speak the language. I don't really know much of anything about being Ukrainian. I don't belong to any organizations or church. I'd feel like an outsider."

"So many of the people who will be at the demonstration are in the same boat as you. Every one of them has one thing in common. Ukraine is in their DNA. The blood of their ancestors flows through their body, just like it flows through yours," Petra said.

"You should have been a preacher," I said with an uncomfortable laugh. It evoked a chuckle from Petra.

"There's just something about being Ukrainian," she said. "It's a candle burning brightly in my soul."

"You should go," Mei urged. "I'm sure a lot of people will be thrilled to meet you."

"You're like a hero to them, especially after your stories on Bucha," Petra added.

I took a deep breath and exhaled slowly. I really didn't want to attend the march. It's not my thing at all, optics aside. But the two women were a force when they lined up against me. It was hard to say no. "I'll go, but I'm keeping a low profile."

"Fantastic," Petra said. "We'll meet in the lobby of my hotel at seven thirty tomorrow morning, grab a coffee, and walk over to Times Square."

CANDY CANE

Captain Detective Spencer had ordered Lamont and Wells to show up at his office early Saturday morning for an update. He was the first to arrive and anxiously paced in the hallway waiting for his team.

"Any news from the lab?" Spencer asked as they walked into the homicide unit, his face wired with anticipation.

"I just got off the phone with the tech. The results are being sent over as we speak," Lamont said.

"The tech tell you anything?"

Lamont refused to make eye contact with her superior. No hint of celebration or bravado registered on her face. She was matter-of-fact. "The DNA collected at Walker's apartment matches Bradford's DNA."

A wide grin spread across Spencer's face. "I knew it. I need to see the security camera footage from the elevator."

The three detectives huddled around Lamont's desk and watched the prime suspect in the Walker murder arrive and depart.

"That's definitely him," Spencer said.

"How can you tell?" Wells asked. "His face is hidden from the camera."

"His size. The way he moves," he said, turning to Lamont. "Make a copy of the video and send it to David Di Adamo at the DA's office."

"What are you going to do?" Jake asked.

"I'm going to call Bradford's lawyer and inform him it would be in his client's best interest that he shows up at the jail first thing Monday morning. After which, I will be holding a news briefing. And Detectives, lips sealed. I don't want any of this to get out until after I deal with Bradford."

"There's something else," Wells said. "Last night, I dropped by to speak to the manager of the escort service Walker worked for. I asked him to give me the names of her clients the night she was murdered. Smug asshole comes back and says the client lists are confidential."

"No cooperation?"

"Not until I read him the riot act. I told him in no uncertain terms I would get a warrant ordering him to supply me with Walker's entire client list from the day she started working there to the day she was murdered. You should have seen the look on his face. Turned over the info right away. On the night Walker was murdered, she had a scheduled rendezvous with Senator Bradford at 9 p.m. Turns out, he was a regular. Made a date with her every month or so."

"Good work, Jake. Write it up."

Wells face broke into a mischievous grin. "There's one juicy tidbit I'm sure will send your mind spinning. Walker had a stage name. It's what she used on the agency's website."

The detective paused for effect. "It was Candy Cane."

Spencer's face lit up. "This just keeps getting better and better."

Before he left the office, he turned to Lamont and Wells. "I repeat. Lips sealed. If any of this gets out before I meet with Bradford and his lawyer on Monday, you'll be back in uniform directing traffic. Got it?"

Wells shrugged his shoulders and slumped down on the chair in his cubicle. "Got it."

Spencer turned to Lamont with a distrustful look on this face.

Lamont looked over at her partner and crossed her eyes. "No worry," she said. "I'll be in church all day tomorrow singing in the Sunday choir."

"Good. I'll be back in the office after my meeting with Bradford and his lawyer. I'll update you then."

VY ROZMOVLYAYETE UKRAYINS'KOYU?

As protests go, this one was massive and impressive. At the very least, 25,000 people moved from Times Square to the UN in solidarity with Ukraine, many waving or draped in the yellow and blue flag of Ukraine. They carried placards denouncing Vladimir Putin as a murderer, a war criminal, a butcher, and a psychopath. Other signs read "Hands off Ukraine," "Stop Russian Aggression," and "I Stand with Ukraine." Strategically placed protest marshals carrying bullhorns shouted chants to get the crowd revved up, not that anyone needed help in that regard.

It took well over two hours for the crowd to walk the one-mile route to the United Nations on East 42nd Street where it was met by a wall of police in full riot gear standing at the ready behind a steel barricade. A makeshift stage had been erected in front of the entrance to the Secretariat: a walkway adorned with the flags of 193 nations.

As twenty-four young men and women dressed in colorful Ukrainian costumes filed onto the stage, the crowd went quiet. A moment later, a choir began singing, first the American anthem, then the Ukrainian anthem. Everyone stood at attention, hands on their hearts. Most joined in the singing. It was incredibly moving.

After the anthems, several federal, state, and city officials, as well as the Ukrainian Ambassador to the United States and leaders in the Ukrainian-American community, addressed the crowd. At the start and end of each speech, the speakers shouted *Slava Ukraini*! Glory to Ukraine! The crowd responded with *Heroyam Slava*! Glory to the Heroes!

After the march, I took Petra to Veselka, a Ukrainian restaurant on the Lower East Side. The place was packed and the mood festive; protesters were enjoying Ukrainian borshch and singing Ukrainian folk songs.

No sooner had we sat down at a table near the window then three women from the protest recognized me and headed over.

"Are you Matt Kozar?" one asked.

"Yes."

"My name is Claudia Tataryn," the older of the women said, reaching out to shake my hand.

"*Vy rozmovlyayete ukrayins'koyu?*" she asked.

I had no idea what she said.

Petra came to my rescue. "She asked if you speak Ukrainian."

"Not a word."

"*Chomu ni?* Sorry. Why not?" Claudia asked.

I could feel my face turning red. "It's complicated," I replied anxiously.

"I didn't mean to offend you," she said, looking somewhat embarrassed. "I want to thank you for your reporting on the devastating situation in Bucha. Many of us in the community were amazed at how you got into the destroyed city, and now to see you taking part in the protest march ... We're all so grateful. We would be honored if you could join us at our table."

"I'm here with my sister. We're sort of catching up on our lives."

Claudia nodded. "We should keep in touch. I would like to invite you to address our organization on the massacre in Bucha. Would that be a possibility?"

"Definitely, but I must remind you I don't speak Ukrainian."

"That's okay. We all speak English. How can I reach you?"

I handed her my business card.

Claudia and her friends then turned their attention to Petra. I had no idea what they were talking about. It was all in Ukrainian. After a minute or so, the women each leaned into Petra and air kissed three times—right cheek, left, and right. The mini entourage then retreated to their table.

"What was that all about?" I asked.

"They were telling me how impressed they were with your reporting on Bucha. You're kind of a hero to them."

"I don't feel like a hero." I said, my voice tinged with sadness.

"They told me they also followed your investigation into the Russian oligarchs stealing American grain meant for Africa—when that Russian gangster almost killed you. That was when they first started to think you might be Ukrainian."

I know I should have been grateful for the praise, but I found myself slightly annoyed.

"I kind of wish people would let that go," I said. "Wherever I am, all I get is 'Hey! You're that guy.' It's really wearing on me."

Petra wasn't going to let me get away with my attitude. She had learned quickly how to push my buttons.

"You're famous, Matt. It's not every day a reporter gets shot by a Russian hitman and lives to talk about it: or in your case, dies and comes back to life."

"Well, I'm here now," I offered lamely.

Once again, Petra had my number, and she changed the subject.

"So tell me. How did you like taking part in the march?"

"I felt like a fish out of water," I told her. "But I have to say I was totally impressed by the passion and intensity of the demonstrators, and seriously stunned by the turnout, and not just Ukrainians. I saw people carrying flags of Poland, Georgia, England, Canada, Germany, France, Italy, Australia, Estonia, Lithuania, Israel, and of course the US."

"The free world is on our side," Petra said with a proud smile.

At this point, after a day of revelations and new insight, I was talked out and hungry. I ordered a plate of pierogies smothered in fried onions. Petra laughed. "Do you know they're called *pyrohy* in Ukrainian? Pierogi is the Polish word, but don't worry. Everyone I know outside of the Ukrainian community calls them pierogies."

"Whatever they're called, they're one of my favorite foods."

Petra ordered a bowl of steaming hot borshch with a dollop of sour cream. We ate in silence.

When we finished, I waved at the server for the bill.

HIDDEN PHOTOS

Wrapped in our thoughts, Petra and I walked for a while and ended up sitting on a bench in a quiet corner of Tompkins Square Park in the middle of the East Village. I was feeling like crap, and Petra sensed it.

"Is something bothering you? You look upset," Petra said.

"I am."

"With me?"

"With me. I acted like a jerk when we first met, and I want to apologize for my behavior. You didn't deserve that."

"You've already apologized, and we're talking now. That's all that matters."

"I know, but my behavior was reprehensible."

"You'll never be a jerk in my eyes," Petra said with a warm smile.

I hit the switch button and asked, "What else are you involved in with the Ukrainian community?"

"Well, two years ago, I signed up with a group of doctors and nurses in Canada on their way to Ukraine to operate on soldiers who were severely wounded fighting the Moscow-backed separatists in Donetsk and Luhansk. The team was led by Dr. Oleh Antonyshyn. He's an amazing doctor from Canada who specializes in craniofacial surgery."

"It must of have been one heck of an experience."

"I loved standing next to Dr. Antonyshyn and his team in the operating room. It tore me apart to see young men, their bodies ripped apart by shrapnel. It was all so surreal. I've seen the craziness of street violence and shootings in Chicago, but this was on a completely different scale."

"You really identify with being Ukrainian," I blurted out. I thought how fortunate she was to have such a clear sense of her roots. I was still floundering, although my trip to Bucha had changed me profoundly, and I was closer than ever to an understanding of what bonded us as a community.

"Yes, of course, but like you, I'm American first and foremost."

"Unlike me, you speak Ukrainian. You know the culture, customs, traditions, and history. You sing the Ukrainian anthem with pride."

"My mom raised me steeped in things Ukrainian. I danced in a Ukrainian dance troupe. That's where I met Stefan. He was my dance partner for three years. Today I sing in a Ukrainian women's choir. I play a bandura, the national instrument of Ukraine. My mom taught me how to make *pyrohy*, *holubtsi*, and *borshch*, how to embroider, and how to write *pysanky*, Ukrainian Easter eggs. So, as you said, I'm the total package," Petra said with a laugh.

"You're like this Super Uke. You do it all. And me? I love *pyrohy*."

Petra burst out laughing and for a few moments couldn't stop. I pointed to a bench, and we sat down. I was about to share something I knew would affect her profoundly, and I wore my concern on my face.

"Text me your cell number," I said. "I'm going to send you something, but don't open it just yet."

Petra nodded with a mixture of worry and anticipation on her face.

I heard her phone ding as my text arrived.

"Last night, I was trying to remember things about my father that I could share with you, and an incident came to mind. It was during the luncheon after his funeral in the basement of the Ukrainian church. Not many people showed up. There was one man watching me. I was sitting alone, and he came over to join me. His name was Jesse. He told me he and my father were best friends throughout high school. I was surprised because in all my seven years on this earth, I'd never met the man. Anyway, he started telling me stories about my father and their close friendship. How my father loved to dance. Not Ukrainian folk dancing—dancing to rock and roll and disco. I kind of laughed at the thought of my father dancing like John Travolta to "Stayin' Alive" in the *Saturday Night Fever* movie. He also told me how all the girls had super crushes on him because he was so cool and handsome and fun to be around. He was always joking and teasing the girls. He played guitar and saw himself one day becoming a rock star. Apparently, he was also quite the jock. He played baseball and football on the high school teams. Baseball was his favorite sport. His position was shortstop."

I was shocked I had all these details to share with Petra. Jesse had filled in the blanks. My father had been a stranger to me up to that point. I must have repressed the discussion and forgotten about it. The details were all coming back to me now, the words tumbling out of my mouth. I couldn't stop talking.

"I asked Jesse why he never came to visit us after Vietnam. He said when my father came back from the war zone, he was a changed man. He drank a lot, had a hair-trigger temper, and was unpredictable. I always remembered that word. Unpredictable.

"As to why dad joined the Marine Corps in the first place, Jesse said he enlisted when he was eighteen, a year after my grandparents died in a car crash. He was alone and penniless. University was out of the question. Dad assumed by enlisting he would learn a trade, become a truck mechanic. Instead, all he was trained to do was kill.

"I never knew any of this, especially that he was an only child and that his parents were killed in a car crash and there were no other family members. No uncles or aunts or cousins. Nobody."

I could tell Petra was lost in her thoughts. She was quiet. A tear slowly rolled down her cheek, then more, until she couldn't stop crying.

I took a deep breath. "Now, I'm going to tell you what I texted you."

She wiped her face with a tissue and refocused.

"Before Jesse left, he handed me an envelope. In it were two photographs. One was of my father at a high school dance with a bevy of girls around him, and the other was of Jesse and my dad, smiling with their arms around each other's shoulders. I broke down the first time I saw the pictures.

"I also have three other images. One is when I was two and sitting on my father's shoulders. We were both smiling. The second is a photo of my father with his parents. He was sixteen at the time and had long hair. The third photo is a portrait of my father in his Marine Corps uniform just after he completed boot camp. I texted you the photos."

"Oh, my goodness!" Petra gasped.

She reached for her purse, her hands shaking as she fumbled with her cell phone. When she saw the photo of her father standing proudly in his Marine Corps uniform, the tears came again and erupted into heartbreaking sobs. I put my arm around her, but I couldn't say a word. There was a huge lump in my throat.

Petra ran her fingers lovingly across our father's face. She gently kissed the photo and hugged the image to her heart.

"Matt, you've given me the missing piece of my puzzle. For so long I wondered about my father. It haunted me, and now I feel such a profound inner peace. I also found you. I'm no longer alone in this world. I have a brother."

We sat quietly for what seemed an eternity. I watched the world go by while Petra flipped back and forth through the photographs. When we finally got up to head back to Mei's apartment, the sun was setting. Hours had passed. I had no sense of the time.

*

On our return, Mei and Petra hugged again. We sat down on the sofa for a brief chat before Petra had to scoot back to her hotel to pack and grab a taxi to the airport. Our moods were vastly improved, our connection now undeniable. We even started finishing each other's sentences.

"How was the demonstration?" Mei asked.

"Absolutely incredible," Petra said.

"The turnout was mind-blowing," I said. "After the march, I took Petra to Veselka."

"I love that restaurant, but if you go there too often you risk gaining a ton of weight," Mei said with a laugh.

"Afterwards, we went to a park nearby and talked about a lot of things," Petra said.

Mei shot me a glance and breathed a sigh of relief when I smiled.

"I'm so happy I found my brother, and it would never have happened had it not been for you. Thank you, Mei. I'm so happy you guys will be coming to my wedding."

"We wouldn't miss it," Mei said.

Petra took a deep breath and turned to me. She had a hesitant look on her face.

"What is it?" I asked.

"I want to ask you a big favor, and I don't want you to feel pressured to say yes. In fact, I'll understand if you say no, and if you do I promise I won't be upset."

"That's one heck of a preamble," I said.

"I want to ask you to walk me down the aisle on my wedding day."

I think for the first time in my life I was speechless.

"It's okay. I understand," Petra said, her voice reduced to a whisper.

"You haven't asked anyone to do this?" I asked.

"Stefan's father asked if he could. I said yes, but that was before you and I met."

I was touched beyond belief, but I was aware enough to ask whether her future father-in-law might be hurt by the change of plans.

"He'll still be standing at the altar with his son. Trust me. He will understand. It'll all be good. I promise."

"Then if he doesn't mind, I'd be honored. However—and I paused for effect—first you have to tell Stefan he has to ask me formally for your hand in marriage. After all, I am the man in the family."

Petra laughed. "I'm so happy I found you."

I thought back to how reluctant I had been to meet Petra and how I was annoyed with Mei. Now I couldn't have been more grateful for her meddling.

"I'm glad you found me, and I'm grateful that Mei kept tenaciously stirring the pot. Boy, we sound like a soap opera."

We all laughed.

*

After Petra left for Chicago, I headed back to my apartment savouring the events of the past couple of days. But it was time to get back to reality and work. I hunkered down to review my notes on the Gail Peterson murder, searching for something in the pages I may have missed. There was nothing; not a single clue I could chase down. The Oath Keepers and the Proud Boys were a dead end. My interview with Mrs. Peterson offered up nothing. I had no idea about my next move, and it was driving me crazy.

A SECOND COUNT OF MURDER

Spencer remained standing while the senator and the lawyer sat across from each other at the table in the prison interview room. It was the detective's signature bad-cop tactic: tower menacingly over the suspect. After a thirty-second pause, he cleared his throat.

"Just a couple of questions," he intoned.

Tate immediately interjected. "I have advised my client not to answer any of your questions."

"Then maybe he should listen," Spencer said. "After which, your client just might want to give his record a spin."

"I have instructed my client not to say a word," Tate repeated.

"Fine. Then I'll do the talking. Senator, when we first spoke in your office you told me you were home alone on the night of Gail Peterson's murder."

"Duly noted," the lawyer acknowledged.

"There is no one to verify your alibi?"

"Is that a question, Detective?" asked Tate.

"Yes."

"Then, no. But you know that. So, what's your point?"

"Senator, do you own a gold Rolex watch? More specifically, an eighteen-karat gold Rolex Yacht-Master?"

"Don't answer that."

"I gather you like baseball, and I'd bet that being from California you're an LA Dodgers fan."

Tate was getting irritated. "What is the point of this line of questioning, Detective?"

"I don't know why your client won't answer two simple questions. When I arrested him, I noticed he was wearing a gold Rolex Yacht-Master. And when I was in his office, I recall seeing a black LA Dodgers baseball cap on the credenza."

"Cut the crap, Detective. Why did you ask for this meeting?"

"Okay. I'll get down to the nitty gritty. Senator, do you know a woman by the name of Janet Walker?"

Bradford turned to his lawyer and whispered into his ear.

"No," Tate responded.

"You don't know Janet Walker? You sure about that?"

"We have already answered that question."

"You might know her by her professional name, Candy Cane," Spencer said, his eyes focused on the senator's face.

Bradford remained tight-lipped, but his right eye twitched. It was the tell the homicide detective was looking for.

"You don't have to say anything. The look on your face says it all," Spencer said with a satisfied smirk.

"Oh, now you're an expert on reading faces, Detective?" Tate shot back.

"Senator Bradford, were you at Janet Walker's apartment on the evening you told me you were home alone? The same night Gail Peterson was murdered when you told me you were home alone?"

"I have instructed my client not to answer."

"He doesn't have to. The senator's fingerprints were found all over Janet Walker's condo and on a bottle of Champagne and a glass on a night table in her bedroom. His DNA, including several strands of his pubic hair, was on her bedsheets."

Tate was jolted by the revelations. His face was ashen. "Detective, this interview is over."

"Not quite, Counselor. Full disclosure. You might be interested to know we have a copy of a video taken by the security camera on the elevator in Ms. Walker's building. It shows your client—a black LA Dodgers baseball cap pulled down to obscure his face—as he enters the elevator from the lobby at precisely two minutes after nine in the evening and exits a few seconds later on the fourth floor. The floor of Ms. Walker's apartment. Apartment 412. Ring any bells, Senator?"

Bradford didn't respond.

"At precisely eleven minutes after ten, you entered the elevator on the fourth floor. You then exited on the main floor nine seconds later. Jog your memory, Senator? You might be certain of the time since you were caught on the surveillance camera checking your gold Rolex Yacht-Master."

"Detective, we're done here," Tate said, rising to his feet.

"Not just yet. I have one more chore to perform. Senator, I'm here to charge you with the murder of Janet Walker, aka Candy Cane."

"Murder?" the senator blurted out.

"We found her body in her apartment on the same morning we found Gail Peterson. Walker was strangled to death in the same brutal manner as Peterson."

"I did not kill her. I swear to you I didn't kill her. And I didn't kill Gail."

"Don't say another word," Tate yelled.

Bradford was in a panic. "To hell with that. I did not kill those women. I swear. I didn't kill them. I admit I was with Candy that evening, but I didn't kill her. When I left, she was alive. I never went to Gail's apartment. I've never been to Gail's apartment. I swear."

Tate was in a state of apoplexy. "Senator! Stop talking," he pleaded.

"Save you touching pleas of innocence for the judge and jury," Spencer said. "I'm here to officially charge you with first-degree murder in the death of Janet Walker. I'll see you in court tomorrow for your arraignment."

The detective rapped on the steel door and signaled the officer to let him out. He had scheduled a press conference for 2 p.m. He needed to preen and prepare.

"Get hold of Matt Kozar," Bradford instructed his lawyer. "Tell him what just happened. Tell him I need to see him right after the arraignment."

Tate signaled the guard to open the door. "I'll see you at the arraignment," he said, without looking at his client.

BLINDSIDED

I was sitting at my desk doodling when I noticed Heather frantically waving at me from her office door.

"Matt! Get over here. Quick. You've got to see this."

"What's going on?" I asked, rushing over.

"Get in here," she said, closing the door.

Heather pointed up at the flat screen on her wall. It was tuned to CNN. A "Breaking News" banner was scrolling across the screen.

The camera zoomed in on a man's face.

"Isn't that the detective heading the investigation into the murder of Senator Bradford's intern?" she asked.

"Yeah. And judging from the smug look on his face, something bad is about to go down," I said.

On the steps outside the DC Police Headquarters, proud and tall behind a black-lacquered wooden lectern laden with a dozen microphones, stood Detective Captain Ron Spencer.

Spencer rapped on a microphone and began in a solemn tone. "Four days ago, the body of a young woman was discovered in her condo apartment. From the ligature marks on her neck, it was apparent she was the victim of a homicide. An autopsy by the medical examiner confirmed the victim had been strangled to death. The victim has been identified as one Janet Walker. She was twenty-four years old."

Spencer paused for maximum effect, staring down at his file. He looked up and continued. "Our CSI team collected several key pieces of evidence at the crime scene including DNA and fingerprints. Our investigators also retrieved video surveillance from a security camera in the condo building's elevator."

Again, Spencer paused for effect.

"This morning, I attended the DC Jail where I officially charged Senator William Bradford with the first-degree murder of Janet Walker."

There was an audible gasp from the contingent of reporters. Several frantically grabbed their cell phones and called their editors.

"As you are no doubt aware, Senator Bradford has also been charged with first-degree murder in the death of Gail Peterson, an intern who worked at his Washington office," the detective added.

The phone on Heather's desk buzzed. She looked at the call display. "It's Doyle."

She answered.

"I want you and Matt in my office. Now," he ordered.

The phone went dead.

"Let's go," Heather said, grabbing her notebook.

Doyle was standing behind his desk watching the live coverage. "I gather from the expressions on your faces you've seen the breaking news item?"

"We have," Heather said.

"Matt, I'm curious," Doyle began. "You've been in direct touch with the senator and his lawyer. Why didn't you have this? Why do I have to learn about the arrest on CNN?"

"I got blindsided," I said.

"No. You got scooped," Doyle said.

That stung.

"And used," Heather added.

Like I needed another nail in my coffin.

"I would think this just about seals the senator's fate," Doyle said.

"Couldn't agree more," Heather said. "I hope he gets sentenced to life."

Doyle looked over at me. "Matt, you're awfully quiet. Have you anything to say for yourself?"

"Yeah, I kinda do. You don't think this is all just a little too strange?"

"The man is a sexual predator and a murderer," Heather spat.

I ignored her interjection and looked straight at Doyle. "Something about this just doesn't add up."

"Look at the facts, Matt," Doyle said. "From what the detective is saying, it appears the senator's DNA and fingerprints were found at this latest crime scene, and a security camera video in the apartment elevator presumably captured him coming and going."

"Mr. Doyle, I want to stay on this," I pleaded.

"Why?" Heather snapped. "Why do you want to waste your time and my time on this lowlife?"

"My gut tells me ..."

"Give me a break with your gut," she shouted, dismissing me with a wave of her hand. "I've got some Gaviscon in my office."

"Get serious," I said.

"I am serious."

Ignoring the testy exchange, Doyle said, "Look, Matt. You have to admit this case looks cut and dry."

"A little too cut and dry. Just give me a week, that's all I ask, and if I don't find anything, I'll drop it."

"I need you on another story now," Heather said. "I'm short-staffed."

I was close to losing it with Heather. "Could you just cool it? I'm not asking for the world here."

Doyle, ever the consummate journalist, acquiesced. "One week, Matt, and if you haven't come up with an iota of evidence showing the cops got the wrong man, it's dropped. Got it?"

"Got it."

Heather shook her head in disbelief. I knew she was ticked off and I knew the best thing I could do was to stay out of her sightline for the next few days.

As I was leaving Doyle's office, my cell phone beeped. The caller ID showed Brian Tate. I answered and retreated to the safety of the men's washroom.

"What in hell is going on?" I asked without saying hello. "I just watched that homicide dick's breaking news sideshow on CNN. The senator swore he was home alone on the night his intern was murdered, and now I get blindsided with this latest shitstorm. Your freakin' client lied."

Tate was not about to shoulder any of the blame. "You think you got blindsided? I'm his damned lawyer. I didn't know any of this until the detective came to the jail this morning to charge the senator. Hell! Bradford never told me he was with another woman. And I don't know why he told Spencer he was home alone on the night Gail Peterson was murdered. He should have kept his mouth shut. Now his alibi is based on a bald-faced lie."

I was steaming. "What exactly do the cops have on Bradford?"

"His DNA on her bedsheets, his fingerprints on a glass and a Champagne bottle, and video from a security camera in the elevator."

"This is bad. Really, really bad," I said.

"Bradford wants to see you tomorrow afternoon after his arraignment on the second murder charge," Tate said.

I didn't respond.

"Will you meet with the senator after the arraignment?" he repeated.

"I'll be there," I said, and I hung up.

*

Once again, the courtroom was packed with heavy-hitters from the Senate and Congress, all wanting a glimpse of the senator turned serial-sex-killer. Absent from the arraignment was anyone from the victim's family.

I was in DC, having arrived with more than enough time to spare before my afternoon meeting at the jail. I decided to stay clear of the courthouse. There was no way I was going into this zoo to gawk at the monkey in the cage. I'd see him later for a one-on-one in the big cage.

From what I caught on CNN while sipping an Americano at a nearby coffee shop, the arraignment was short, lasting no more than fifteen minutes. There was no grandstanding, no attempt by Tate to obtain bail for his client. The charges were read out and the senator pleaded not guilty.

The prosecutor requested that the murder charge be attached to the Peterson case. Tate offered no objection, and the judge made it so. Bradford's request for a speedy trial remained in effect, and he was led out of the courtroom shackled.

DISCREET ENCOUNTERS

The senator was in the interview room when I arrived at the jail. He was sitting on a metal chair with his arms tightly folded across his chest. Tate was a no-show.

Bradford looked like a defeated boxer. It was round two and he was down on the mat. The question was, would he be counted out or would he manage to get to his feet for round three? He could see I was ticked off and that the chance of my continuing to waste another minute on his behalf was hovering just above the zero mark.

Breaking the tension, I asked, "Your lawyer drop you?"

"I'm his meal ticket whether he wins or loses. He's prepping for the trial."

"You look like hell," I said.

"Believe me, I feel far worse than I look."

"I have to say, Senator, I didn't appreciate being blindsided with news of this second murder charge flashing on CNN. In fact, I'm seriously pissed. You made me look like an idiot in front of my boss."

"That was not my intention. I had no idea this woman had been murdered until the detective showed up here yesterday morning."

"Was Tate here when Spencer charged you?"

"Of course."

"Why didn't he call me and at least give me a heads-up?"

"I told him to call you."

"Well, he did. Right after Spencer's nation-wide news conference. Your lawyer's a jerk."

"I guess with all that happened, it slipped his mind."

"I'm sure that's exactly what happened," I responded sarcastically. "Let me cut to the chase. Why did you lie about your whereabouts on the night your intern was murdered?"

"Because I was with this other woman."

"And yet you told the cops, your lawyer, and me that you were home all by your lonesome, knowing full well it was a lie."

"I didn't want to tell the detective I was with her."

"Why not? She was your alibi," I pointed out. "Now she's not. By the way, what was she to you? Were you two having an affair?"

"No, it wasn't anything like that."

"Well, don't hold back on my account. Who was Janet Walker?"

The senator nervously cleared his throat. "She was an escort."

"An escort? Oh, shit. You mean a prostitute? I don't believe it. Heather is going to go ballistic."

"Who's Heather?"

"National editor of the *Tribune* and my boss. This will just add fuel to her fire."

"Mr. Kozar, as I have told you, I am being framed. I did not kill anyone. I did not kill these women."

"First time we met, you claimed you were being framed by the Oath Keepers or the Proud Boys. Well, I sat down with a couple of those whack jobs the other day and they laughed when I repeated your accusation. Bottom line, these halfwits dance like giddy pigs at the trough every time you mention their names. Apparently, you give them the attention they crave. It's free advertising for their cause. For them, any attention, good, bad, or ugly, draws in a slew of new recruits from the far-right lunatic fringe. In fact, they're hoping I write that you're fingering them as murder suspects."

"Are you going to?"

"No. I'm not going to give them a platform. Let them pray at the altar of Fox News."

"There's Putin," the senator repeated.

I shook my head and sighed. "Yeah, sure. I mean, seriously? You think the Russian president might be behind the murders?"

"I've been hammering at him from the day that murderer invaded Ukraine. He's a vengeful psychopath. He's known to throw tantrums when things don't go his way, and he gets even with anyone who stands in his way or dares to criticize or malign him."

"Scores of politicians around the world have been slamming that asshole on a daily basis over Russia's invasion of Ukraine. What makes you so special?"

"I suggested in a recent speech that Putin's irrational behaviour could be the result of neurosyphilis infecting his brain. He certainly exhibits all the disorders associated with it: psychosis, delusion, impaired judgement."

"So what?"

"And that his mother dumped him when he was a child."

"That could trigger a visceral reaction," I conceded, still not convinced.

"And that he was nothing but a wimp throughout his teenage years. Always picked on and bullied by his schoolmates. That he turned into a bully while working as an agent for the KGB. It gave him a chance to get even. Now this little man is bullying the free world."

"I heard the speech you gave at Georgetown University. I'm sure if Putin was made aware of it, he might blow a gasket. But to frame you by ordering the murders of two women is so way, way out there."

"It's more than a hunch. Keep in mind I chair the Senate Committee on Appropriations."

"How does that play into Putin's orbit?"

"With our president's strong and unequivocal commitment to Ukraine, we've directed nearly fifty billion dollars in emergency funding to support Ukraine's efforts to repulse Russian aggression. In that package we've allocated more than three-and-a-quarter billion dollars in military assistance to Ukraine so it can stand up to Putin's military. I've been the driving force behind this effort."

"Look. I'm not about to call the Russian embassy to ask if Putin had two women murdered to shut you down. I'm persona non grata at the embassy, and after my recent trip to Ukraine I've been banned from travel to Russia. Even if they gave me the time of day, they certainly wouldn't give me the truth."

Bradford slumped in his chair. A look of arrant defeat swept across his face. I was about to throw another coal on the fire.

"I also spoke with Mrs. Peterson."

Bradford's eyes snapped wide open. "Why in hell would you do that?

"I needed to ask her something."

"What could you possibly ask her that might help me?"

"First, I'm not doing this to help you. I'm doing this by the book. As I told you when we first met, if I find out you killed Gail Peterson, and now Janet Walker, you're toast."

"I got that. What did you ask Gail's mother?"

"If her daughter ever told her that you had been inappropriate with her."

"What did she say?"

"That Gail never mentioned you coming on to her. But there's more to this."

With a look of concern on his face, Bradford asked, "What do you mean?"

"It seems Detective Spencer tried to convince her to get on the witness stand and drive the final nail in your coffin by saying Gail told her you came on to her. She refused to go along with it."

"What the hell? Wait till Tate gets hold of this."

"What will he do with it? I doubt Mrs. Peterson will talk to him or corroborate what she told me. I also doubt the prosecutor will ever put her on the witness stand."

"I knew the detective was a sleaze," the senator growled.

"Let's get back to this second murder charge," I said. "How long have you been seeing this woman?"

"Off and on about two years."

"If I'm not mistaken, you're married."

"Yes."

"Man, I hate to say it, but every time I ask you a question and you give me an answer, you dig yourself deeper into a hole."

"You think I don't know that? I'm being vilified in the media. My political career is over. My family is shattered. My life is totally fucked. But there is no way I want to spend the rest of my life in prison for two murders I did not commit."

"Your lawyer told me the cops found your fingerprints and DNA in the woman's apartment."

"Yes."

"And a security camera in the apartment elevator captured video of you coming and going on the night she was murdered."

"Yes."

At this point I wanted to toss in not only the towel but the entire linen closet. Clenching my fists, I pressed on. "So, you had occasional sessions with the hooker. Then what?"

"I would leave and go home."

"On the night she was killed, did you go straight home?"

"Yes."

"When you left, the hooker was alive?"

"Yes."

"How did you meet her?"

"A colleague told me about a website."

"Another senator?"

"Let's leave it at a colleague."

"What website?"

"Discreet Encounters. It had this photo array of women and when I saw Candy's photograph ... well, I stupidly asked for a date."

"Candy? Who's Candy?"

"Janet Walker. She went by the name Candy Cane."

"You have got to be kidding. I can just see the headlines when that gets out."

"It'll get out?" Bradford asked nervously.

"Trust me. It will make headlines real soon along with the fact she was a prostitute. And if anything, I'll bet Spencer is primed to get it out."

"Spencer is enjoying every minute of this."

"Why wouldn't he? A case like this is every cop's wet dream. He's become an overnight national celebrity at your expense and he's playing it to the max. I watched his news conference. The way he acts, the way he mugs for the cameras, the guy's a certified media slut."

"He came in here with this tough guy attitude. I don't know what the hell he was thinking. That maybe he could intimidate me and bully me into a confession."

"Spencer was playing the bad cop. What did you expect? That he would defer to you because you're a senator? Like I said, you're this guy's prize catch."

"All he wants is to get me. He's not interested in searching for the truth," Bradford shot back.

"I hate to tell you this, Senator, but Spencer has you by the short hairs. He's gathered enough evidence for the DA to put you away for life. That's your reality."

Bradford said nothing.

"What did she charge?" I asked.

"Who?"

"Who else? Candy Cane."

"Is that important?" the senator asked.

"Yeah. Because it will get out. Believe me."

"One thousand dollars for an hour."

"Wow! A grand. And you never knew her real name?"

"No. She could have called herself Marilyn Monroe for all I cared. It was about the sex. I had no intention of striking up a relationship with her. She was a prostitute. I never asked her anything about herself. I didn't care about her private life, and she knew never to ask anything about me. My name and resume were off limits."

"She could have figured it out. I mean, you're on television more often than Jimmy Swaggart," I noted.

The senator grimaced. "I seriously doubt she watched television. Certainly not anything to do with news and current affairs. She was a social media addict. TikTok, Snapchat, Instagram. That's all she ever talked about."

"When you were together, what did she call you? Sir? Honey?"

"John. I told her my name was John."

I said nothing.

Bradford ran his fingers roughly through his hair, at one point grabbing a chunk and yanking at it. "This whole thing is so totally insane. I mean, why would I want to kill these women? I had no reason to kill them."

"I'm sure the DA will come up with a rock-solid motive," I said.

"There is no motive," the senator shouted.

"Well, I can give you two motives the DA might come up with right off the top of my head. The hooker found out who you really are and set out to blackmail you, so you offed her. As for your intern, you made an inappropriate move on her. She threatened to go public, and you offed her."

"Candy never tried to blackmail me, and I never made a move on Gail or any other woman on my staff. Ever!"

"I'm just telling you how I think the DA will present the case to the jury," I offered.

I stared down at my notebook. The page was as blank as my mind. My brain was screaming at me to bail. My gut was urging me to stay the course. The trouble was, I had no course, no road map. Not a single clue. All I had was the word of a confessed liar vehemently professing his innocence.

"This is really bad," I said.

Bradford sighed and slumped back in his chair. "Don't you think I know that? What I need to know is will you keep on this?" he asked, his voice barely audible.

Staring directly into the senator's face, I replied, "I don't know."

"You can't give up on me," he pleaded.

"Look, you haven't given me much of anything to work with. First you lie to the cops about the night your intern was murdered. Now the woman you were with that night ends up dead. And you were the last guy seen leaving her apartment."

The senator's hands started to shake.

"To top it off, the media is roasting you like a stuffed pig on a spit."

"And you?"

"My problem is I have no idea where to go from here. All you've given me is 'I didn't do it' and maybe it was the Oath Keepers or the Proud Boys, and if that doesn't pan out, then maybe Putin is behind it."

The senator stared up at the ceiling, a look of desperation etched on his face.

I continued. "I need to find a patch of loose dirt that I can stick a shovel into. I need to dig up something. So far, all I'm hitting is solid concrete."

As I got up to leave, I added, "You should know my editor is pressuring me to drop this."

"Are you giving up?"

I didn't respond.

"Then can I ask you this? Do you believe me when I say I did not murder these two women?"

I closed my eyes for a moment and then looked at the senator.

"Yes. I believe you."

Just as I was about to bang on the door to catch the guard's attention, an idea struck. It was way out there, but it was worth a try.

"I need to ask you for a big favor," I said.

"What is it?"

"I want you to tell Tate to gather up all the forensic evidence collected at both crime scenes. And I mean all of it including the full report from the State lab that tested the DNA."

"Why?"

"I want to go over it. I also want all DNA specimens taken from both crime scenes sent to another lab for an independent analysis."

"What lab?" Bradford asked.

"Forensic Analytics Inc. in New York City. I have a friend who heads the DNA analysis unit there. She's top notch in her field. It will cost you."

"I don't care about the cost. I'll do it."

"One last thing: Instruct Tate to inform the people at Forensic Analytics to share all their findings with me. Tate will no doubt balk at that, but I need to stay in the loop. No more blindsiding. He's got to agree to this. I need to see every single piece of evidence, or I swear, I will pull out of this."

"I'll do that, and he'll do what I instruct him to do," Bradford said.

"What if he doesn't?"

"I'll fire him and get another lawyer."

*

When I stepped out onto the street, I stared up at the cloud-filled sky and wondered why the hell I let myself get roped into this. I had no idea how I was going to prove the cops got the wrong guy. They had rock-solid evidence pointing to the senator, whereas I had not turned up a scintilla of evidence to prove otherwise. And yet, my gut told me Bradford was innocent.

I was halfway down the block when I noticed a man in a cheap beige suit approaching. His pace was deliberate, and his eyes were focused on me. I immediately recognized him.

Stepping in front of me, he introduced himself. "Mr. Kozar, I'm Captain Detective Ron Spencer, DC Homicide."

I smiled and shook my head. "Tell me, is this a coincidence or were you lying in wait for me? And let me just say, Detective Spencer, I don't believe in coincidences."

"I was hoping we could have a little chat."

"Well, let's start off by how you knew I was here," I said.

"I make it my business to know who's in town."

"And I'm making it my business not to chat with you."

"Word is you're working for the senator," Spencer charged.

I knew he was on a fishing expedition and didn't respond.

"Just a word of caution. Don't get fooled by his 'I've been framed' bullshit. The man is as guilty as sin and you're going to look like a complete ass when it comes out you've hitched your wagon to a sexual predator and a serial killer."

"Wow. I must admit I'm touched by your concern for my reputation and the fact that you came all the way out here to warn me."

"The man is guilty. We've got him dead to rights," Spencer said firmly. "So, I suggest you go home and report on your little stories in New York and not waste your time on my turf."

"It's my time and I'll do with it what I choose, and as a point of clarification, your turf, as you put it, belongs to the American people. At least it did last time I looked."

"I don't appreciate you poking your nose into my investigation," the detective warned.

"Poke is what I'm paid to do. And if you're so certain you've got an iron-clad case against the senator, why would you be worried about little ol' me doing a little poking? Did you forget to cross a t or dot an i somewhere along the road?"

"Oh, take my word on it. I am not the least bit worried. I just find it odd that a so-called investigative reporter of your alleged fame would waste his time on a killer."

I turned to walk away. Spencer blocked my path. His face was inches away from mine. I thought if we hadn't been on a busy street in daylight, he would have roughed me up. I stood my ground.

"You went to visit Gail Peterson's parents."

I met his threatening stare and didn't respond.

"You people are like vultures. No respect for the family of the victim. All you care about is getting a news hit."

"Okay. We're done here," I said, brushing past him.

I hated when anyone tried to tell me how to do my job, or even worse, tried to intimidate me. All that ever accomplished was to tick me off, and Spencer had succeeded in doing just that. What I couldn't figure out is why he confronted me. Did he forget to cross a t? I was now more determined than ever to find out.

*

I parked myself at the far end of a quiet café and ordered an Americano. I took a sip, turned on my cell phone, and looked up Discreet Encounters. The website was high gloss and polished, offering up a bevy of gorgeous dates for well-heeled gentlemen with discerning tastes. There was no mention of sex for money, but you'd have to be a child not to figure out what was for sale. Color photos of a dozen voluptuous young women in tantalizing, sensuous poses dotted the menu section along with a summary of their attributes and specialties. I scrolled through the date offerings and was surprised when I came across Candy Cane's photo. She had been dead for four days, and no one at the escort service had bothered to remove her profile from the website. I flipped through her photo spread.

Candy was a knockout. In the fantasy world of most straight men, she rated a ten across the scoreboard. She had long, flowing, auburn hair, warm brown eyes, and an infectious, come-hither smile. She wore a lacy, blood-red negligee that left little to the imagination. She oozed sensuality and poise.

I tapped the Discreet Encounters phone number on my keypad. After five rings I was shunted to voicemail.

"My name is Matt Kozar. I'm a reporter with the *New York Tribune*. I'm hoping I can speak to someone who knew Janet Walker, also known as Candy Cane. I will keep your identity private."

I left my cell number. It was a long shot, but I was a firm believer in the age-old adage: if you don't try, nothing will happen.

*

Half an hour later, my cell phone beeped. It was the senator's lawyer, and he was steaming mad.

"What the hell do you think you're doing?" Tate demanded.

"Can you be more specific?" I asked.

"I just spoke to the senator. When did you suddenly become a forensics expert?"

"I never said I was an expert. Get to the point."

"You instructed my client to have the state's lab results sent to an independent lab," Tate charged.

"What about it?"

"Why on earth would you do that? The state's lab is unquestionably one of the best in the country," Tate pointed out.

My response was terse. "Sometimes labs make mistakes. You of all people should know that."

"You also told the senator you want the DNA samples and the lab report sent to this Forensics Analytics lab in New York."

"Yes."

"What's your cut?"

"I've got two words for you, Tate."

"What I find far more objectionable is you insisting that the findings from this forensics lab be sent to you. Who are you to make such a demand? I'm his lawyer. I represent him. Not you!"

"I'm investigating the senator's claim that he's been framed. I think it's important I see all the evidence gathered by the cops in the two murders."

"Oh, give me a break. I don't expect any lab, no matter how good it is, to come to a different conclusion. The DNA at both crime scenes is a hundred percent match to the senator's DNA."

I was stunned. "Wow. Sounds like you'll be pushing the senator to take a plea bargain."

"Do you have a better idea, smart guy?"

"What if he's innocent? What if, as he claims, he's being framed?"

"Between you and me, I don't believe in fairy tales."

"Between you and me, if I'm ever in a pot of boiling water, I won't hire you to rescue me."

"You couldn't afford me."

With that, Tate hung up.

*

With a bit more than an hour to spare before my train rolled into the station, I took to Google for a search on Putin and just how far he would go to exact revenge. There were sites awash with reports of more than a dozen prominent Russians who met their end under mysterious circumstances, all after the dictator ordered the invasion of Ukraine. Virtually every investigation conducted by Russian police concluded that the victims committed suicide. The most intriguing and seemingly preferred form of suicide, in which the victims supposedly leapt to their death from high-rise windows, was referred to in whispers among the Russian elite as "sudden death syndrome." Among those exiting through windows were a top official with the Russian Ministry of Defense, a diplomat, a scientist, a gas-industry executive, the head of a ski resort, a railroad magnate, an aviation official, a shipyard director, the editor-in-chief of a newspaper, two doctors, and a sausage tycoon.

The one unmistakable link in these alleged suicides was that the victims all made one of two critical errors. They either criticized Putin's invasion of Ukraine or questioned his mental fitness.

As I shut down my laptop, I began to wonder if the vengeful dictator had targeted the senator. No matter how hard I tried, I couldn't buy into it.

CLIENT 62

As my train approached the station, my cell phone beeped. I looked down at call display. It flashed No Caller ID. I don't usually answer unknown callers. Far too many of them are scammers offering to clean my air ducts. I figure if some unknown entity really needs to get hold of me, they'll leave a voice message. They never do.

My phone continued to buzz. As I stared at the screen, something told me I should answer.

It was a woman. She didn't identify herself. She spoke in a low, nervous whisper like someone afraid of being overheard.

"I won't give you my name. I heard the message you left. Janet was my friend. I'm devastated by what happened to her."

"Can we meet?" I asked.

She was hesitant. "Only if you promise never to say you ever met me."

"I promise."

"I checked you out online. I got a feeling you're someone I can trust. But you have to promise never to say you ever spoke to me."

"You have my word. I'm still in DC. Can we meet maybe in an hour?"

"Six o'clock at the Lincoln Monument."

"Can you tell me what you look like?"

"No. I know what you look like. I'll find you."

*

Abraham Lincoln, the sixteenth president of the United States, sat majestically on a classical ceremonial chair at the western end of the National Mall. Gazing up at the colossal statue, I wondered what he would think of his

Grand Old Party were he alive today—a party awash in conspiracy theories and lies and infested by a cabal of elected misfits who refused to stand for truth to power.

From the corner of my eye, I noticed a tall, striking black woman lurking nearby. She was wearing sunglasses and a black, belted wrap coat. She seemed nervous, cautiously peering over her shoulder. I knew it was the contact. I walked over and introduced myself.

"I thought about turning around and heading home. You have to understand, I'm really scared," she said in a whisper.

"There's no need to be scared."

"Seriously? Janet was murdered. I don't want to be next."

"Why would you think that?" I asked, hoping she'd feed me a tangible fact.

"Just a feeling."

"Can you tell me your name?"

"I go by Caramel."

"Okay. Why don't you tell me what you know?" I asked in a calm, reassuring voice.

"Well, for one thing, a homicide detective came to the office the other day and talked to the manager."

"At Discreet Encounters?"

"Yes."

"Do you know what they talked about?"

"He asked Robbie—he's the manager—who Janet was meeting the night she was murdered. At first Robbie refused to tell him. Then the cop said he would get a warrant that would give him access to all of Janet's clients. That got Robbie shitting his pants, so he gave the detective the rundown on Client 62."

"Client 62?" I asked.

"The names of our clients are top secret, and I mean top secret. We are never told their real names and we're warned never to ask."

"Do you know the identity of Client 62?"

"I do now. That senator who was arrested for killing Janet."

"What kind of work do you do for Discreet Encounters?"

"Same as Janet. I'm an escort, and for the record, I like my job. No one is forcing me to do what I do, and I take offence at being called a hooker or a prostitute. I'm also offended Janet is being labeled a prostitute by the news media."

"Okay. You're an escort."

"Does what I do offend you?" she shot back.

"No. Not at all, as long as you're doing what you want, and no one is forcing you."

"I make a lot of money. I date an elite clientele, and I've never once had a bad date."

"Your friend Janet obviously did."

"That's what I want to talk to you about. Will you keep your promise never to say you ever met me?"

I nodded. "Did Janet ever complain about Client 62?"

"We have a buddy system. Janet and I were buddies. We kept in close touch with each other when we went out on a date. Janet and I always called each other after every date."

"What did she tell you about Client 62?" I asked.

"She told me he was a dashing older man. Dashing was her word. Said he was always polite and always brought a bottle of French Champagne. She also told me he was a little kinky. Nothing new there. Most of the men we date have a kinky side. Janet said 62 liked it a little rough. I don't mean being rough with her. He liked it when Janet got rough with him."

"Did Janet ever say she was scared of him?"

"Never. We always reported how each date went to Robbie. It's part of our protocol. The owners don't want any of us to get hurt. It's not good for business."

"Or to get murdered."

"It's the first time that's happened. I broke down in tears when the police came to the office and told us about Janet. I had a feeling something bad had happened to her because she didn't call me after her date. I called her cell phone like a dozen times, but she never picked up."

"Did you tell that to the detective?"

"No. None of us spoke to him. Robbie told us to lay low and not say anything. And if we were asked about Janet, he told us to act dumb."

"Did Janet ever mention that the senator had a dark side?"

"No. She said he was always a gentleman, and he always paid with cash. Never by credit card."

"Did she ever confide in you that she found out the real identity of Client 62?"

"No. Why do you ask?"

"I was wondering if maybe she found out he was a US senator and tried to blackmail him."

Caramel's eyes narrowed. "That would never happen," she said firmly. "Janet was not that kind of person. And she knew if she ever tried that it would be the end of her."

"What do you mean by that?"

"Use your imagination."

"What else did the manager tell the detective?"

"Not much else to tell."

"And you?"

"Never came near the detective. I hid in a back room."

"If you got a chance to talk to the detective, would you have been able to shed some light on Janet's murder?"

Caramel hesitated. I could tell from her expression I'd hit a nerve.

"You won't say you got this from me. Promise?"

"Totally."

"Janet and I got together for drinks three weeks before she was killed. She was all giddy. Said she bought a new car. A red Mazda Miata. Paid cash. I was happy for her. And then she tells me one of her dates asked her to do a small favor and gave her twenty-five thousand dollars."

My radar kicked in. "Who was this date?"

"Don't know. But I do know he didn't come through the service. Janet was freelancing. The guy met her at a bar. Said he knew what she did. Said she came highly recommended by a friend who had dated her."

"Did Janet say what the favor was?"

"No. Well, not exactly. Just that it was something a little kinky. A prank he wanted to pull on a friend who also happened to be one of her regular dates."

"Twenty-five thousand dollars is an expensive prank."

"That's what I thought. I warned her to be careful and not get drawn into anything illegal."

"She never told you what he asked her to do?"

"No. She was sworn to secrecy."

"Any idea who this guy was?

"Like I said, dates never give us their real names, and we don't ask."

"Did Janet know who the guy's friend was?"

"Yes. But she never told me."

"Did she say what the guy looked like?"

"Yeah. A six-footer, handsome, very strong, and very fit. She said he had blond hair and piercing, dark brown eyes."

"Tall, blond, and handsome, and yet he has to pay for sex. Weird."

"Not really. Some men like variety, especially bored, rich, married men who don't want the drama or the complications of an affair."

"Anything else about the guy?"

"No. Anyway, what does it matter? The detective told Robbie he is a hundred percent certain the senator killed Janet."

I could see Caramel was becoming jumpier with every passerby. But I had more questions. I wanted to know about Walker: where she came from, how she got into the business, if she had family. I pressed on.

Caramel had no idea where Janet was from. "As a rule, none of the girls ever talk about their private lives. It's off limits. But judging from her accent, I figured someplace down south, maybe Texas or Tennessee."

"Janet never told you anything about her family?"

Caramel closed her eyes and scoured her memory. "One time we were at a bar and Janet had a bit too much to drink. There were these men ogling us and she snapped, calling them holy hypocrites. That kind of threw me for a loop. I asked her where that came from, and she went off about her parents and two older brothers. She couldn't stand them. Apparently, they're hardline evangelical Christians, so she packed her bags and ended up here. Then all hell broke loose. Some guy from their church was in DC on business and, get this, just happened to be trolling sex sites on the internet. He hit on Discreet Encounters and Janet's photo and profile."

"Let me guess," I interjected. "He brought it to the attention of Janet's parents." Caramel nodded. "The oldest brother comes to DC with a letter from mom basically saying Janet was excommunicated from the church and dead to the family. She never heard from them again. That was about two years ago."

I asked how Janet got recruited by Discreet Encounters. Caramel said Robbie, the manager, would troll upscale bars in DC looking for potential. Most times, she noted, Robbie was told to get lost. Then there were those few women who were taken by Robbie's rugged looks and convincing sales pitch—especially the money, the class of clientele, and the guarantee of a safe working environment.

"We make a lot of money. I mean a lot of money," Caramel said with a convincing smile.

I was about to thank her for meeting with me when suddenly she began to cry. I didn't know what to do. I just stood there feeling uncomfortable. Caramel pulled a tissue from her coat pocket, dried her eyes, and caught her breath.

"Janet was my friend. In fact, she was my bestie. I loved her, and now she's gone. I need you to do me one favor."

"If I can," I said.

"Could you find out if anyone has claimed her body? If not, I will. I will give her a proper funeral."

"I'll do what I can."

Caramel gave me her cell number. Then she turned and slipped away.

*

Rather than head back to the train station, I decided to stay another day in the capital to do a little more digging. Caramel's revelation about Candy's mysterious freelance date got me thinking about the prank. Was it what got her killed? Or was it a red herring? I had no idea how in hell I could ever find out what it was. I decided to retrace the steps of the homicide detectives, hoping I might trip on something they missed.

While I mulled over my next move, I decided to call DC Police headquarters, hoping to collar Alyssa Lamont or Jake Wells for a brief update on the Walker murder. I was put through to Detective Lamont. When I introduced myself she immediately instructed me to call media relations. I continued my pursuit.

"I don't want to ask questions about your investigation. I spoke with a close friend of Janet Walker. She's devastated about what happened to her. She wants to know if anyone has claimed the body. If not, she will. She wants to give her friend a proper burial."

Lamont was silent for a moment. She asked me to meet her in twenty minutes at a Starbucks a few blocks away. When I entered, she waved me over to a table at the back of the café.

Detective Lamont stared at me. She was sizing me up.

"I don't want to be quoted at all. Got that?"

"Got it."

"Also, I am not going to say anything about the investigation. Ask me one question about it and I leave."

"No problem there."

"I mean it."

I nodded.

"Janet Walker's body was identified by her brother, Andrew Walker, and released. He had a funeral home pick up the deceased for cremation."

I looked down at the table and shook my head. "I'd hate to think what he'll do with the ashes."

"I can tell you this. Janet Walker's brother is a cold, self-righteous man. The way he looked at his sister said it all. He was disgusted with her. However, he was keen to find out whether she had a will."

"Did she?" I asked.

"Not that we could find, and we went through all the paperwork in her condo. However, we did find a life insurance policy for half a million dollars. The beneficiary is a woman, and from what I can determine, she is probably not family."

"What do you mean?"

"She is probably Black like me."

A lightbulb snapped on in my head. Did Janet Walker make Caramel the beneficiary? I asked Lamont if she would give me the woman's name.

"Why?" she asked.

"I have a feeling I might have talked to her. Trouble is, she wouldn't give me her name."

Lamont retrieved a notebook from her purse and flipped through the pages.

"The beneficiary is one Latisha Williams."

I pulled out my cell phone and called Caramel. She answered on the first ring. I told her Janet Walker's body had been claimed by her brother and that she had been cremated. There was silence on the other end.

"I have some interesting information, Latisha. You are Latisha Williams?"

The mention of her name drew a sharp and instant response. "How did you get my name?"

"Calm down. It's all good. I'm sitting here with Detective Alyssa Lamont. I'm going to give her your cell number. She has some incredible news to share with you, and I mean incredibly good."

"What is it?" Caramel asked.

"Just stay by your phone. The detective will call you."

I wrote Caramel's phone number on a napkin, handed it to Lamont, and left.

A WOMAN SCORNED

Senator Bradford winced when his name blared out over the prison's public address system. The dreaded moment had finally arrived and there was no avenue of escape.

"Visitor."

Bradford knew who it was. His only saving grace was that the confrontation would not be in person. The visitor would be sitting on a stool in a cubicle at the Video Visitation Center in a building adjacent to the jail. He would be in a plexiglass stall on the second floor of the prison.

Bradford rose from his cot and shuffled over to the cell block control center. An officer escorted him to the visiting station. He felt like a prisoner being led to his execution. After taking a deep breath, he sat down in front of a screen, picked up the receiver, and hesitantly pressed the enter key. A moment later, Margaret Collins-Bradford, his wife of sixteen years, flickered onto the screen. She looked haggard. Her eyes were so bloodshot it was impossible to determine their color. Her long, blonde hair was tousled, and she had abandoned the stylish clothing and the makeup she was never without.

The senator could feel her eyes boring into his skull, clawing at his brain. It was a tense stand-off as each waited for the other to speak.

Margaret finally blinked. "You bastard. You bloody bastard. Do you know what you've done to our family? To me? To the children?"

A barely audible "I'm sorry" was all Bradford could manage.

"Sorry? That's all you've got to say? Go to hell with your 'sorry.' You have the gall to pass yourself off as a Christian family man. I'm home in Santa Monica taking care of the children, and you're in Washington fucking some high-priced whore. And then murder? You go and kill two women?"

The senator stared down at the counter, knowing the worst was yet to come.

"I don't accept your pathetic apology. Not now, not ever. You have no idea the humiliation I've had to suffer."

The senator closed his eyes. He could feel his pulse pounding in his ears.

"Look at me when I speak, you coward. Look at me," she yelled.

Bradford obeyed.

"I had to take the children out of school. They're devastated. Have you any idea the names they've been called? The way all the kids look at them? Most of their friends have stopped calling. They're being bullied on social media. I had to close all their online accounts and take away their iPads. William Junior doesn't want to live anymore. All he talks about is wanting to die. I had to take him to a psychologist. Michael won't come out of his room. He just lies in his bed staring at the ceiling. And Libby hasn't stopped crying. You were her world. You destroyed her world."

"Margaret, I know you won't believe me, but I did not kill those women. I swear, I didn't kill them."

"Save it for the judge, because I don't believe you."

"I swear, I didn't kill those women."

Margaret ignored his claims. "Just seeing you sickens me."

"You don't believe me?"

"I don't believe a single word that comes out of your mouth."

The senator could feel rage building in his gut. "Then why the hell did you leave the kids and come here? You could have sent me a Dear John letter."

"I came here to tell you to your face that I hate you. I came here to tell you I hope you rot in prison for the rest of your life for what you did."

"I understand why you feel the way you do, but …"

"Bill, go fuck yourself. Don't give me this 'I understand' bullshit. I'm not one of your stupid constituents. You destroyed my family. You destroyed my life, and after you go to prison, I'm changing the children's family name to Collins. When I get back to Santa Monica, I'm filing for a divorce. I never want to see your disgusting face or hear your name again."

Margaret Collins-Bradford suddenly jumped and swung around. A female officer had tapped her on the shoulder.

"What?" she snapped.

"Ma'am, I have to ask you to leave,' the officer began. "You were instructed when you arrived that foul language and disruptive behavior will not be tolerated. You have to go. Now."

The officer pulled the phone out of Margaret's hand and switched off the video.

"Fine. I said all I had to say," Margaret shouted as she was escorted out of the visitation center. "I'm done with that bastard. You'll never see me here again."

APARTMENT 412

It was just after 9 a.m. when I yanked open the front door and entered the nine-storey apartment building where Janet Walker had been murdered. I had no expectation of finding the slightest clue to help my investigation. The cops had been through the condo with a fine-tooth comb. But I had to start somewhere.

I waved at the security camera on the ceiling of the elevator and headed for the fourth floor. There were twelve units on the floor. I began knocking on doors. At each apartment, I got more or less the same response. No one heard a thing on the night of the murder. No one saw anything suspicious. Oh, and "Hey, you're that reporter … The one who got shot."

At apartment 409, a surly, balding, forty-something guy answered after a couple of knocks. I identified myself and his fuse tripped.

"You're not a police officer."

"I never said I was a police officer. I told you my name and the newspaper I work for."

"Why the fuck are you bothering me?" he asked.

"I'm sorry if I'm bothering you. I just wanted to ask if you had heard or seen anything …"

"Not *if* you're bothering me. You *are* bothering me."

"Like I said, I just wanted to ask you about the …"

"Murder. I've spoken to the police, and I don't speak to reporters. You journalists are all the same, digging up shit and spreading fake news."

"I take it you saw and heard nothing."

"Fuck off, asshole."

"Again, I'm sorry to have bothered you," I said, as he slammed the door in my face.

Directly across from 409 was Janet Walker's apartment. It was impossible to miss. Bright yellow police tape with *Crime Scene Do Not Cross* in bold black letters criss-crossed the door. After making some notes, I was taking a few creative photos with my iPhone when I heard the elevator ding and the door open. Two uniformed DC cops exited and came right for me.

"Who are you?" badge number 1683 demanded.

He was six feet four inches tall, muscular, and he probably tipped the scales at 220 pounds. He was right in my face. I could smell the frosted chocolate donuts on his breath.

"Matt Kozar from the *New York Tribune*," I said, backing up a tad. "I have ID."

I pulled out my wallet and handed the officer my press pass.

1683 examined it and then handed it to 1214, who was wearing dark plastic sunglasses and a scowl on his face no doubt meant to intimidate.

"We received a number of complaints you've been harassing some of the tenants," 1683 said.

"I doubt it was a number. At most it was one, the occupant in 409. And for your information, I was polite at all times, because I have tact."

"What?" 1683 asked.

"Tact. I have tact."

"He's a smartass," 1214 said, stepping into my space.

"I suggest you leave the premises," 1683 advised.

"I've still got a couple more apartments to go and then I'll leave."

The duo stared at me. I stared back. It was a classic face-off. They blinked.

"We get another complaint, we'll take you in," 1214 warned, the index finger of his left hand in my face.

"Thank you, officers. Have a good day."

By the time I got to the last apartment on the floor, I was thirsty, peckish, and out of steam. Unit 412 was at the end of the hallway. Janet Walker's unit was kitty-corner on the left. On the right was an industrial metal door with a red sign attached to it that read "Emergency Stairwell."

I knocked on the door of 412. A minute passed and I knocked again. A few seconds later, I heard footsteps clacking on a wooden floor. A woman who looked to be in her mid-fifties answered. A wide smile spread across her face. It was instant recognition.

"You're that reporter. The one who was shot. You're famous," she gushed.

"I'm Matt Kozar."

"I know. I know. Nice to meet you. My name is Deborah Simmons. Come in. Come in."

"I won't keep you long."

"Don't you worry about me. I'm not going anywhere. I have a pot of fresh coffee. Would you like a cup?" she asked.

Before I could answer, she ushered me into the kitchen.

"Have a seat. How do you take your coffee?"

"Black, please. No sugar."

"Do you like cookies? They're chocolate chip. I baked them myself."

"Thank you," I said with a smile, reaching for the biggest one.

"What brings you up here? Wait. Don't tell me. I bet you're looking into Janet's murder."

"I am. Did you happen to know her?"

Mrs. Simmons' eyes instantly filled with tears. She reached for a tissue on the counter. "We talked from time to time. She was very sweet and absolutely gorgeous. I could never understand why she did what she did for a living. I asked her one time if she ever got scared. She said never. Said all her callers were gentlemen."

"Well, as the saying goes, never say never."

"Janet told me she was always careful, and the company she worked for screened all her clients."

"I was wondering. On the night Janet was killed, did you see or hear anything suspicious?"

"I wasn't even in the city. I was away visiting my daughter and my new granddaughter in Boston. I got back two days ago and heard about what happened from one of the neighbors. I'm sick about it. I found a business card under my door from a Detective Wells asking me to call him at my earliest convenience. I phoned him yesterday and when I told him I had been away, he thanked me, and that was that."

I winced. I had totally struck out. Everyone I'd spoken to claimed they saw or heard squat. I had no next move.

"I want to thank you for your time. I'm sorry if I disturbed you," I said, getting up to leave.

"I wonder what is going to happen with her new car?" Mrs. Simmons asked. "Is it here?"

"I saw it this morning in the underground parking garage when I went to get something out of my trunk."

The garage would be my next stop. I thanked Mrs. Simmons again and headed for the door. As I made my way, my eyes suddenly fixed on an odd contraption attached to the back of her door.

"What is that?" I asked.

"It's a security camera."

I closed my eyes for a moment, trying to recall what was on the front of the door. There was a peephole. An ordinary apartment peephole. There was nothing on it that suggested a security camera. I opened the door and checked. I was right. Dead center was a cheap, old-fashion peephole. I closed the door and turned to the woman.

"That is some interesting-looking security system you've got there."

"My son-in-law installed it about a year ago," Mrs. Simmons said. "He's a computer whiz. My daughter was worried for my safety what with the male callers visiting Janet at all hours. It's for my protection."

"Have you had trouble with any of these so-called gentlemen callers?" I asked.

"No. Never. But my daughter was adamant about putting in a security system. She worries about me living here alone. I'm a widow."

"How does this setup work?" I asked.

"When anyone walks by my apartment or knocks on the door, the motion sensor goes on. Whoever is out there pops up on my iPad so I can see who it is before opening the door. I checked to see who was at the door when you knocked."

"When anyone walks by your apartment? What do you mean?"

"My apartment is adjacent to the emergency stairwell on the right. Some of Janet's callers use the stairs. I figure it's to avoid being caught on the security camera in the elevator because they're married."

"So the motion sensor is triggered when someone simply walks past your door?"

"Yes. Once it's activated, it continues to run for about thirty seconds. Most of the time, whoever it is usually ends up at Janet's door."

I crossed my fingers, whispered a quick prayer, and asked: "Does your security system save the video data?"

"Yes. My son-in-law linked the camera with something called Bluetooth that goes straight to my iPad. He told me to keep everything for a month before deleting the contents."

My pulse began to race.

"Have you checked to see if there was any activity while you were in Boston?"

"No need to. Like I said, it's just for security in case someone tries to break in or cause trouble. I've never bothered to check it ever since it was installed because nothing has ever happened."

I held my breath for a moment. "Have you erased any data recently?"

"I haven't erased anything. Haven't got around to it."

"Would you mind if I take a look at what's on your iPad?"

"I'll bet you want to look at the night Janet was murdered."

"Yes."

"I hate to tell you, but I don't think you'll find anything."

"Why's that?" I asked, feeling my mood take a nosedive.

"From what I read in the paper, the police have the security camera surveillance from the elevator on the night Janet was killed. I was told by the superintendent that it shows the senator coming into the elevator on the main floor and getting off on this floor. Then sometime later, he left using the elevator. None of his comings and goings would have been picked up by my motion detector because he never came near my door. He was out of range of the motion detector."

"Well, I'd still like to have a look, if it's okay with you."

"It's okay with me. Come back in. I'll get my iPad."

I followed Mrs. Simmons into a guest bedroom where a white IKEA desk faced the window. She logged onto her iPad, opened the security folder, and handed me the unit.

"You could sit right here. Would you like another coffee?"

"That would be nice."

"And a cookie?"

"Sure, why not? They're delicious."

Mrs. Simmons smiled. "I'll be back in a jiffy."

I quickly moved the cursor over to the date column and clicked on the day Janet Walker was killed. There were two hits triggering the motion sensor that night. The first occurred at 11:06 p.m., capturing a man entering the floor from the emergency stairwell. I hit the pause button to get a closer look. The camera caught the side of the man's face. He was clean shaven, and his blond hair was slicked back. His nose was slightly bent like the curved beak of a hawk. I hit play and watched as he made his way down the corridor. He was wearing a black raincoat. I figured him to be a little more than six feet tall and about a hundred and eighty pounds. I bolted upright in my chair when he stopped in front of Janet Walker's apartment and knocked. I held my breath. A moment later, the door was opened. and he entered. Before it closed, Janet Walker stuck her head out and glanced up and down the hallway.

"Holy shit," I muttered under my breath. My heart was slamming against my ribcage. Janet Walker was alive after the senator left.

Thirteen minutes later, at precisely 11:19 p.m., the motion sensor was triggered once again. It was the same guy who had entered Walker's apartment. Of that I was certain. Black raincoat, hooked nose, and blond hair. This time the camera got a clear shot of his face.

As he approached the stairwell, he stopped and looked directly at Mrs. Simmons' peephole. He rapped on the door and waited. Twenty seconds later he knocked again and put his ear to the door. Then he peered into the peephole. Suddenly, startled by something behind him, he turned and disappeared into the stairwell.

I sat staring at the computer screen in stunned silence, trying to calm my nerves. Janet Walker was alive for more than an hour after the senator left her apartment. There was no way Bradford murdered her, and I had the proof. But who was this mystery man?

"Are you finding anything?" Mrs. Simmons asked, placing a coffee mug and a dessert plate with two chocolate chip cookies on the desk.

"I just got through the day Janet Walker's body was discovered," I said, trying to appear calm.

"I heard it was a crazy day," she said. "I'll let you get back to your work. *Judge Judy* is on, and I never miss an episode."

As she turned to leave, a cold shiver shot through my body. What might have happened had Mrs. Simmons been home that night and answered the knock on her door?

There was no activity on the security camera until the next morning. At precisely 10:53 a.m., there was a loud rap on her door. Detective Wells' face popped up on the screen. Wells stood in front of the door for about a minute before knocking again, this time shouting out, "DC Police. Homicide." After another minute, he dug into his jacket pocket, retrieved a business card, jotted something on it, and appeared to slip it under the door.

I got up and went to the living room. Mrs. Simmons was engrossed in Judge Judy's rambling verdict on the alleged attack on a DoorDash driver by a deranged Chihuahua. I waited. When the segment ended and went to a commercial, she looked up.

"How did it go?"

"Well, for one thing, once the police arrived it was a total zoo. There was certainly a lot of action in front of your door. Your motion sensor went into overdrive with cops going into and out of the stairwell."

"I guess that was to be expected."

"Would you mind if I made a copy of the video data on your security system? I've got a USB stick with me," I said, pulling a 64gb memory stick from my jacket pocket.

"What are you going to do with it?"

"I want to take a closer look at all the material, which will no doubt take a few hours, and I'm sure you have things to do."

She shrugged her shoulders. "I don't see a problem."

Before leaving, I made one more request.

"Could you make certain not to erase anything from your iPad? I'm sure at some point the police are going to want to take a look at it as well."

That sparked a look of concern on her face. "Is there something I should be worried about?" she asked.

"No. And if I find anything important to the case, rest assured, I'll bring it to the attention of the police. You have my word."

*

I was about to press L for lobby when I remembered Janet Walker's car. I tapped P1 and headed for the parking garage. A red Miata convertible stood out among the rows of silver and black cars. Walking around it, I noticed a sticker on the bumper advertising Capital Motors Mazda. I opened my Uber app and typed in my pick-up address and my destination: the dealership.

At the car lot, it didn't take long for an eager, metrosexual salesman in a perfectly cut suit to bound out of the showroom.

"Sweet car," he said, pointing at a metallic green Miata.

"Yeah, it is. But it's definitely a chick car," I noted.

"I could see you in the MX-5 RF. Now that's a cool sports car. Definitely a chick magnet."

"Actually, I'm not here to buy a new car. I was wondering if you knew a woman named Janet Walker."

"Yeah. Hard to forget a woman like that. I sold her a red Miata about a month ago. Heard she was murdered. Real tragic."

"Could you tell me if she leased it or bought it on a finance plan?"

The salesman stepped back and looked me over. "You a cop?"

"I'm a reporter. Have the cops come around to ask you about the car?"

"No. Why are you asking about the car? Was it stolen?"

"No. I was just over at the condo where Janet Walker lived, and I saw the car in the underground parking garage with the Capital Motors decal on it."

"I should go and check it out. I'd buy it back. It would resell in a second," the salesman said.

"Can you tell me anything about Janet Walker?"

"She was a real looker. Drop-dead gorgeous. I read she was some kind of an escort, like for rich dudes."

"Yeah. Can you tell me how much she put down for the car?"

"She bought it outright. Paid for it in cash with crisp one-hundred-dollar bills."

"You didn't find that a bit odd?"

"Not really. We've had arrogant rich kids whose parents are diplomats come in here and pay cash for a car. And Arab and Russian kids with a ton of money to blow."

Realizing I wasn't going to get much else out of the guy, I thanked him and called for an Uber.

*

My next stop was the apartment building where Gail Peterson lived. There was a sign on the lawn for a one-bedroom apartment to let. The superintendent was in the lobby chatting with a tenant. When he saw me, he opened the door and invited me in.

"I am Juan Diego. You here to look at the apartment?" he asked with a welcoming smile.

"Actually, no. My name is Matt Kozar. I'm a reporter with the *New York Tribune*. I was wondering if I could talk to you about the Gail Peterson murder."

"God bless her soul. Look, I don't want to be quoted. Management wants us to put all that behind us," he explained. "It's her apartment that's for rent, but I'm not having much luck. People lookin' to rent get cold feet when I tell them it's available because the previous tenant was murdered it in. And the law says I have to tell them. I guess they're scared it might be haunted."

"A lot of people believe in ghosts. But I'm not here to quote you or get you into any trouble. I just want to find out a bit about Ms. Peterson. What kind of person she was, that kind of thing."

"Gail was a sweetheart. Only way to put it. Always polite. Always with a smile. I still can't believe her boss did what he did."

"Do you know if she had a boyfriend?"

"Not that I ever saw. She was a workaholic. I don't think she ever had anyone over to her apartment for drinks or dinner."

"Did you ever see her boss, Senator Bradford, drop by on business or for a friendly visit?"

"The detective asked me that. I told him I never saw the man. Weird guy, that cop," he added bitterly.

"What do you mean by weird?"

"Just the other day he came by. He showed me a photograph of the senator and asking me in an almost threatening manner, 'Are you sure you never saw this man?' It was like he was trying to get me to say I did when I never did."

"Was that Detective Spencer?"

"Yeah, that's him. Arrogant. Walked around here like he owned the place. Rubbed me the wrong way. I instantly did not like him."

"What else did the detective ask you?"

"Well, for one thing, on the day they found Miss Peterson, he got really pissed at me when he asked about the security camera," Diego recalled, pointing up to a camera mounted on the ceiling with its lens aimed at the entrance.

"What about it?"

"When he saw it, he asked if it was working. I told him it was about to be repaired. Well, he takes a flying shitfit like it's my fault. Says he's fed up with all these security cameras that don't work or are there just for show, and then dismisses me like I'm some kind of flunky."

"Why wasn't it working?" I asked.

"If that cop had asked me, I would have told him. The night before Miss Peterson was killed, someone spray-painted the lens."

My radar kicked in. "Until that happened, was it working?"

"Yeah. Just fine."

"Do you have the video leading up to the moment the camera got sprayed?"

"Sure do. Want to look at it?"

"If it's no problem."

The super led me into his office. He pulled a disc from a filing cabinet and inserted it into a playback unit.

"See here? It's twenty-six minutes after eleven. There, that guy in the black raincoat. He walks in behind Mrs. Nelson. She lives in apartment 1007. She gets into the elevator, and he stays back. He keeps his head down, making sure you don't see his face. Then he moves out of range of the camera and a second later, boom … paint spray hits the lens. He had to be the one who did that."

I hit freeze frame and studied the dark figure. From his height and build, there was one thing of which I was certain: He was not Senator Bradford.

"When did you realize the camera was sprayed?"

"When the cops got here and found Miss Peterson's body. I went to the office to see what was on the security tape. That's when I saw nothing but black."

"You didn't tell Detective Spencer about this?"

"Never got the chance. Like I said, after I told him the camera wasn't working, he walked away in a huff, cursing me under his breath like it was my fault."

"Any of the tenants say anything about the night Ms. Peterson was murdered?"

"Nobody heard anything. Nobody saw anything. One of the cops in uniform said Miss Peterson must have known the killer."

"An officer told you that?"

"No. I overheard him tell another cop there was no forced entry. Said the detective figured she must have known the person and let him in. Anyway, they caught the guy. Too bad DC doesn't have the death penalty. The guy who did this deserves to fry in the chair."

Diego let me take a copy of the footage. I thanked him for his time and left, more certain than ever that Bradford not only did not kill Janet Walker, he also did not murder Gail Peterson.

*

On the train back to New York, I held onto the memory stick like it was an eighteen-karat gold nugget. Once in the city, I made a beeline for the Trib and parked myself in my cubicle. I spent the next five hours reviewing two months of motion detection outside Mrs. Simmons' apartment and made another chilling discovery. The same man who entered Walker's apartment on the night she was killed visited her four weeks earlier. He entered the fourth floor via the stairwell and remained in the flat for ninety-two minutes before leaving, once again taking the stairs.

"Who is this guy?" I asked myself. "A customer? Or someone far more sinister?" My gut was betting on the latter.

FIVE STRANDS OF HAIR

"I owe you a dinner," Mei announced with a smile and a warm hug as I arrived at her apartment.

"What for?"

"For referring the Bradford case to us for a re-test of the DNA."

"You're welcome. You can take me out to Gallagher's for a steak."

"You got it," Mei said. "What I find curious, if not somewhat disturbing, is that we've been instructed by Senator Bradford's lawyer to share our findings with you."

"I'm not disturbed by that. I have a critical eye," I said.

"You know nothing about DNA. You can't even pronounce deoxyribonucleic acid let alone spell it or tell me what it is."

"That's why I have you to Dick and Jane all the scientific mumbo-jumbo for me. And if you're not around, I always have Google."

"Explain how you managed to convince Bradford's lawyer to go along with this request to retest the DNA findings."

"Let's just say Bradford's lawyer is not a happy camper, but the senator overruled him."

"No doubt because of something you said."

"I simply placed a kernel of doubt in the senator's bonnet. I told him I had a bad feeling about the test results."

"Based on what? Another one of your gut instincts?" Mei asked with a wry grin.

"Spinning inside me like a whirling dervish."

"And Bradford bought it?"

"What does he have to lose? Right now, the cards are heavily stacked against him."

Mei shook her head in disbelief. "Let me just say the lab that did the original tests is top notch. One of the best in the country. I know some of the technicians over there. I went to university with a couple of them. There is no way they would slip up. And given what I've discovered in my quick read of the lab report, I would say the senator's goose is cooked."

"But you will retest everything, right?"

"That's what we're being paid to do. So, yes."

Mei paused and looked into my eyes. She was searching.

"You should know by now I can always tell when you're up to something or when something is bothering you. What's going on?"

I hesitated. "You won't believe this. I have absolute proof Bradford did not murder Janet Walker."

Not one for jumping to conclusions before weighing the evidence, Mei calmly asked, "What is it?"

"A video. That's all I can say for now. I need to do some more digging."

"You just told me you have absolute proof. What more do you need to dig for?"

"I need to find proof the senator did not murder Gail Peterson."

"Well, while you're working on it, I'll be working on the lab results.

*

Late the following afternoon, I received a terse text message from Mei: "We need to talk. See you at my place around seven p.m."

If there was one thing that rattled my cage, it was getting a voice or text message from Mei that began with the words "we need to talk." It usually meant I did something wrong, said something stupid, or forgot an important date in our relationship. And now she was leaving me to stew for a few hours over what it was we needed to discuss.

When I arrived at her apartment, the tendons in my shoulders were in reef knots and my temples were throbbing.

Mei greeted me with a smile and a warm hug. I knew instantly I wasn't in hot water. My shoulders relaxed. The head trauma abated.

"You won't believe what I've ..."

I cut her off. "Before we get into whatever it is you want to discuss, could you please do me a favor?"

"Certainly, my love. What is it?"

"Please stop using those four words. All they do is trigger a tidal wave of acid in my stomach and make me worry I did something to tick you off."

"What are you going on about? What four words?"

"The 'we need to talk' words."

"Well, if you didn't do something to annoy me then there's nothing to be worried about. Is there something you feel you need to get off your chest?"

"No. Just please stop with the 'we need to talk.'"

"You can relax, Matt. What I have to tell you has nothing to do with any transgressions you may or may not have committed."

"There are no transgressions," I shot back.

"That's good to know. Now to the issue at hand. It's about the Bradford case. It's early stages, so what I have to tell you is off the record."

"Then don't tell me. I swore an oath when I became a journalist never to deal in off-the-record comments. They handcuff me from doing anything with them."

"How about, as you've so aptly put it at times, 'not for attribution'? And you never, ever say that I told you. Ever!"

I nodded. "I'd go to jail for life to protect you as my source."

"Oh, stop with the drama," she said. "I got a call from a tech at the lab who did the DNA tests for the prosecution in the Bradford case. He told me something in strictest confidence. Something extremely disturbing."

My curiosity was piqued. "What is it?"

"He told me there's a lot of pressure on the lab to get the testing right."

"What's the problem with that? I would hope they'd get it right."

"Except the lead detective and the prosecutor showed up at the lab for a quiet chat with the director. The tech said they were unwavering in their resolve that the senator murdered these two women—that they'd caught a serial killer."

"What else would you expect from them? They believe they got their man."

"And therein lies the problem. The tech said he felt they were meddling in the process. He was really uncomfortable with them pushing their theory on his boss."

"Are you saying the prosecutor and the detective are trying to skew the findings, that maybe what the cops found is not Bradford's DNA?"

"No, nothing like that. The senator's DNA was definitely collected at both crime scenes. No doubt about it."

Shaking my head, I said, "I don't get what you're getting at."

"It's the evidence package the lab sent over on the Peterson case. There were five strands of hair—blond hair—in it. Three have roots and appear to have been pulled from the scalp. Problem is, I couldn't find any paperwork that the hair had been tested for DNA. I called my contact at the lab. He told me he was instructed by his boss to ignore the hair. She told him the hairs weren't germane to the case, that they were most likely left behind during an earlier tryst."

"Who came up with that scenario?" I asked.

"According to the tech, the lead detective."

I could feel my pulse rate kick up a notch at the mention of the strands of blond hair. The sole image flashing in my mind was the man leaving Walker's apartment the night she was killed. He had blond hair.

"Bradford has dark brown hair," I pointed out.

Mei nodded. "I know. Anyhow, we tested the hair and got a solid DNA read. It belongs to a male. I ran it through CODIS, the combined DNA Index System, and struck out. No match. So, I went a step further. I decided to run a test for ethnicity."

"The thing you had done with my DNA?"

"The same. You won't believe this. It turns out the DNA from the hair sample tested seventy-nine percent Russian and fourteen percent Chechen."

I stopped breathing. I stared at Mei in disbelief. She had just put the prosecution's entire case against Senator Bradford in jeopardy. For the first time, I was convinced, as the senator always maintained, that he was innocent ... that he was being framed. I was also certain the blond hair collected by the CSI team in Peterson's bedroom belonged to the blond man I saw on the video leaving Walker's apartment. The problem was connecting the pieces. I had no idea who the man was.

I turned to Mei. "Don't do anything with this yet."

"I wasn't intending to. We have more tests to carry out and then there's the report we have to submit to Bradford's lawyer and, of course, you. Have you told your editor about the video you uncovered?"

"Not yet. I'm going to hold off until I can figure out my next step in the Peterson murder."

Mei shook her head in disbelief.

I shrugged. "I just need a couple of days."

"Fine. I'll let you know what we find when our tests are concluded," she said.

*

I now possessed what I firmly believed was ironclad evidence proving Senator Bradford did not murder Janet Walker. But I knew if I submitted the story at this stage, it would unleash a media frenzy. The journalists with their sights on the Peterson case would start working the possibility that Bradford didn't kill his intern. I had to stay ahead of the story. I had to make certain I would not be scooped on my investigation, especially now that I had come so close to solving the Peterson murder. In my mind, Mei's DNA test proved Gail Peterson's killer was the same guy who murdered Janet Walker. But I had no idea who the killer was, who he worked for, or whether he was still in Washington. More importantly, I had no DNA sample from him to determine if it matched the hair samples found in Peterson's bedroom. If he'd already flown the coop, all I had was circumstantial evidence, albeit powerful exculpatory evidence that might result in the charges against the senator being dismissed at best, or, at worst, stayed. Whatever the court and prosecution ruled, Bradford would be followed by a dark shadow for the rest of his life, with many people believing he got off on a technicality.

I pored over my notes with the senator's voice echoing in my ears, reciting a list of enemies who, in his mind, had motive and the ability to hatch a plot to frame him for murder. The one I had discounted as fantasy was the one I was now buying: Russia's president was the puppet master behind the plot to destroy Bradford. That scenario now seemed so plausible, although I was still far from proving it. I needed a credible source who could lend credence to the Putin plot and steer me to a clear track. I scanned Google and Twitter. The sites were inundated with political pundits spouting opinions and hypotheses on Vladimir Putin and his war against Ukraine.

After a four-hour search, I found a strong candidate who didn't opine but called it as he had experienced it firsthand; a man who had inside knowledge of the arcane world of Russian intelligence. I got his cell number from the Trib's Washington bureau chief, called him, and asked if we could meet to talk about Vladimir Putin. Without a moment's hesitation, the man invited me to his home in Langley, Virginia, for a backgrounder.

NO 007

Nils Aaberg was a former senior officer with the CIA who spent seventeen years as the Moscow station chief before retiring two years earlier. His resume as a top agent in the spy biz was impressive. He was considered an authority on Vladimir Putin, having watched him rise from a lieutenant colonel in the notorious KGB to a brutal dictator. He understood Putin far better than most pundits and he was always on tap to share his knowledge.

When Aaberg opened his front door, he threw me for a loop. He was no James Bond. He carried a belly the size of a pumpkin, and the buttons on his creased white shirt strained to pop free. His pants were held up just below his stomach by red, white, and blue striped suspenders. He sported a comb-over; a scraggly beard covered his double chin.

After warmly shaking hands, Aaberg escorted me to his study at the back of the two-story, yellow-brick house. Floor to ceiling, oak bookcases lined two walls. From a quick scan of titles and authors, I noticed most of his books dealt with the world of espionage. His preferred genre was spy fiction, and his favorite author, judging by the prominent, eye level position of the novels on his bookshelves, appeared to be John le Carré, followed by David Ignatius, Mick Herron, and Helen MacInnes.

"Mr. Kozar, how can I help you?" he asked, pouring himself a glass of twelve-year-old Macallan and adding a splash of spring water. He offered me a glass, which I politely declined. It was 11:05 in the morning.

I got right to the point. "I've read a lot about Putin going after people who criticize or belittle him, and that a lot of them end up dead."

Aaberg peered over his silver-rimmed reading glasses and leaned back in a black leather club chair. He took a sip of the Scotch, swirled it in his mouth, and swallowed.

"Russia is notorious for targeting enemies both at home and abroad," he began. "It has a long history with what I call the dark arts, which include assassinations referred to internally as 'executive actions' or 'liquid affairs.'"

"When you refer to executive actions, who would be giving the order?" I asked.

"In today's Russia, no one gets liquidated without Putin's approval or direction."

"Especially if his target happened to piss him off?" I ventured.

"Putin has no hesitation in going after anyone who crosses him," Aaberg said flatly. "The man is thin skinned and vengeful."

I cleared my throat and fired my next question. "Would he send a hitman to the United States to kill someone?"

It didn't take him long to gather his thoughts. "I don't know if you're aware of the attempted assassination of Aleksandr Poteyev. He was the former deputy head of Directorate 'S' of the Russian Foreign Intelligence Service, the SVR."

I shook my head. I had no idea who the man was.

Aaberg continued. "Around 1999, Aleksandr Poteyev began secretly working with the CIA to reveal a clandestine network of Russian spies operating in the US. In 2010, we had to extract him from Russia.

"We set him up in Miami. On February 14, 2020, Hector Alejandro Cabrera Fuentes, a Mexican national, was confronted outside Poteyev's gated residence by a security guard. Two days later, Fuentes was stopped by Border Security agents at Miami International where he was about to board a plane to Mexico City. On his cell phone was a photograph of the license plate of a car belonging to Poteyev. While in custody, Fuentes spilled the beans about his role in a plot to eliminate Poteyev, and he identified his handler at the Russian embassy in DC. The SVR was using Fuentes' wife, who is a Russian citizen, and his daughters, as bait, refusing to let them leave Moscow unless he carried out his assignment."

"Was Putin behind it?"

"Putin was very likely the mastermind. He made no attempt to hide his fury at Poteyev, who he felt betrayed his country. Poteyev's actions led to the arrest of ten sleeper agents living undercover in the US."

I wondered aloud what would have happened if this Poteyev character had been assassinated by a Russian hitman.

Aaberg's eyes narrowed. "It would have been seen as an extraordinary breach of American sovereignty. There would have been serious repercussions."

"So, you don't think Putin would dare send a hitman here?"

I waited for Aaberg, who was weighing his response while staring wistfully across the room at a signed, framed photo of Sean Connery as 007 in *Dr. No.* "I no longer put anything past that psychopath."

The spymaster's response to my next question was crucial. "If Putin hated someone here and wanted to nail him, is it possible he'd use other means?"

"No doubt in my mind," Aaberg said. "Putin has a lot of tools in his arsenal to take revenge on whomever he perceives as a threat."

"Like what?"

Dragging his fingers through his beard, Aaberg said, "Putin would find a way to destroy the individual by placing him in a compromising situation— one that would lead to the complete destruction of his career, his reputation, and everything he holds dear. The manufactured evidence against him would be devastating and virtually impossible to disprove."

I couldn't believe what I was hearing. Aaberg had just described the dire situation in which Senator Bradford was ensnared.

I took a deep breath and let it out slowly. "Hypothetically, if Putin wanted to take revenge on someone here, would he use a hitman from the Russian mafia in New York or Miami?"

"I highly doubt it," Aaberg responded. "Too many links in the chain. Dangerous links. The Russian mafia in New York is a bunch of thick-skulled thugs. They would follow orders from Moscow, but they couldn't be trusted to keep their mouths shut. Pour a few shots of cheap vodka down their throats and their lips start flapping. They love to brag. So, to answer your question, if Putin wanted someone put down using your example, the only people in the know would be the head of Unit 29155 and the hitman."

"What is unit 29155?" I asked.

"It's a secret unit within Russia's GRU tasked with foreign assassinations and other activities aimed at destabilizing Western nations. We only became aware of its existence in 2019."

"GRU is short for what?"

"It's the acronym for *Glavnoye Razvedyvatelnoye Upravlenie*."

"Easy for you to say," I joked.

"It's Russia's chief intelligence office."

The next question, as I considered the options, would be the tipping point. If it all came together, I would have my roadmap. "If Putin ordered an assassination in the US, how would his henchman get into the country?"

"These days, with all the sanctions in place, the only way a Russian could enter the US is through diplomatic channels. No tourist visas are being issued by our embassy in Moscow."

"What do you mean by diplomatic channels?"

"The individual would probably come here on a diplomatic visa. The Russian embassy would use some ruse like saying they need the individual to fill an important post or work on a specific project, and they'd ask the State Department to clear him for a visa."

"And that person could be an agent within Russia's spy network trained and primed to do whatever Putin orders?"

Aaberg chuckled. "Most of the diplomats at the Russian embassy are not diplomats by any stretch of the imagination. They're spies. The lot of them."

Staring at me inquisitively over his reading glasses, Aaberg asked, "Do you think Putin has you marked for exposing Russia's involvement in the international food aid scandal?"

I made no effort to dissuade him of the assumption. I didn't want him to connect my visit to my investigation of the Bradford case. But I needed answers. "You never know. I mean, a Russian hitman tried to off me on two occasions."

"Well, be vigilant," he warned. "That's all I can say."

I ventured cautiously with my next question. "What about a politician?"

"What about it?"

"Would Putin order a hit on a US politician?"

"It would cross a red line and would definitely trigger serious retaliatory measures, and I mean serious. Putin knows it. Again, while I highly doubt it, I wouldn't bet my life on it."

"What if it was a politician who really got under his thin skin, as you put it?"

"As I mentioned earlier, he'd probably order his people to find a way to destroy the individual."

Aaberg's eyes suddenly snapped into focus and burrowed into my face. "You're here about Senator Bradford."

He caught me. All I could do was nod. Then he stunned me with his response.

"I will say this about the matter. At first, I thought Senator Bradford killed his intern. I mean, the evidence is overwhelming. Then came the second murder. The same MO on the very same night. I've looked at this case from every angle, and I couldn't come up with a sane explanation as to why Senator Bradford would go to a hooker, pay her a thousand dollars, have sex with her, and then strangle her to death leaving his DNA all over her apartment. Then head straight to his intern's place, force himself on her, strangle her to death, and leave his DNA all over her bedroom. Unless the senator is some sort of psychopath, none of this makes sense, and I always say if it doesn't make sense, then something else is at play. Trouble is, I don't know how you can go about proving his innocence."

I didn't respond. Aaberg had given me pretty much what I needed, and I knew exactly who to tap next for help. My only problem? He told me a few years back never to contact him again.

NEVER A SOURCE

On the ride back to DC, I opened the contact list on my cell phone and looked up Ross McDougall, a senior foreign service officer at the US State Department. Ross wasn't a source in the true meaning of the word, and if he ever found out he was on my contact list, he'd have a royal fit.

A few years back, McDougall and I met on the hot desert sands of Eritrea after his boss ordered him to bail me out of a dicey situation brought on by my investigation of international food aid shipments to Massawa. When I returned to the US after being expelled from Eritrea, I managed to convince him to give me a not-for-attribution, deep dive into food aid. He turned out to be an invaluable resource.

Once my story hit the front page of the *Tribune*, the State Department launched a full-scale, department-wide search for my source. After almost being fingered, McDougall made me promise never to call him again. I kept my word. Now I had no choice. I needed his help.

I knew McDougall wouldn't answer his phone if he saw my name on call display, so I switched off my ID and tapped in his number. I was hoping he would answer because he would never respond to my message. To my surprise, he answered after four rings.

"Hey, Ross. It's Matt. Matt Kozar."

"Didn't I tell you never to call me?" he asked in a tense whisper.

"I know, but I miss you."

"Cut the crap. Why are you calling me?"

"It's a matter of life and death."

"Sounds rather extreme," McDougall said. "Then again, you've always been prone to hyperbole."

"Hear me out, I'm in an Uber heading to DC from Arlington. Can we meet up this afternoon for a few minutes?"

"No."

"I'll buy you a beer."

"No.

"I'll light a candle for you in church."

"You don't go to church. There's not a religious bone in your body," McDougall said.

"I just need you to explain the procedure for foreigners applying for visas to travel to the States. It's a simple request," I pleaded.

"One thing I learned in my limited dealings with you is that nothing is as simple as it sounds."

"Actually, it is. Come on. I haven't seen you in a dog's age. It would be nice to catch up."

"You are so full of it, Kozar," McDougall said. "Look, after what happened to you getting shot and all, most everyone in DC knows your face. If I'm seen within a block of you, I'm finished."

"I'll be wearing dark sunglasses and a red Make America Great Again ball cap."

"Like I would ever be seen with a moron wearing a MAGA cap," he shot back.

"Okay, how about a New York Yankees cap with the brim pulled over my face? Come on, Ross. Let's say we meet at the same bar we met at last time. It's dark. It's out of the way. And no one there will ever remember your name."

There was no sound on the other end of the line. I thought McDougall had disconnected.

"Is anybody out there?" I called out.

McDougall cleared his throat. I knew right then I had him baited and hooked. He was a bureaucrat through and through, but he had a fault line in his tough mantle: curiosity. He needed to know what I was up to.

"What time?"

"Let's say we meet at four."

*

When I walked into the bar, I spotted McDougall tucked into a booth at the back. There was no smile, no warm greeting, no handshake, and lamentably no hug.

"I must say it's nice to see an old friend," I said with a silly smirk.

"We're not friends."

"So, how's life been treating you?"

"Let's see. I'm stuck here in DC twiddling my thumbs and pushing paper while incompetent, butt-kissing airheads get plum assignments at our embassies abroad. That's how life's been treating me," McDougall said.

"I feel your pain."

"No, you don't. So what is it you want?"

"I need you to explain the process of getting a visa to come to the States."

"Any numbskull could find that information on the State Department website."

"What if the individual is from a country in turmoil?"

"I'm in no mood to dance," McDougall said. "From where?"

"Like Russia."

"Damn it, Kozar. If you had mentioned Russia on the phone, I would have hung up."

"I'm just asking about the visa process."

McDougall was silent for what felt like an eternity. I knew he had the information, but I wasn't sure he was going to share. At last, he spoke.

"It's like any other process for people applying to enter the US as a tourist or on business from any country requiring a visa."

I pushed the red button. "With all the sanctions the US government has imposed against Russia for its invasion of Ukraine, what's the situation like for Russians obtaining a visa to come here?"

"And now we stumble from the pothole and tumble into the murky abyss. What is it you really want?"

I knew right then I had to give him something or he would shut me down.

Hesitantly, I asked, "Are Russians still being allowed into the US?"

"Does this have anything to do with your trek into Bucha?"

"No."

"Why don't I believe you?"

"I swear. It has nothing to do with Bucha. All I want to know is whether Russians are allowed to come into the US given Putin's invasion of Ukraine."

McDougall shook his head. I knew he didn't believe me, but it didn't matter. He offered a measured response. "About six weeks ago, the US embassy in Moscow suspended its non-diplomatic visa services owing to the Russian government prohibiting the embassy from employing foreign nationals, including Russians, in any capacity. The Russian government made it impossible for our office to continue offering non-diplomatic visa services in Moscow."

"So no Russians getting in."

"I didn't say that. Diplomats are exempt."

Nils Aaberg had pointed out the same loophole. "Have any come in lately?" I asked.

"I don't know. It's not my area. I would assume one or two may have entered at the request of the Russian embassy. Why?"

I ignored the question. "What's the process when they arrive?"

"They go straight to the line earmarked for diplomats at the airport. We check their credentials, take a photograph, and say, 'Welcome to the United States of America.'"

It was music to my ears. I discreetly pulled an envelope from the inside pocket of my blazer. "I've got a couple of photographs of a guy I'm pretty certain is Russian, and I'm wondering if maybe he entered the US as a diplomat," I explained, sliding two photos toward him.

McDougall glared at me. "Why in heaven's name did I agree to meet you?"

"I gather from your tone that would be a rhetorical question."

Glancing down at the photos, McDougall shrugged. "You're asking me to look for a needle in a haystack."

"Not if just a handful of Russians have been issued visas to enter the States in the past few months."

"What are you really up to?"

"I'm playing a hunch."

With a look of distrust, McDougall took a deep breath and exhaled slowly. "What is it you're working on?"

"Like I told you, this is extremely important. I swear I wouldn't steer you wrong. It's all I can say. Look—I know it's a long shot, but if you could just have a look …"

"If you don't tell me exactly what you're working on, you can eat my dust as I leave this joint."

From the look in his eyes, I knew he meant it.

McDougall had me up against the wall. I decided to spill, knowing he'd never tell anyone at the State Department what I was about to reveal. If he did, he'd have to explain his meeting with me, and that would cause him no end of grief.

"I'm investigating the murder of two women, allegedly by Senator Bradford. I'm fairly certain the guy in the photos committed the murders."

"That's quite the allegation. What evidence do you have? From what I've read, the prosecutor has his case locked and loaded."

"Ross, I know I'm right on this. I know I am. I need your help. An innocent man needs your help. Just do me this one favor. It's all I ask. If not for me, for Senator Bradford."

McDougall stared down at the photos, then he closed his eyes and pursed his lips.

Without another word, he slipped the photos back in the envelope, put the envelope in his breast pocket, and walked out of the bar.

**

I was surprised when McDougall called me ninety minutes later. I could tell from the sound of traffic in the background he was not in his office.

"His name is Anton Kuznetzov," he said, spelling out the name. "He entered the US five weeks ago on an A-2 diplomatic visa. He's supposedly an IT tech, here, as an embassy official wrote on the application, 'to perform duties which take place at the Embassy of the Russian Federation.' Let me just say, if this guy is a computer expert, then I'm a NASA astronaut."

My pulse started to race. "Is he still in the country?" I asked.

"There's no indication he left. We have him listed as staying at the hotel directly across from the embassy."

"This Anton Kuznetzov is definitely the guy in the photos I gave you?"

"It's a perfect match. Blond hair with a face that can freeze vodka. He looks like one dangerous SOB. Dead eyes."

"Can you tell me the exact date he entered the US?"

"I can't. It would lead back to the department, and I don't need another witch hunt."

"Thanks for this, Ross, and I mean it."

"Matt, like I told you once before, don't ever call me again, and once again, I mean it."

"But you'll miss me."

"This is no joking matter. Whatever it is you're working on, watch your back," McDougall warned. "Remember what happened to you last time. These guys don't play nice."

Before I could respond, the line went dead.

THE ASSASSIN

I flagged a taxi and headed to the hotel across from the Russian embassy. In the lobby, I picked up the courtesy phone and asked to be connected to Anton Kuznetzov's room. The phone rang five times before being re-routed to voicemail. I hung up and parked myself on a faded green leatherette sofa with a clear view of the entrance. Less than an hour later, I spied the Russian crossing the road. I pulled out my phone, hit video, and placed the phone to my ear with the camera lens facing the entrance. I pretended to be talking to a friend. As he neared the revolving door, he took one last drag on his cigarette and stuffed the butt into the sand of an ashtray to the right of the entrance.

The Russian walked past taking no notice of me. As soon as he disappeared into the elevator, I pulled a tissue from my pocket, rushed out, and took a photo and a video of the ashtray. His was the only butt sticking out in the sand. I retrieved it and dropped it gingerly into the baggie I always carry in my breast pocket. I could tell the filter was wet with the man's saliva. I hailed a taxi, headed to the train station, and called Mei.

"I should be back in New York no later than a quarter after nine tonight. I need you to test a cigarette butt for DNA."

"I can't do it tonight. I'll do it first thing tomorrow. Matt, make certain you keep it properly contained. I don't need contamination."

"It's carefully contained in plastic."

"Are you coming over tonight?" she asked.

"I'm going to my apartment. I've got a lot to do on this investigation. I'll see you in the morning at your office."

*

At exactly 8 a.m., I was pacing outside the office tower where Forensic Analytics was headquartered. Mei arrived an hour later.

I was annoyed. "Is this what you call first thing?"

"And good morning to you," Mei responded with a smile.

"I need this really, really fast," I pleaded, handing her the baggie.

"What are we looking for?" she asked.

"Once you've isolated the DNA, compare it to the DNA from the hair you tested. I'm betting you'll find they match. Then call me, please. I'm heading to the newsroom to write my story on the Walker murder."

*

I was at my desk, pounding on my keyboard and anxiously anticipating Heather's reaction once she read the lead. She would have to eat crow. As for Doyle, I figured all I might get from him were two words: good job.

I jumped when Heather came up behind me and began to read the lead paragraph over my shoulder.

> *The sex worker US Senator William Bradford is accused of killing was alive almost an hour after he left the woman's Washington, DC, condo, according to a security video obtained by the New York Tribune.*
>
> *The video shows a man who is clearly not the senator entering the fourth-floor apartment of the victim, Janet Walker, at 11:06 p.m. A moment later, Walker sticks her head out of the door and checks the hallway.*
>
> *The unidentified man appears to gain access to the floor by using the emergency stairwell. He is seen leaving the victim's apartment at 11:19 p.m., again using the stairwell to exit the building.*

The time code on the elevator security camera obtained by DC homicide detectives captured Senator Bradford arriving at the victim's floor at 9:02 p.m. and leaving the condo at 10:11 p.m.

Heather drew in a sharp breath. "Matt, you'd better have all the facts right, because this is explosive. We need to send this to Doyle right now."

"I'm not even close to finishing my copy," I countered.

"Just send him the first three paragraphs and keep writing. He'll want the publisher, the editor-in chief, and our lawyer in on this right away."

Two hours later, I was done. I pressed the send key with encrypted copies going to Doyle and Heather. It didn't take long before I was summoned to the managing editor's office.

"Good job," Doyle said as I walked in. "However, you're missing reaction from two important parties: the prosecutor and the DC police."

"They can react after they've read the story," I said.

"It's called due diligence, Matt. Our lawyer is also concerned that what you have in your possession is crucial evidence in a murder investigation. He says if we run the story without first turning over the evidence to the prosecutor and the police, you might be charged with obstruction of justice," Doyle explained.

"So, let them charge me."

"It's not going to work that way. You are going to contact the DA and the lead detective and provide them with a copy of the video," he instructed.

I fired back. "Then they'll move like hell to shut me down, or even worse, hold a press conference announcing they've come into possession of new evidence in the Walker case and release the information to the entire Washington news corp."

"They won't have that opportunity. We'll be set to go with your story the moment you turn over a copy of the video. Make certain to document all your conversations and interactions," Doyle said.

"Yes, sir."

I marched out of his office and booked the 7 a.m. express train to DC to hand-deliver copies of the video to Detective Spencer and federal prosecutor David Di Adamo.

OBSTRUCTION OF JUSTICE

On the two-and-a-half-hour train ride, I called the prosecutor every fifteen minutes, leaving an urgent voice message on his phone. When I reached DC, I called again. This time his assistant answered. She said her boss was busy and would get back to me when he had a free moment.

"Could you please tell Mr. Di Adamo it's urgent? It's about the Walker murder."

After a fifteen-minute wait, I called back.

"Mr. Kozar, I have placed your message on his desk. As I told you, he will get back to you when he has a moment," the secretary snapped.

I also called Detective Spencer. He answered and disconnected the moment he heard my name. I called back, but his phone went to voicemail.

I left a message. "Detective Spencer, this is Matt Kozar," I began. "I just got into Washington. I need to speak to you about the Walker murder. It's urgent."

I decided to head straight to DC police headquarters. On the way over, I called the prosecutor again. This time his assistant didn't answer.

*

At DC police headquarters, a sergeant manning the front desk paged Spencer and informed him of my presence. A moment later, the red-faced detective charged into the lobby like a bull on steroids.

"I specifically instructed you not to interfere in my case," he bellowed.

"First of all, I'm not deaf, and second, I'm not interfering," I said calmly. "As I told you when we first met, I'm an investigative reporter doing my job, and I came here to inform you that I found evidence which I believe will change the direction of your case against Senator Bradford in the Walker murder."

"What the fuck would you know about investigations?"

I stood my ground. "Do you want to hear what I've dug up or not?"

"I don't have time for your fantasy theories. I deal in facts, and you wouldn't recognize a fact if it was right in front of your face."

"There you go again with the insults."

"There's the door. Don't let it hit your idiot ass on the way out."

"So, I take it you don't want to hear what I've uncovered. I swear it will change the entire direction of your case against Senator Bradford in the Walker murder."

"What I've uncovered as a veteran homicide detective shows unequivocally that your friend is a serial rapist and a cold-blooded murderer."

"For the record, the senator and I are not friends."

"How much is he paying you to lie for him?" he asked, his voice filled with disdain.

"He's not my employer, and I'm not getting paid by him. The *Tribune* pays my salary. And I don't lie for anyone."

"Yeah. The *Tribune*. The New York beacon of truth," he said.

I stepped back and waved the envelope containing a USB drive in his face. "All I ask is that you look at what I've found. It's all I ask."

Spencer yanked the envelope from my hand and stormed back toward the inner offices. As he pulled the door open, he tossed my offering into a trash bin. When the door closed, I walked over, calmly retrieved it, and waved at the security camera.

The desk sergeant was grinning, "Well that was certainly a performance. Don't take it to heart. Spencer doesn't like most people."

"Well, he certainly doesn't like me," I said as I left the building.

*

My next stop was at the Robert F. Kennedy Department of Justice Building on Pennsylvania Avenue. Specifically, the Homicide Section where federal senior prosecutor David Di Adamo had his office. I was immediately confronted by a beefy security guard who wouldn't allow me to cross the hallowed threshold unless I had an appointment. I handed him my press credentials and he called Di Adamo's office. After a short conversation, the guard came back and instructed me to leave.

"Mr. Di Adamo's assistant informed me that he is not in the office," the guard said, pointing to the exit.

"Could you please take this and make certain that Mr. Di Adamo gets it? It's extremely important," I said, handing the guard an envelope addressed to the prosecutor. In it was a USB drive. The accompanying note instructed, "Watch this video NOW! It concerns the murder of Janet Walker. Look at the date and time codes. Please call me with your reaction because this will be the subject of the lead story in tomorrow's *New York Tribune*."

My cell phone number and email address were at the bottom of the page.

The guard took the envelope and logged the delivery date and time on a computer. "I'll see it gets to Mr. Di Adamo's office right away."

With my legal requirements completed, I called Heather.

"I've done my due diligence. I met with Detective Spencer, handed him the USB stick, and he basically told me to eat shit."

"He actually said that?" Heather asked.

"Well, not exactly in those words. It was the gist of his confrontation with me," I explained.

"I hope you kept your cool," Heather warned.

"I was as polite as I could be."

"Well, I'm sure he'll call once he's seen the video," Heather said.

"I very much doubt that," I countered.

"Why?"

"Detective Spencer never opened the envelope. He tossed it in the garbage can."

"What did you do?"

"I retrieved it. After that, I went over to the Department of Justice. Freakin' place is like Fort Knox. Security called Di Adamo's office. His assistant told the guard her boss wasn't in the office. I gave the guard an envelope with the USB stick in it, along with a note telling the prosecutor it was extremely important he get back to me ASAP. I also phoned him a dozen times leaving messages on his voicemail and with his assistant, saying it was urgent I speak to him about the Walker case."

"Good. You covered the bases. I'll let Doyle know," Heather said.

"Will the story be running in tomorrow's paper?" I asked.

"Yes."

"On front?"

"What do you think? When are you heading back?"

I told Heather I was staying in DC for the night. "I have one more accountability to do."

"What are you talking about?"

"On the murder of Gail Peterson."

"What about it?"

"Soon as I find the guy I'm looking for, I'll file." I hung up.

SHIT HITS THE FAN

David Di Adamo's face went red when he turned on CNN to catch the headlines at 7 a.m. Below the "Breaking News" banner and a full screenshot of the *New York Tribune*'s front page, the headline in bold lettering screamed,

US Senator William Bradford Alleged Murder of Call Girl in Serious Doubt.

A quick recap of the story by the news anchor sent the prosecutor's blood pressure soaring into the danger zone. He knew instantly his case was in jeopardy.

Three minutes into the newscast, Di Adamo's phone rang. It was Judge Hamilton's law clerk. The instruction was terse.

"His Honor wants you in his chambers this morning at ten o'clock sharp. Do not be late."

Di Adamo hung up, scrolled down the list of police contacts on his phone, and dialed Spencer. After five rings, the call went to voicemail.

"Spencer, it's Di Adamo. Call me ASAP. It's urgent," the prosecutor said.

After his fifth attempt to raise the detective, Di Adamo's voice messages went from anger to desperation.

"Spencer! I know you're there. Pick up the damn phone. I need to talk to you. Pick up the damn phone."

Before he headed out to door, the prosecutor opened his desk drawer, pulled out a bottle of antacid, and popped a handful of pink tablets into his mouth.

Minutes before entering the judge's chambers, Di Adamo tried one last time to reach Spencer, and again his call went straight to voicemail.

"I know you're avoiding me. I want you in my office at eleven o'clock sharp," the prosecutor shouted.

*

Detective Ron Spencer downed two extra-strength Tylenol gelcaps to ease the pounding in his temples. Two copies of the *Tribune* were spread out on his desk. A third copy was strewn across the floor where he had thrown it in a fit of rage.

The detective knew he was in serious trouble when Di Adamo began calling him at 7:15 a.m., and every fifteen minutes after that until 9:45 a.m. Each time he left a message, yelling like a man possessed.

Spencer ignored the calls. He was lying in wait for Detectives Lamont and Wells. The duo arrived at 10:15 a.m. looking like nervous lambs. Both had caught the jarring CNN wake-up call before heading in.

"Tell me, please, how the hell you missed this," Spencer snarled.

With his hands in his pockets and his eyes focused on the floor, Wells accepted the blame. "I went to the Simmons apartment when we canvassed the condo. She wasn't home. I left my card under her door and a day later she called. She said she was out of town visiting one of her kids and hadn't been home the night Walker was murdered."

"And you left it at that?" Spencer asked.

"Yes."

"Do you have any idea the pile of shit we're in?"

"Yes."

"You two imbeciles blew the Walker case. Don't expect to be in homicide much longer. Get to your desks, read the fucking paper, and write up a report on how you fucked up this case. I want it in my hands in an hour," Spencer yelled as he tossed copies of the *Tribune* at his two detectives.

*

Brian Tate also received a call from Judge Hamilton's law clerk ordering him to be in chambers at 10 a.m. He had just woken up and wondered what the judge wanted. When he turned on the television, he knew.

"I'll kill that son of a bitch," the lawyer shouted at the screen. "I'll kill him."

*

At 9:55 a.m., the defense lawyer and the prosecutor faced each other in the waiting room. There was no polite morning greeting, and no words were spoken. There was only intense, angry glaring.

*

Tate and Di Adamo stood in silence in front of Judge Hamilton's desk like delinquent schoolboys in the principal's office. They knew they were in serious trouble but for different reasons. The judge sat behind his 200-year-old oak desk, poring over the front page of the *New York Tribune*. Slowly and deliberately, he turned to the second page and continued reading. He was making the lawyers sweat. When he was done, he leaned forward and glared at the prosecutor and the defense attorney.

Hamilton first focused his wrath on Di Adamo. "What is this, Counselor?" he boomed, waving the paper in the prosecutor's face.

"Your Honor, I only learned about this when I tuned in to CNN this morning."

"Really? Can you explain how the homicide detectives missed this one crucial fact? It appears from what this reporter alleges that Janet Walker was alive when Senator Bradford left her apartment. Let me repeat that. She was alive, not dead. There's a video showing she was alive more than an hour after the senator left her apartment, and that's because she received another caller."

"Your Honor, I will be speaking to Detective Spencer the moment I leave your office. I've been trying to reach him for the past two hours. He isn't picking up his phone."

"You're damn right you'll be speaking to him, and I expect a full report on my desk no later than ten o'clock tomorrow morning. You got that?"

"Yes, sir."

The judge then turned his attention to the senator's lawyer. "Mr. Tate, tell me. This reporter, Matt Kozar … Is he working for you?"

"In a way but not really," Tate responded.

"What in hell does that even mean? Does Matt Kozar work for you or not? Yes or no!"

"Your Honor, against my advice, Senator Bradford personally asked Kozar to look into the allegations against him."

"Is the reporter being paid by the senator?"

"No, Your Honor. Kozar made it clear that any investigation he does is strictly in his role as an investigative reporter for the *New York Tribune*."

Holding up the front page of the *Tribune*, the judge asked, "Did you not think it prudent to inform the court of his findings before they were splashed all over the newspaper?"

"Your Honor, I swear I knew nothing about it. Kozar never mentioned he had the video, and he didn't see fit to inform me that the story was coming out. If he had, I would have immediately called Mr. Di Adamo and informed the court."

"I better not find out you had a hand in this," the judge warned. "I do not take kindly to being bushwhacked."

"Your Honor, I swear I had no hand in this whatsoever. Kozar never informed me of any of this."

The judge turned to the prosecutor. "Ten a.m. sharp tomorrow. I want a full report on my desk."

"Yes, Your Honor," Di Adamo said.

"And I want you to consider charging Mr. Kozar with obstruction of justice. It is obvious he withheld crucial information from your office and the police on a homicide investigation. Now both of you, get out."

*

When Di Adamo arrived at his office, Spencer was standing over the prosecutor's desk thumbing through several messages from Kozar. He took notice of one word on each message: Urgent.

"What the fuck do you think you're doing? That's private information." Di Adamo grabbed the pink message stubs out of the detective's hands.

"Did you bother to call the jerk back?" Spencer asked.

"None of your business. Why didn't you call me back? I left you a dozen messages. And don't bullshit me. I know you were ignoring my calls."

"I needed to talk to my detectives first. They're the ones who fucked up the Walker investigation."

"They may have fucked it up, as you put it, but you're the lead detective. The buck stops at your desk."

The detective didn't respond.

"Bloody hell, Spencer! How did your people miss this?" Di Adamo asked, flinging a copy of the *Tribune* across the room. "We look like a gang of incompetents. I can just imagine how the media is going to play this. I've already received a slew of calls from reporters from Boston to LA wanting me to respond to the *Tribune* article."

"How do we even know the time code on that woman's security camera is correct?" Spencer argued.

"You really want to go down that rabbit hole? Be my guest. You want to question that time code? All you need do is compare the times on the night Walker was murdered to the time when one of your detectives was recorded knocking on the woman's door the next morning."

Spencer grabbed for a straw. "We still got the senator on the Peterson murder, and that's a fact."

"Do we? Is that, as you put it, a fact?"

"The DNA evidence is rock solid."

"I'm not dealing with the Peterson case right now. The judge wants to know how you bungled the Walker murder investigation."

"I didn't bungle the investigation. Detectives Lamont and Wells were working the Walker case."

"Don't you dare pass the buck on this one, Spencer. You signed on as lead detective in this case. Lamont and Wells report directly to you. Your job is to look over their reports. Did they even bother to canvass the condo?"

"They told me they canvassed the entire fourth floor."

"How did they not find the video of a man entering Walker's apartment long after the senator left? A five-year-old could have done a better job."

"They slipped up," Spencer offered in defense.

"Slipped up? You mean fucked up. This is shoddy police work. It's inexcusable. The judge is on the warpath and I'm sure he's going to recommend I bring a motion requesting the charges against the senator on the Walker murder be dismissed."

"What about the charges on the Peterson murder?"

"They stand. For now, that is, unless there is something, anything you haven't told me that I should know." Di Adamo said.

"We've got the creep on that one. I personally headed the investigation on that case from start to finish. It's ironclad. You have nothing to worry about."

"You've given me more than enough to worry about. Now, I have one more task at hand. The judge suggested I consider charging Matt Kozar with obstruction of justice. He had key evidence of a serious crime which he deliberately withheld. Evidence he should have brought to our attention. I'm going to issue a warrant for his arrest."

Spencer shifted nervously in his seat and cleared his throat. "I'd hold off on that if I were you."

"What now?"

"Late yesterday morning, Kozar showed up at headquarters. He asked to speak to me. He muttered something about having uncovered information that would impact the Walker case. I told him I didn't have time for his fantasy theories and told him to leave."

"That's it? So, what's the problem?"

"He handed me an envelope. He said it contained a USB stick," Spencer explained, his gaze dropping to the floor.

"What was on the stick?" the prosecutor asked.

"I don't know."

"What do you mean you don't know?"

"I tossed it into a waste basket."

"What the hell were you thinking, Spencer? The judge is going to go ballistic when he hears this."

"Do you have to tell him?"

"Are you insane? Of course I have to tell him. Better me than the judge hearing it from Kozar on the witness stand in a courtroom packed with journalists."

"Why should we take his word on what was on the USB stick? It could have been recipes for cupcakes for all anyone knows."

"The problem with that inane excuse, Detective, is you didn't even bother to find out. When the media gets hold of this, you're finished."

Spencer didn't respond.

The prosecutor shook his head. "I want you to double-check everything on the Peterson case. I don't want to walk into the courtroom tomorrow and get blindsided by another damning revelation. Do you understand me?"

"I said I personally handled the Peterson case. I can guarantee there won't be any damning or unforeseen revelations."

"I hope so, for your sake and mine," Di Adamo said.

The prosecutor glanced down at the left side of his desk, his eyes focusing on a tiny pile of yellow Post-it notes and an envelope addressed to him. URGENT was handwritten in black capital letters. The *Tribune* logo was imprinted on the upper left-hand corner. His hands began to shake as he flipped through the urgent messages. They were all from Kozar, starting at 9 a.m. the previous day. Each had been placed on his desk by his assistant, and each one read, "Matt Kozar, *New York Tribune,* called. He keeps repeating it's urgent regarding the Walker case and asks that you call him ASAP."

Before his assistant left work for the day, she had placed the envelope on his desk with a note: "Matt Kozar dropped this off at the security desk at 3:45 p.m. Security wouldn't let him in without an appointment. Per your instruction, I said you were not in the office."

Di Adamo swallowed hard. He looked at the Post-its and swore under his breath, ripping them into pieces before tossing them in the waste basket.

"What was that?" Spencer asked.

"Nothing."

"From the look on your face, I'd say it's definitely something."

"I have work to do."

When the detective left his office, Di Adamo ripped open the envelope. It contained a USB stick. He plugged it into the port on his computer. When he finished watching the video, he vomited into his waste basket.

BROKEN CONDOM

Mei was sitting at her desk at Forensic Analytics Inc. and staring at her computer screen. She looked tense. Rarely had I seen her so worked up. Her hands were shaking as she opened a file labeled "Janet Walker Crime Scene Investigation Report."

"Matt, I've never come across a case like this. It's deeply troubling, and I can tell you it's going to have serious ramifications right across the country. I know it."

"Well, you've definitely got my undivided attention."

"Before I tell you what we've found, I want to say I am so very proud of you."

"Okay."

"I also want to say that it was what you said the other day about a possible link between the Peterson and Walker cases that led me in this direction."

I held my breath.

Mei continued. "I'll begin with the results of our findings on the DNA evidence gathered by the CSI team at the Walker crime scene. First, the autopsy showed she had sex two hours prior to her death. However, no semen was found in her vagina, which says to me the participant probably used a condom. That said, Senator Bradford's DNA was found all over the bedsheets. Pubic hair, skin cells, and saliva. Then there are his fingerprints on a Champagne bottle and a glass."

"The senator admitted he was with Janet Walker that evening," I noted. "But as you know, I now have indisputable proof that Janet Walker was alive when he left her apartment."

Nodding her head in agreement, Mei placed the Walker case file on the side of her desk and opened a file labeled "Gail Peterson Crime Scene Investigation Report."

"Now this is where things go seriously sideways. While the senator's DNA, in the form of pubic hair, skin cells, and saliva, were all over the Walker apartment, none of this was present at the Peterson apartment. Not a trace. All that was found was a used condom with the senator's semen in it, as well as his semen on the victim. There was something about this that bothered me, so I went back and looked again at the DNA evidence gathered at the Walker crime scene. Again, no semen inside her vagina."

"Meaning the senator used a condom," I interjected.

"I then reviewed the DNA results from the State lab in the Peterson case. Semen was swabbed from the victim's abdomen. What I found troubling was that an internal swab of the victim produced no semen. Not a trace."

"Because the killer used a condom," I repeated.

"Yes, which apparently broke, depositing semen on the victim's abdomen. I asked one of my techs to examine the condom under a microscope. He found the reservoir at the tip of the condom had a hole in it which caused the semen to leak onto the victim."

"A defective condom. It happens," I said.

"However, upon close examination under a microscope, the tech found the reservoir had been cut, most probably with a small pair of scissors."

I was now perched at the very edge of the chair.

Mei continued. "I swabbed the internal surface of the condom and it yielded DNA originating from the male participant, Senator Bradford. I then swabbed the external part of the condom and isolated a sample of female DNA." Mei paused as she studied the results.

"And?"

"This is where the prosecutor's case against the senator totally collapses. The female DNA on the external part of the condom did not match Gail Peterson's DNA. We triple-checked the results. It definitely was not Peterson's DNA. Then an idea hit me. The senator admitted to you that he had sex with Janet Walker. So, I tested her DNA sample and ..."

"Let me guess! It matched the DNA on the outside part of the condom," I said.

Mei nodded. "To be absolutely clear, Walker's DNA was on the external part of the condom found on the bed at the Peterson crime scene."

I leapt to my feet. "Absolutely freakin' amazing."

Mei held up her hand and waved at me to sit down. She was not finished.

"Now we get to the blond hair found on the bed in Peterson's apartment," Mei continued. "What I'm going to tell you is very disturbing. You have to be very careful how you use it because I don't want to jeopardize my relationship with the tech at the State lab."

I assured her the tech would remain anonymous.

"The technician who did the initial DNA tests on the evidence gathered at the Peterson crime scene told me he was instructed not to bother testing the blond hair samples for DNA.

"He told me in the strictest confidence that the detective and the prosecutor said they had all the evidence they needed to convict the senator. He told me they were convinced the blond hair was from an earlier encounter with a boyfriend and testing it would not alter the fact that the senator killed Gail Peterson."

"Quite the assumption," I said.

"Still, the tech offered to test the hair samples but never got around to it. The lab director shuffled him off to another rush case."

"That is not going to look good when it comes out," I said.

"What troubles me about all this is the perfunctory manner in which this crucial piece of evidence was treated by the police and the prosecutor. They seemed to be so convinced of the senator's guilt, and somehow they convinced the lab to ignore the evidence."

"And now for the icing on the cake," Mei said, opening a third file. "First off, remind me where you retrieved the cigarette butt."

"In an ashtray in front of the entrance to the hotel in DC."

"Did you see who put it there?"

"Yes. I even have a video of the guy with the cigarette in his mouth before he stubbed it out in the ashtray. Why all the questions?"

"Whoever this guy is, his DNA matches the DNA from the hair follicles found in Peterson's bedroom."

"Holy shit! Do you know what this means? The senator is totally innocent. He didn't kill the women. It's like he was swearing all along. He was framed, and now we have the evidence to prove it."

"Do you have any idea who this man is?" Mei asked.

"His name is Anton Kuznetzov. He flew in from Moscow a few weeks ago, supposedly to work on some computer issue at the Russian embassy."

"Matt, you have got to go to the prosecutor and the police with this."

"The first thing I have to do is write this up and get it into tomorrow's paper. I also have to confront the Russian embassy and, with any luck, the killer."

"You know what happened last time you faced off with a Russian killer. You almost died."

"Don't worry. This time I'll be extra careful."

"This has become extremely dangerous," she warned.

As I got up to leave, I asked Mei for a small favor.

"Matt, no favor is ever small with you."

"Could you hold off sending the results to Bradford's lawyer until … let's say six this evening?"

"Too late. I've already emailed the report to him."

"Damn. You should have held off."

"I don't play favorites, and I don't play games. My instructions were clear. You both get the results. I don't need any fallout if the lawyer finds out I withheld the report so you could get an edge on him."

"I'll be really pissed if Tate does an end run on me."

"Matt, you're ignoring what I said. This has become too dangerous. You should drop this now and turn it over to the police."

"Look, Mei. The lead dickhead didn't want to listen or even look at the stuff I uncovered on the Walker murder. He's got his head stuck in the sand. Nothing I say will convince him that he nailed the wrong man."

"If the Russians are behind the killing of those two women, they won't think twice about shutting you down, and this time I don't think they're going to miss."

"I've got a better cell phone this time."

Mei grabbed hold of my hand. "This is no time for jokes. I'm scared for you."

"I'm not going to back down because some Russian assassin under orders from Putin might come after me."

"Will come after you."

"Look, I'm being extremely careful. I look both ways before I cross the street."

"Stop with the wisecracks. This Russian is a cold-blooded killing machine."

"Mei, I'm just doing my job."

"Your job is to report. It's not to become a dead hero."

"I'm not doing this to be a hero, and I certainly don't want to be killed doing my job. But I'm sure as hell not going to run for the hills because the situation is getting hot."

"I don't want to see you in a coffin."

"You won't. You've just got to get out of that dark place you're in."

"I can't help it. I love you, and I don't want to lose you."

"You won't lose me. I've got a guardian angel watching my back."

*

When I left Mei's office, I felt like I was treading barefoot on broken glass, worried sick that Tate would steal my thunder once he read Mei's report. But I had to let it go. There was one important question resonating in my brain. A question only the senator could answer. I called the DC jail and asked the duty officer to have Bradford get in touch with me as soon as possible, adding that it was extremely urgent. I started walking down 5th Avenue armed with the indisputable evidence that not only did the senator not murder Janet Walker, he also did not kill Gail Peterson. I kept staring down at my cell phone, wishing it would buzz. Twelve minutes later, it did.

"Matt, first off, I want to thank you," Bradford began, his voice tinged with excitement. "Your article caused quite the stir. But I want to warn you that Tate is on the warpath."

My stomach knotted. "Is it about the Forensic Analytics report?"

"What? No. He called to tell me the DA is looking at charging you with obstruction of justice for withholding the video on the Walker case."

"Well, I can say this with confidence. We're definitely not going to be cellmates. However, that's not why I asked you to call me. There's something

I need to know. The evening you were with Janet Walker, it appears from her autopsy you used a condom."

"I always used a condom with her."

"Do you remember what happened to it?"

"To what?"

"The condom."

I could almost hear the wheels spinning in the senator's head as he thought back to the encounter.

"Come to think of it, Candy removed it. I thought it was kind of odd because she never did that before. She told me to relax, handed me a glass of Champagne, removed it, and scurried off to the washroom. A few seconds later I heard the toilet flush, and then she was back in the bedroom. Why are you asking me this?"

I kept the reason to myself. I was worried Bradford would immediately inform his lawyer and my investigation would be blown out of the water before I could get it into the paper.

"It's for an angle I'm working," I said.

"Have you found more evidence to clear me?" he asked. I could sense the anticipation in his voice.

"I'm working on it. Let's leave it at that for now."

I disconnected the call, smiled, and shouted at the morning sky. "Solved it! I freakin' well solved it."

*

At the office, Heather rushed over to my cubicle. Doyle wanted to see us.

As we entered his office, Doyle was beaming. "The reaction to our story on the Walker murder case has been overwhelming. We've got news media outlets from coast-to-coast begging to get an exclusive interview you."

"I'm don't give interviews."

"Your choice." Doyle continued. "I just heard from our lawyer that Judge Hamilton is apoplectic. I'm told he hauled the prosecutor and Bradford's lawyer into his chambers this morning and exploded, demanding to know how the police messed up the investigation into the Walker murder. Both lawyers have to appear before him in open court tomorrow at two o'clock. Now, what I need to know is whether there's a follow up to today's story."

"There is, and if you think today's story was explosive, wait till you read what I've found."

"What do you have?"

"Absolute proof that Senator Bradford did not murder Gail Peterson."

"Do you know who did?" Heather asked.

I paused for effect. "The man who murdered Gail Peterson *and* Janet Walker is Anton Kuznetzov. He entered the US on a diplomatic visa two months ago. His visa indicates he's a technician sent to the Russian embassy in DC to update its computer system. He's the guy on the video going into Walker's apartment an hour after Bradford left. He's also the guy whose hair was collected by the CSI team in Gail Peterson's bedroom."

Doyle looked perplexed. "How do you know for certain the hair belongs to this man?"

I smiled. "I got his DNA off a soggy cigarette butt he discarded in an ashtray outside the hotel he's staying in across from the embassy. The DNA extracted from the cigarette butt is a match to the hair from the Peterson crime scene."

Doyle shook his head. "I don't believe it. This is incredible. When can you write all this up? We'll need to send it to our lawyers ASAP."

"I've written most of it. It's slugged 'Putin's Assassin.'"

Heather's face lit up. "I love it."

"I'll fire it off in a few minutes. Then I need to get back to DC to get the last piece of the puzzle," I explained.

"What last piece?" Heather asked.

"The accountability. I'm grabbing the noon high-speed train to DC. I should be there no later than three o'clock. I'll file an insert from there."

PERSONA NON GRATA

The final piece of the puzzle meant a face-to-face confrontation with the bad guy, Anton Kuznetzov. I had to admit I was scared out of my mind given what happened the last time I confronted a Russian hitman. But this time, I had worked out a plan to approach my target in a very public place, which I hoped would provide me with a modicum of physical safety. That was, if Kuznetzov was still in the country. I was worried he could have been ordered to hightail it back to Moscow once the Russian ambassador or one of his senior flunkies read today's *Tribune*.

From the guest phone in the hotel lobby, I called up to Kuznetzov's room. There was no answer. I pulled out my cell phone and tapped in the number to the Russian embassy. My fingers were shaking. I managed to get the right number after four fumbled attempts.

"Embassy of Russian Federation," a woman with a thick accent announced.

"I would like to speak to Anton Kuznetzov," I said.

"Who is calling, please?"

"Matt Kozar. I'm a journalist with the *New York Tribune*."

"You will hold, please."

A moment later, the woman was back on the line. "There is no one here with that name."

"Are you sure? Blond guy, about six feet two inches tall, a hundred and ninety pounds. Wears a black suit," I said.

"No."

"Funny. Just the other day I watched him enter the embassy. Let me repeat his name. Anton Kuznetzov. I'll spell it if you'd like."

"I have told you we have no one here with that name."

"Then would you pass me to the person who deals with the news media?"

"You will hold, please."

Not five seconds later, a high-ranking embassy official was on the line.

"I am first secretary Grigoriy Belov. I must inform you, Mr. Matthew Kozar, you are not welcome to have any business to do with Russian Federation. You have been declared persona non grata."

"I don't know what that means," I said, feigning ignorance.

"You are not welcome in Russia."

"Well, I'm not in Russia, and let me just say for the record, I have no intention of going there, ever. I simply would like a word with Anton Kuznetzov."

"There is no one here with that name."

"Seriously? He entered the US about six weeks ago on a diplomatic visa as some kind of computer technician. Ring any bells?"

"I do not know of what you speak."

"Look. I know he's there, and you know he's there. So, I would appreciate it if you would pass on a message to him. Let him know that I know precisely where he was on the evening of May 27. In fact, I have a video of your Mr. Kuznetzov entering Janet Walker's apartment and exiting several minutes later, leaving her dead on the living room floor. Strangled."

There was stone-cold silence on the other end.

"Are you still on the line, Mr. Belov?"

He said nothing, but I could hear him breathing.

"I've also got rock-solid evidence placing your Mr. Kuznetzov at the apartment of Gail Peterson later the same night. She too was strangled to death. Ms. Peterson was an intern with US Senator William Bradford, who has been charged with the murders of these two women. But I'm sure you know that."

Again, silence.

I continued. "In fairness to Mr. Kuznetzov, I feel it is incumbent on me to at least get a comment from him before we go to print. And let me add, whether he talks to me or not, the story will be in tomorrow's paper."

"Mr. Kozar, we have nothing to say about these allegations which I must point out are totally false. I also wish to note that Mr. Kuznetzov was here at a meeting on that night."

I held back a laugh. "I thought you said there was no one by that name at the embassy."

Without uttering another word, Belov hung up.

I looked at my phone. It was 3:53 p.m. At precisely 4:08 p.m., Kuznetzov leapt out of a black SUV bearing diplomatic plates, stormed into the hotel lobby, and headed to the banks of elevators where he repeatedly punched the up button like a crazed drug addict. Nine minutes later, he was back in the lobby toting a carry-on suitcase, and I was standing in his way.

"Mr. Kuznetzov, my name is Matt Kozar. I'm a reporter with the *New York Tribune*. I'd like to ask you …"

I didn't see the left hook coming, but I felt it slam into my right temple like a sledgehammer, followed by a straight right into my forehead. I went down for the count, out cold. Several minutes later I came to on a sofa in the lobby. The doorman was splashing cold water on my face. Standing behind him was the hotel manager, looking distressed.

"Sir, are you alright?" she asked.

I grabbed the sides of my head in a futile effort to stop the pounding. "Aside from the ringing in my ears and a splitting headache, I think so."

The doorman grimaced. "I hate to say it, but you don't look good. Your left eye is starting to swell up bad. It's the size of a golf ball. You're going to have one heck of a shiner."

I pushed myself up on the sofa and scanned the lobby with my good eye. "The guy who clocked me. Did you see where he went?"

"He ran across the road and took off in a black limo that was waiting for him," the doorman said.

"What was this about?" the manager asked.

"Political differences," I said.

"Do you want me to call the police or an ambulance?"

I shook my head. It was a big mistake. A jolt of pain shot through my skull. On wobbly legs, I headed for the washroom and reeled in horror at my reflection in the mirror. I looked like I had run face-first into a battering ram. I pulled out my phone and called Heather. I think I mumbled something about accountability.

"Matt, are you okay?" she asked.

"I got … confronted the Russian …"

"Matt, you're slurring your words."

Shutting my eyes tightly, I tried to loosen the cobwebs.

"I confronted the hitman. Thing is, I only managed to stay on my feet for three seconds of the first round."

"What do you mean? Are you hurt?"

"When you see me, you'll know what I mean. Once I clear my head, I'll file an insert on my interview with the spokesperson at the Russian embassy and my run-in with Kuznetzov."

"I'll see you in the office tomorrow," Heather said with a hint of hesitation in her voice. "Matt, before I let you go, let me just say this is absolutely amazing work. I also want to say I'm sorry for my actions in trying to push you off the story. It was totally irresponsible of me."

"You can buy me a beer and it'll be water under the bridge."

ASSUMPTIONS

Judge Hamilton glanced up as David Di Adamo and Brian Tate shuffled into his chambers. He looked like a guided missile, locked and loaded.

"I have never, ever seen a case so bloody messed up as this one," Hamilton began. "It's like the Three Stooges are trying to out-do each other. Have you read this morning's installment in the *Tribune*? You can't miss it. It's plastered right across the front page."

"Yes, Your Honor," the prosecutor and defense lawyer responded in unison.

"And?"

"I'm still trying to wrap my head around it," Di Adamo said.

"I suggest you get your head into it, not around it," the judge barked. "What in hell is going on? I cannot understand how a reporter can find crucial exculpatory evidence that a team of highly trained veteran homicide detectives appear to have missed. My question is: Did the detectives miss this, or did they find it and decide to hide it?"

"Your Honor, I do not believe the detectives deliberately hid anything," Di Adamo countered.

"Oh, and you know that for certain?"

"Well, no, Your Honor."

Hamilton glared at the prosecutor. "Let us assume for the moment that nothing nefarious is going on. What you are saying, then, is these homicide detectives are a bunch of incompetent country bumpkins."

"I wouldn't go that far, Your Honor."

"Really? Then I beg of you, enlighten me. How far would you go?"

"I don't know."

"Have you spoken to the lead detective?" Hamilton asked.

"I spoke to him yesterday about the video."

"What did he tell you?"

"He told me the two detectives assigned to the case confirmed they did not interview the woman whose security camera captured the event. At least, not face to face."

"What does that mean?" the judge asked.

"She was out of town when Walker was murdered. Detective Wells spoke to her by phone when she returned. He assumed she knew nothing."

"The detective assumed. Brilliant. But the reporter didn't assume, did he?" the judge barked.

Di Adamo shook his head.

"As I suggested yesterday, have you considered charging the reporter with obstruction?" Hamilton asked.

"Yes."

"And?"

"Can't."

The judge snapped. "Stop with the monosyllabic crap. Why can't you?"

"Detective Spencer informed me that Matt Kozar came to see him the day before yesterday's story ran in the *Tribune*. The reporter told him he had evidence that would clear the senator in the murder of Janet Walker."

"I have a bad feeling about where this is going," the judge said, rubbing his forehead.

"Detective Spencer dismissed Kozar out of hand, but before the reporter left, he handed the detective an envelope containing a USB stick."

"What was on it?" Hamilton asked.

"I put that very question to Detective Spencer. He said he didn't know."

"I am afraid to ask. Pray tell, why not?"

"He tossed the envelope into a trash can."

"That said, the reporter should also have brought the evidence in the Walker case to your attention," the judge pointed out.

Di Adamo cleared his throat. "Your Honor, I had several messages on my desk from Mr. Kozar asking that I call him ASAP. He told my assistant it was urgent and had to do with the Walker case."

The judge interjected. "Let me guess. You didn't bother to call him back."

Beads of sweat were forming on the prosecutor's forehead. "Your Honor, in my defense, I had dozens and dozens of messages from reporters on my desk, all wanting to ask questions about the case. I didn't call any of them. I was extremely busy preparing for the trial."

"The Justice Department is chock-full of assistant attorneys and researchers. Did it not enter your mind to ask one of them to call this reporter and ask what it was that was so urgent?"

"My focus was on the case."

The judge shifted uncomfortably in his chair. "Why do I get the feeling there's something you're not telling me?"

Di Adamo took a deep breath. "Mr. Kozar showed up at the Justice building right after he left the police station. He asked to see me. I was busy and instructed security to escort him out. Kozar handed the guard an envelope."

The judge winced. "It contained a USB stick."

"Yes, Your Honor."

"And did you bother to look at what was on it?"

"Yes, Your Honor."

"May I ask when you looked at it?"

"Yesterday morning, after I left your office."

Shaking his head in disgust, Judge Hamilton moved on to Matt Kozar's latest revelations. "And now we have this morning's edition of the *Tribune*. The security camera at the Peterson apartment was rendered useless because the lens was spray-painted the night before. Was Detective Spencer aware of this?"

"I don't know, Your Honor. I haven't spoken to the detective today. I've called him several times but he's not picking up. I've left messages for him to call me. I said it was urgent."

"Let me ask you this. Do you honestly think Senator Bradford visited Gail Peterson's apartment building the night before she was murdered to spray-paint the lens on the security camera?"

"No, Your Honor."

"Now I come to the evidence that is the most damaging to your case in the Peterson murder: the blond hairs found on or near the victim's bed. I gather, having seen the senator in my courtroom, he is not blond."

Di Adamo's hands were shaking. "Correct."

Hamilton looked down at the paper. "According to this article, the hair allegedly belongs to this Russian, this Anton Kuznetzov, the *Tribune* reporter managed to track down. It turns out he is the man who was captured on video entering and leaving Janet Walker's apartment on the same night Gail Peterson was murdered."

The prosecutor yanked a handkerchief from his jacket pocket and wiped his face.

"Mr. Di Adamo, for the record, were you aware of this evidence? I'm referring to the hair," the judge said.

"I was aware of the hair, yes. Detective Spencer assumed it was from a boyfriend who had visited the victim sometime earlier."

"The detective assumed. Did Detective Spencer follow up on his assumption?"

"Not that I'm aware of, Your Honor. Detective Spencer was of the opinion that Senator Bradford sexually assaulted the Peterson woman and then killed her. He felt it was a waste of time to pursue the matter of the blond hair."

"What action did you take?"

"I concurred with Detective Spencer's assessment."

"What you mean to say is you also assumed."

"Yes, Your Honor."

The judge shook his head in disbelief. "What about the lab that carried out the initial DNA tests for the state? Did it test the hair?"

"Not that I'm aware. Detective Spencer was pushing the lab for the results on the semen found on the victim and in the condom. This was his sole focus."

"You were aware of all this?" the judge asked.

"Yes, Your Honor."

"You are in big trouble, Counselor. Big trouble. Do you realize how this looks? A reporter finds out that hair collected at the crime scene was not tested for DNA. He wonders why and decides to have the hair sent to an independent lab for analysis. And surprise, surprise. Through this so-called ethnicity or ancestry process, the reporter discovers the hair comes from the scalp of a male who is Russian and Chechen."

Judge Hamilton continued. "The reporter puts one and one together, tracks down a suspect, manages to get a DNA sample from the individual, and boom. It took a reporter who *assumed nothing* to solve the case."

David Di Adamo was at a loss for words. He looked like a mouse trapped in a maze. He understood his case was a bust. Senator Bradford did not kill the two women. He also knew his career as a prosecutor was over.

The judge then turned his attention to the defense attorney who had been sitting quietly. "Now, Mr. Tate. You're not getting off easy on this, and I warn you not to play coy with me. Were you aware of the evidence this reporter collected which is now splashed all over the front page of this newspaper?"

"I was not, Your Honor. I first found out about it when I got a phone call this morning from a colleague," Tate said.

"Can you explain how this reporter managed to get his hands on the lab results before you, and why, I gather, he kept you out of the loop?"

"Mr. Kozar doesn't like me. He doesn't like lawyers. Or politicians. In fact, I don't think he likes many people."

"Are you being glib?"

"No, Your Honor. Mr. Kozar is driven by one thing: beating the competition. He told the senator that if he found evidence either exonerating him or proving him guilty, his first and only obligation would be to his newspaper."

"Did this independent Forensic Analytics lab have the courtesy to send you a copy of their findings?"

Brian Tate hesitated.

"Looks to me like you're trying to formulate an excuse," the judge suggested.

"Your Honor, I received a detailed copy of the report from Forensic Analytics yesterday morning in my email account."

"And?"

"I was up to my neck in alligators and didn't get around to it until I read the online report in the *Tribune* early this morning."

"Were you in the Florida Everglades?" the judge asked.

"I don't understand, Your Honor," Tate said.

"You said you were up to your neck in alligators."

"It's a figure of speech, Your Honor."

"I know what it is," the judge snarled. "I also know that you are the criminal defense lawyer in a double homicide involving one of the more powerful senators in the United States of America. One would think that if a crucial forensic report on the individual you are representing popped up in your email box, you would read it without delay."

"Sir, I was busy ..."

"Don't give me this 'I was busy' crap. Get out of my office, both of you. Mr. Di Adamo, I suggest you find a quiet place, confer with your colleagues at the DOJ, and come up with a plan for dealing with this mess. We will reconvene in my courtroom at precisely two o'clock this afternoon. And I warn you both, I will not tolerate any shenanigans."

*

Tate scurried off to the DC jail to brief his client on the latest developments.

Senator Bradford looked calm and relaxed. In fact, he was smiling when he was led into the interview room by a guard.

"I gather you heard about the story in the *Tribune*," Tate said.

"I read it online. The head guard handed me his iPad this morning opened to the front page of the *Tribune*," the senator began. "You have to admit, Brian, that my decision to bring Matt Kozar on board was sound."

The lawyer did not respond.

"Cat got your tongue? A reporter won your case for you. You should be dancing an Irish jig and calculating what cut of your exorbitant fee you'll be donating to Matt Kozar's favorite charity," Bradford added.

Tate ignored the barb. "My thinking is Di Adamo is going to file a motion this afternoon to dismiss all charges against you."

"And?"

"Hopefully, you will go free."

"Not so quick. I want that little weasel to file a motion stating clearly and unequivocally that I am innocent of all charges. Merely dismissing them does not clear my name in the eyes of the public. I want it stated in court that I am innocent. Do you understand me?"

"That's not how it works, Senator," Tate countered.

"Then make it work. And make sure my suit is freshly pressed. I am not entering the courtroom in this jumpsuit or in handcuffs."

"I can't do anything about the clothes or the handcuffs."

"Why not?"

"Because I don't know for certain that the prosecutor will file a motion to dismiss. He may request you remain in custody until he has fully reviewed the latest developments."

"He does that, and I'll make sure he'll be chasing ambulances when I get out of here."

"I think that's a forgone conclusion," Tate mumbled.

*

David Di Adamo skulked into his office to find Spencer waiting for him.

"What the fuck, Spencer? What the fuck?" the prosecutor yelled.

The detective did not respond.

"I just met with the judge. He ripped my throat out. He's ordered me to appear before him in court today with a plan for how I'm going to deal with the findings in the *Tribune*."

"What are you going to propose?" the detective asked.

"The only thing I can do. I'm going to put forward a motion to dismiss all charges against Bradford," the prosecutor said.

"You can't do that," Spencer said desperately.

"Did you even bother to read the second installment of the *Tribune* this morning?"

The detective shrugged.

"You should. Your entire investigation is fried."

"I told you, even though Bradford may not have killed the hooker, he definitely murdered his intern. You know that. The evidence is solid."

"Get yourself a newspaper and read the findings from this Forensic Analytics lab in New York. And then face the facts. You messed up big time."

"You can't let him off. He's a killer!"

"Take off the blinders, Spencer. The senator is innocent. There is no doubt in my mind about that, and there is no doubt in my mind that you and your team fucked up the investigation."

"Fuck you, Dave. I can't believe you're bending over and taking the word of a two-bit hack over me. What if he got it wrong? Ever think of that? What if this is nothing more than a heap of fake news? Do what the fuck you want. I'm out of here." Spencer got up, heaved a chair against the wall, and stormed out.

As he left the building, the detective was ambushed by a half-dozen reporters. With his jaw clenched shut, he pushed his way through the crush and made a dash for an awaiting police car.

"Detective Spencer! What is your reaction to the story this morning in the *New York Tribune?*" an NBC reporter shouted.

Big Foot did not stop to respond.

Moments later, the prosecutor emerged only to be chased down by the champing herd.

"Mr. Di Adamo, what steps is your office taking on the report in the *New York Tribune?*" a CNN reporter asked.

"The only statement I am prepared to make is that my office has read the report in the *Tribune,* and we are processing it. I will appear before Judge Hamilton at two o'clock this afternoon to make a motion on this matter."

"Is the investigation by the *Tribune* factual?" a *Times* reporter asked.

"I've given you my statement," said the prosecutor as he began to walk away.

"Did DC Homicide and your office drop the ball on the investigation?" a CBS journalist shouted out.

Di Adamo kept walking with the newshounds hot on his heels, peppering him with questions. He gritted his teeth and kept mum.

MOTION TO DISMISS

"Holy crap! You look like you went ten rounds with Wladimir Klitschko. Your face is a mess," the managing editor said with a whistle when I walked into his office.

"It feels far worse than it looks," I said. "But you should see the other guy."

"You've ignited one hell of a firestorm, Matt," Doyle said. He was smiling.

"Well, at least I didn't get shot this time around."

Heather slipped warily into the office. "Matt, I owe you a big apology. I'm sorry I got caught up in the frenzy to convict the senator. You did a good thing here."

"Stop already with the apologies," I said.

"The court should be in session in a few minutes with a live feed. Grab a coffee and we'll watch the proceedings from my office," Doyle said, as he reached for his remote. "This should prove to be one interesting and, might I add, historic day in court."

*

It was bedlam outside the DC courthouse. A dozen news vans were parked on the street. Scores of journalists were on their phones, touching base with their editors and producers at news outlets across the country. Everyone had a copy of the *Tribune* in their hands. Inside the courtroom, the air was thick with anticipation and tension.

Di Adamo sat at his station keeping his head buried in documents. He looked shell-shocked. Absent was his retinue of junior State attorneys. Conspicuously absent was lead detective Ron Spencer.

At 2 p.m. sharp, Senator Bradford was escorted into the courtroom by two sheriffs and led to the defense table where his handcuffs were removed. His lawyer smiled and shook his hand.

"Any word on what the prosecutor is going to do?" the senator asked.

"He's going to put forward a motion to dismiss all charges against you. In a short while, you will be a free man."

"What about declaring me innocent of all charges?"

"Senator, you know this as well as I do. Even if a person is found innocent of a crime, the court does not declare that person to be innocent," Tate explained. "Keep in mind that from the moment you were charged you were presumed innocent until proven guilty."

"I want to be declared innocent."

The senator turned and scanned the courtroom. Several of his colleagues greeted him with a thumbs-up gesture.

"Where's that jackass detective?" Bradford asked.

"Probably handing in his resignation as we speak," Tate said.

As the judge made his entrance, the courtroom fell silent. Everyone rose. Hamilton's expression was resolute. He sat down and looked straight at the prosecutor.

"Mr. Di Adamo, I take it you have a motion to make."

The prosecutor rose reluctantly. "Yes, Your Honor. In light of new and compelling evidence recently brought to my attention, I am formally submitting a motion for the dismissal of all charges without prejudice against Senator William Bradford in the murders of Gail Peterson and Janet Walker. I move that Senator Bradford be released from custody immediately."

The spectators reacted in a frenzy.

"Order in my court! Order!" the judge shouted, slamming his gavel repeatedly on the dais. "Order, or I will clear the courtroom."

With a semblance of decorum restored, Judge Hamilton focused his attention on the accused. "Senator Bradford, please rise. Having been fully apprised of new evidence that has come to light in this matter, I am in agreement with the prosecutor. All charges against you in the case of Gail Peterson and in the case of Janet Walker are hereby dismissed without prejudice. You are to be released immediately."

Before the judge could bring the gavel down, the senator called out, "Your Honor!"

"What is it, Senator?" the judge asked.

"I would request the prosecutor declare me innocent of all charges. Merely dismissing the charges will leave doubt in the minds of many who will think I got off on a legal technicality or because of high-powered back-room maneuvering."

The judge looked over at the prosecutor. "Mr. Di Adamo, do you wish to rebut?'

Appearing addled, Di Adamo stood and stared at the judge like a forlorn dog begging for a reprieve.

"Well, Mr. Di Adamo? I think the senator has a right to a response after what he has been put through," Judge Hamilton noted.

"Your Honor, the law clearly states that every person accused of any crime is presumed innocent until proven guilty. In light of new evidence brought to my attention, I brought forward a motion to dismiss all charges against the senator without prejudice."

The senator was not about to concede. "Your Honor, if I may. From the moment I was arrested and jailed, I have been vilified in the news media. There was no presumption of innocence afforded me, only calls for a lynching. Throughout this ordeal, I did not hear a peep out of the prosecutor about the presumption of innocence. I don't want any ambiguity as to why the charges against me were dismissed. Therefore, I want the prosecutor to state unequivocally for the record that the new evidence brought to light in the *New York Tribune* exonerates me of all charges and that I am innocent. It's a simple and fair request."

The prosecutor shot back. "The presumption of innocence is a legal principle that ..."

The senator cut him off, shouting, "Am I innocent of all charges? Is that so difficult for you to admit? Am I innocent? Answer the question."

Di Adamo knew he was caught between a rock and a hard place. In a raspy whisper, he surrendered. "Senator, you are innocent."

Like a herd of spooked horses, the reporters bolted for the door to file their reports.

Beaming, Tate turned to his client. "I'll pick you up in about an hour in front of the jail."

"You do that. I also want you to let the reporters know I'll be holding a press conference in front of the courthouse immediately upon my release."

FREE AT LAST

With a solemn expression on his face, the chief of the Metropolitan Police Department of Washington, DC, appeared on the steps outside police headquarters.

"My comment will be brief," the chief began. "I have ordered a full and independent investigation into the handling of the Gail Peterson and Janet Walker murder investigations. I want answers and I will leave no stone unturned."

"Will heads roll?" a CBS reporter shouted out.

"I have asked for and received the resignation of Homicide Detective Captain Ron Spencer."

"What about the other detectives involved in the homicide investigations?" a *Washington Post* scribe asked.

"They have been suspended pending the outcome of the independent investigation," the chief said. "That is all I can say about the matter at this time. However, I would like to take this opportunity to publicly apologize to Senator William Bradford for the pain he has suffered and the damage that has been inflicted on him, both personal and professional. I hope he will agree to meet with me in the near future to discuss this matter."

*

Minutes after his release, Senator Bradford stood on the steps of the courthouse facing a swarm of reporters.

"I want to begin by offering my deepest condolences to the family of Gail Peterson."

The senator paused for a moment and looked up at the sky. He cleared his throat and continued.

"While I was in my jail cell, Gail Peterson never left my thoughts. She was a wonderful and dedicated member of my staff. She was a bright light shining in the office. Always upbeat, always on her toes with insightful questions and ideas. I could see she was forging a remarkable life for herself, but tragically, brutally, her life was cut short. Like everyone on my staff, I was devastated when I was informed of her death. I will never forget her. May she rest in peace."

The senator paused once again to gather his thoughts. "I want to apologize to my wife and children for my contemptible and disgraceful behavior. It was the action of a foolish man. I wish I had possessed the strength to resist and act like a decent human being. I am praying my family can find it in their hearts to forgive me, and I promise I will work hard to rebuild their trust and earn back their love."

Bradford slowly scanned the crush of journalists as if he were looking for someone in particular. With disappointment registered on his face, he continued. "I also want to thank the one person who fought hard to prove my innocence. Matt Kozar of the *New York Tribune*," the senator pronounced.

"When Mr. Kozar and I first met while I was in custody, I knew he had serious reservations about my innocence, but he listened to my pleas, and rather than give up, he started digging. He did what the homicide detectives should have done from day one: investigate this case from all angles. It was my misfortune that the lead detective, Ron Spencer, went into this investigation with an intractable mindset and steadfastly refused to deviate from it. He was on a mission that had little to do with being a professional police officer. Detective Spencer was chasing celebrity at the expense of an innocent man.

"I also want to point out that Matt Kozar did what each and every one of you here today failed to do as journalists. His job. Had Mr. Kozar not dug for the truth, I would not be standing here today. I would be serving a life sentence in prison for two murders I did not commit. Mr. Kozar not only proved I was innocent, but also tracked down and identified the real killer, the assassin sent here by Vladimir Putin to destroy me.

"I hope the so-called journalists who spent the past several weeks vilifying me in the media will now report that I was found innocent of all charges brought against me. The new evidence the prosecutor referred to in his motion to dismiss the charges against me totally and unequivocally exonerates me from the murders of Gail Peterson and Janet Walker."

Senator Bradford looked up from his notes and stared out at the throng of media people.

"Tomorrow morning, I will be asking the president to order the closing of the Russian embassy and expel every single Russian diplomat from American soil. The embassy knowingly harbored a hitman who came here on a diplomatic visa to carry out Putin's dirty work.

"Now, I will take a few questions."

A Fox reporter was first off the mark. "Senator, you are critical of the police, but surely you must agree the evidence against you was incredibly overwhelming," he shouted out.

Bradford scowled. "The media took the so-called evidence handed to you by Detective Spencer at face value without question. You decided he was right, and I was guilty—a sexual predator and a serial killer. There were calls, reported by many of you, to hang me from the nearest tree. You all bought into the narrative fed to you by the police, and you forgot a paramount principle of law: Every person charged with an offence has the right to be presumed innocent until proven guilty in a court of law. You were no better than a lynch mob."

The next question came from CNN. "Will you be resigning?"

With his brow furrowed, Bradford chose his words carefully. "I was elected by my constituents to serve them and to serve the country. I still have two more years to carry out my mandate. I have decided not to resign."

"Despite the fact that you were caught, as they say, with your pants down?" the Fox reporter interjected.

Not missing a beat, the senator shot back. "Tell me. Can you find the balls to ask that very question of your lord and master, Donald Trump?"

With that, Senator Bradford turned and left.

*

When I walked into Mei's apartment, she rushed to give me a hug but stopped short when she saw my face.

"Matt! What happened to you?"

"I confronted the hitman at his hotel. He responded with a left hook and I think a straight right. That's all I remember before the lights went out."

"Are you okay? Was he arrested?"

"I was told he jumped into a black limo that sped away."

"So, he's free and clear," Mei said.

"Looks like it," I said, pulling out my phone. "On my way over, I got a text from my Washington contact. Here's what he wrote: 'AK boarded Turkish Airlines flight to Istanbul last night at JFK.'"

"You believe Putin set all this up just to destroy the senator," Mei said.

"It's his modus operandi. All you have to do is follow the trail of bodies. Anyone who dares to criticize or question his actions or his mental state ends up with their name etched on a tombstone."

Mei shook her head. "It's all so Machiavellian." After a moment, she asked, "Why didn't Putin simply order his assassin to kill the senator?"

"That's the twist. Had Bradford been assassinated, and it was proven to be on Putin's orders, it would have triggered a huge and dangerous international incident. Think about it. A US senator executed by a Russian hitman on American soil. The repercussions would be immense. My thinking is Putin ordered the head of the FSB in Moscow to hatch a plan that would be far, far worse than death for Senator Bradford."

I closed my eyes and thought back to the day I met Deborah Simmons and spotted the makeshift security camera attached to the back of her apartment door. One serendipitous twist of fate led to the complete unraveling of a police investigation that had all but convicted an innocent man.

I ran my fingers lightly over my left eye. It was sore and badly swollen.

Staring at my face, Mei softly stroked my cheek. "How are you feeling?"

"I'm okay. And don't worry. The doctor promised I'll have my roguish looks back in a few weeks."

"You're such a goof. Your face is a badge of honor. Well, actually, a few badges. I'm proud of you, Matt."

EPILOGUE

When the Turkish Airlines flight landed in Istanbul, Anton Kuznetzov was taken into custody by nine Turkish intelligence agents and escorted to a private hangar. There he was turned over to six stone-faced agents from Russia's FSB special ops directorate. He was handcuffed and placed aboard a private jet. No words were spoken. The assassin understood his life was over. He had botched his assignment and brought international scorn and scrutiny on the Russian president.

The jet landed on an isolated airstrip outside Moscow. When the assassin got off the plane, he was bundled into the back of a black SUV. From a dusty road outside Moscow, he was led to a freshly dug grave in a rocky field. He was asked nothing, and he said nothing. He was shot in the back of the head and buried.

*

Early the next morning, Petra called me on WhatsApp. Standing in the background were her fiancé, Stefan, and his family. They were holding a handmade poster that read "Congratulations!"

"We're all so proud of you," Petra said. "I'm so happy to be your sister."

The Holuk clan applauded and yelled, "*Vitayemo*! Welcome to the family."

I was wearing dark sunglasses, but not because I thought of myself as some kind of rock star. I looked like hell, and I didn't want to shock them.

"Thank you for this," I said. "Mei and I will be seeing you soon. And Stefan, I don't know if Petra has told you, but according to tradition, you have to ask the man in her family for her hand in marriage. So, before she walks down the aisle, we need to talk."

Stefan laughed. "You better say yes. I mean, you will say yes, right?"

"We'll see."

Acknowledgments

I want to thank Sonia Holiad for her diligence, tough critiques, and insightful edit of *Putin's Assassin*. She is one razor-sharp editor. I would also like to thank Sandie Rinaldo for her suggestions and creative support throughout the writing of this novel.

ABOUT THE AUTHOR

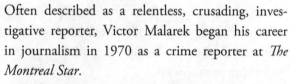

Often described as a relentless, crusading, investigative reporter, Victor Malarek began his career in journalism in 1970 as a crime reporter at *The Montreal Star*.

In 1976, he was hired by *The Globe and Mail*, Canada's national newspaper, where his work garnered an unprecedented three Michener Awards for meritorious public service journalism.

In 1990, Malarek was recruited by CBC to co-host its current affairs show, *the fifth estate*, where he was awarded a Gemini in 1997 as Canada's top broadcast journalist, and a fourth Michener Award in 2000. A decade later, he joined CTV's *W5* as its senior investigative reporter where his documentaries won four Canadian Screen Awards. He retired in 2017.

In his 27 years in television, he has worked on more than 325 investigative documentaries. Malarek has reported from across Canada, the United States, Australia, and the European Union, as well as Ukraine, Afghanistan, Iran, Kurdistan, Ethiopia, Somalia, South-East Asia, and Central and South America.

Malarek is the author of six non-fiction books including his internationally acclaimed *The Natashas: Inside the New Global Sex trade*, which has been published in 2003 in a dozen countries and 10 languages, and: *The Johns: Sex for Sale and the Men who buy it*; released in Canada, the U.S. and the UK in 2009.

His first book: *Hey ... Malarek!* hit the bookstores in 1984. It documents his troubled and tumultuous childhood and teenage years. In 1989, it was made into a feature movie called *Malarek*.

A second feature movie, *Target Number One*, starring Josh Hartnett in the role of investigative reporter Malarek, was released in July 2020 in Canada, the US, Britain, and France.

In 2014, Malarek decided to go independent, publishing his first fiction, *Orphanage 41*, with FriesenPress. His second fiction, *Wheat$haft* was published in 2021.

www.ingramcontent.com/pod-product-compliance
Lightning Source LLC
La Vergne TN
LVHW040023291224
800108LV00006B/80